The Barking Gods

A Harry Dolan Thriller

Cameron MacBeath

PublishAmerica
Baltimore

First printing

ISBN: 1-4137-7030-4
PUBLISHED BY PUBLISHAMERICA, LLLP
www.publishamerica.com
Baltimore

Printed in the United States of America

To all those who fight against hatred and bigotry the world over, and a big thank you to Stephen Vogt, Bruce Craft and Nigel Winter for their stories and information about life as a U.S. Army Ranger in Vietnam. Another thanks to my brother Mark for his colorful language contributions and his unique viewpoints of life. May he enjoy life on the Other side.

Chapter One

Harry Dolan glanced at his notes sparingly as he paced before the packed classroom. This semester he was doing something a little different by expanding the chapter on human dentition, the study of teeth.

"When I went back to Vietnam to help ID bodies, we had to rely on dental records and old fractures or anything else that might make an individual unique. Now, of course, DNA has proved us wrong a few times, but who would think that people would have identical dental work?" He strolled around the classroom laying teeth of various types on desktops. There were molars, pre-molars, incisors and canines from both sexes, both upper and lower teeth, and both left and right sides of the jaws. A packet ten pages long was passed round the room until all students had one.

"In the past, I've just skimmed over the chapter on dentition, but since many of you have no plans to take the Human Osteology course, I thought this would be fun and a learning experience. We'll just do two weeks on teeth, but when we're done I think all of you will have a little more respect for forensic anthropologists."

Dolan held up the copy of his field manual, *Human Osteology* by William Bass. "If any of you major in physical anthropology you'll see the names, Bass, Ubelaker and Moore-Jensen many times. They are giants in the field. The samples I've placed on several of your desks can tell us many things about the people who once used them. When I give the test, I will put specimens on a table and you will tell me the name of the tooth, where it came from and whether it is deciduous or adult." He smiled at the harmonious groans that filled the room like a warped version of the "Hallelujah Chorus." It was a sign that he was doing his job as a teacher.

"Questions?"

"How hard are you going to grade this test?" Rob Clark, an archeology major asked.

"Like I usually do." Harry smiled, his teeth pearly white next to his bright red, chapped lips. Gray peppered his dark brown hair and the tan corduroy blazer made Harry look more like an English professor than a medical investigator.

"That's what we were afraid of," Rob replied as he glanced around at his fellow students.

"You will have plenty of time to familiarize yourselves with the beautiful specimens before you." Dolan waved his hand over a molar that perched on Cindy Gaston's psychology book. "Take about ten minutes and read the handout I gave you, then we'll have a pop quiz. I need to run upstairs for a minute then I'll answer any questions before the test."

It had been eighteen months since the hit in Argentina. Nolan hadn't intended to kill the drug lord Molina, but he had let his emotions get the best of him. The government paid him for two jobs, the second of which Harry donated to the French order of nuns in Blanco. He still chuckled and wondered how long Sister Marcella had been suspicious of him. It was fortunate that she had not been a soldier. Harry had also eliminated his last pedophile just over a year ago and he felt a profound sense of justice that a least a few more children would be safe in the world.

Final exams were three weeks away, but Dolan didn't give comprehensive finals. The last test was simply the last test of the semester. He rarely put essay questions on his tests, as they were not objective and difficult to grade. Life did not have to be complicated and Harry was determined to keep it that way.

Dolan had never forgotten the moron who taught his anatomy and physiology class years ago. The entire physiological portions of the test were essays. Why would anyone do that to the students or himself? Subjective grading in science classes completely contradicted itself.

Harry entered the liberal arts office to check his mail which was kept in slots on one wall. A bundle of papers was jammed into the slot marked, *H. Dolan*. He pulled them out and sat in a one of the chairs placed before a coffee table. The furniture was all twenty or thirty years old and uncomfortable. It was mostly junk mail concerning the full-time faculty, so Harry wished they wouldn't bother him with it at all. Dolan leaned back in the black vinyl-coated chair to while away ten minutes and tossed the papers into a small trash can next to the chair.

———————•—•—•———————

"Okay! Any questions before we start?" Dolan rubbed his hands together. The students remained silent. "Get out a piece of notebook paper and write your name in the top right-hand corner, then put your phone number and major in that order. When you're finished, pass them up front." Baffled expressions and the shuffling of feet made Harry laugh. "No. You didn't miss anything, but at least I know that you took the time to read the handout. Sorry, I had a high school teacher do that to me and I just had to try it!" He retrieved his backpack from under the table at the front of the room and placed his notes and Bass manual into it. "Let's cut out a little early tonight. It's supposed to sleet tonight and it's raining out there now. Remember, you've got one more week to get your projects turned in, see you next Wednesday!"

———◦———◦———◦———

The air was chilly and the rain cold as the night students hurried across the grass toward the parking lot near the stadium. Wichita State University had no football team, but the stadium remained as an elaborate border around the track. Harry had voted against the football team as a student, alumni and instructor over the past fifteen years. It made no sense to do without academic journals such as *The New England Journal of Medicine* to support athletic teams. Quality education had to come before research and sports at a university, though Dolan knew the issue was a hot one. Wet asphalt glistened under the street lights as Harry half jogged to his white Suburban. He still liked the rain, even after spending many months being drenched in Vietnam and Cambodia. There had been no relaxing and listening to the rainfall there as it never stopped the Viet Cong. Charlie had no sense of Western battlefield honor and he did not play fair. The monsoons poured so hard it was difficult to keep your eyes open or to hear anything beyond the sound of water beating down the vegetation.

The raindrops were cold, but Dolan titled his head to the clouds and took a deep breath of fresh air, only mildly concerned with his safety. Wichita State was located in a bad neighborhood and someone had already lost her life in a drive by shooting not long ago, but Harry had been in much worst places.

The headlights of the Chevy lit up the porch of the Dolan house and the stormy sky made the house appear gothic. He really wished that his mother and grandmother had lived to see him own it, as they both had loved majestic old houses. The last owner was an eighty-year-old woman named Susan Decker who had a wonderful flare for decorating. Harry hadn't changed anything, as her taste was pleasant and elegant.

The large windows in front still had the original stained-glass border like the panes in the heavy oak door, and there was a window seat in the dining room that reflected the yellows and reds of the glass. The house had five bedrooms and a bath upstairs. Downstairs consisted of a huge living room with a fireplace, a library, dining room, utility room and a kitchen large enough to have an island in the middle. The old house was Dolan's pride and joy. The flashing red light on the answering machine was prominent in the dark living room. Harry flipped on the light and hit the play button as he hung up his blazer in the front closet. The first message was from a nervous sounding young man.

"Um, Mr. Dolan? I'm Tim Walker. My reserve unit is going to Bosnia and I need to take the final earlier if I can…sorry, I just found out. My number is 555-7895, uh, thank you." Harry shook his head as his listened to the anxious young student. Bosnia would be another waste of lives just like 'Nam.

After a beep the second message played. "Harry! Hey, we finally got to buy that Simmons property, you know, the one that's been caught up in probate for years? I could only afford four-hundred acres, but oh, Harry! Jesus, call me back will ya?"

It was Blake Gayle, a guy Harry had met in Vietnam. Dolan took a bullet in the thigh in the Plain of Reeds area of the Mekong Delta and young Captain Gayle had removed it for him in a shitty field hospital. The two men had much in common and had kept in touch through the years. Blake had retired from the army as a major and settled in Idaho. The land he was referring to had been fought over by three brothers for over a decade until two of them had been hit head on by a dump truck.

Suddenly the battle was over and the surviving son divided the land into sections and sold it off. The Gayles bought the land that abutted their own. The third and fourth messages were hang ups. It was probably more of those telemarketer assholes trying to sell Dolan crap that he didn't need. It was too late to return Blake's call, so Harry took a long hot shower then emerged in sweat pants and a tee shirt bearing the statement, SNIPER: If You Run, You'll Only Die Tired! He made a big glass of ice tea, and toast with crunchy peanut butter. Instead of watching the news Dolan turned to *Law and Order* on the A&E channel and dropped into his blue recliner. Harry grabbed the remote just as his new Basset hound crept up to the arm of the chair. She was named "Orphan" after the Orphan brigade of the Civil War, which found itself belonging to no one when Kentucky joined the Union. The moniker fit the dog, as both litters she had whelped produced spinal deformities, which made the pups drag their hind legs. Orphan wasn't wanted for breeding and the buyers didn't want a spayed pet, so Dolan paid twenty dollars for her. He liked not being the only mammal in the house. She barked while jumping up and down on her front legs, floppy ears swinging with the motion. Orphan's bowl must be empty and that was a situation that the dog did not tolerate well despite the fact her belly nearly polished the floor.

Chapter Two

Hagar, Idaho was in Idaho County, Idaho, between the towns of White Bird and Gospel Peak, an elevation more than eight thousand feet. The county residents were spread out over the densely wooded hills. Hagar was rustic and catered to fishermen and hunters that journeyed northwest in search of their pioneer past. The majority of them left for home with no trophies, no ammo and a realization that their ancestors may have been shoemakers in Boston.

The people there were very conservative, football and apple pie types. It was America, right or wrong to the beer drinking, flannel shirt and blue jean crowd of Hagar. The laws were based on the Bible and applied to all except niggers, kikes, fags and anyone else that would not be invited to join the Klan. The locals basically tolerated the tourists, which is how Hagar men viewed the soft, city types that wanted to play mountain man for a few days a year. For the sake of the economy, Hagar citizens put up with the upper-middle class yuppies, their Bravados, their cell phones, barely used rifles and brand new, authentic mountain man attire. Many were proud to have a Viking cartoon in the Sunday paper with the same name as their town. But those that believed the name Hagar had a Norse background would have been disappointed to learn that the town's name in Hebrew means, forsaken.

Dr. Gayle loved the wilderness. He loved the way the clouds drifted down and settled on the tall pine trees, giving them a smoky, noble appearance. The air was fresh, clean and scented with pine, and Blake looked forward to getting up each day to see patients in the local clinic with his two partners. The doctor had fallen in love with the country after years of gazing at his wife Laura's pictures of her native Washington State. His father-in-law had been assigned to the Puget Sound area when in the Navy and remained there after he did his six-year hitch. Laura worked on her husband for twenty years to convince him they should retire in the Pacific Northwest and not his native New Jersey. He wasn't a hard sell. As a boy Blake's favorite author was Jack London with his tales of the rugged northwest. After years of being stationed in tropical ports with no seasons and hot, humid temperatures, the rough weather of northern Idaho was a welcome change. Of course, Gayle didn't run into the exotic viruses that he had in the army, but there was always a tradeoff of some sort in life.

Gayle had long coveted the land that bordered his own to the east. The Simmons brothers fought for years over the property though none of them liked to hunt or fish. It was almost virgin territory, as the land had been posted to trespassers for more than fifteen years; nearly two decades of forest area untouched by human hands and an enormous lake with fish that had never seen a lure; it had cost Blake plenty, but it was worth it. He hoped to get Harry up there in the spring to help him explore it.

The doctor also wanted Dolan's company because he **had** not made many friends since moving to Hagar almost a decade ago. It seemed that he or Laura was always saying something to alienate the local population and they had little in common with them. The only friend Blake had made so far **was** the veterinarian, Tom Tannahill. Tom had grown up in the area, but had trouble dealing with the new white supremacist attitudes of his childhood playmates.

Laura was experiencing some of the same difficulties with the people that Blake had, though not to the same degree. The women in town were more open-minded than the ones that lived scattered about the hills, but not much more. She was not used to the ignorance these women displayed, or to the blind way many of them obeyed their husbands. It wasn't easy for Laura to take it all seriously. Women in the area were not as vocal with their ethnic opinions, but it hung around them like polluted auras.

Many of the local boys assumed that because Gayle was ex-military that he would be consumed with weaponry, the white race and Christianity. Hunting and the killing should be sacred pastimes for him. These ignorant clods knew nothing about what it meant to be a soldier. Harry would not like most of the citizens in Hagar, but maybe they could just avoid them. All Blake wanted was to enjoy his stress free practice and the beautiful land his family owned. He had no interest in any Aryan cause.

Five months later near the end of April, Dr. Gayle's waiting room was swamped with sniffing, coughing patients. He was expecting Tannahill to meet him at the clinic so they could go do a cursory survey of the property. Tom had never been on the land either, as the Simmons family had possessed it for generations and did not believe in sharing it. It didn't look as if Blake would make it, as this Friday afternoon everybody in town seemed to have some sort of ailment. The outing would have to wait until the next morning.

Most of the snow had melted from the clinic parking lot when Tannahill stepped into the warm waiting room. It had not snowed for two weeks and he was looking forward to checking out Gayle's new playground. He flipped his blonde hair around to knock off the snow blown into it from the clinic roof and surrounding trees. The rectangular room was full of coughing, sneezing patients and kids fighting over magazines. At least dogs didn't grumble about old copies of *Newsweek*. "Is he busy?" Tom asked with a sarcastic smile.

The receptionists peered over wire-framed glasses. "Why no, we've been bored stiff all day…he's taping in his office now. If you hurry you might catch him before he disappears into an exam room." Helen Wright still retained her Scottish accent after two decades in the states. She was an older woman with boundless energy and meticulous organizational skills. Doctors Gayle, Michaels and Spindle would be lost without her.

Blake put down his pocket tape recorder then leaned back in the swivel chair, massaging a sore neck. He glanced sideways as Tannahill entered the small office.

"I should have gone to med school, then I could have sat on my ass all day!" The vet pulled up a chair across the large desk from his friend.

"I'd rather be staring at strep throat than shoving my finger up a cat's ass." Gayle spun around to face Tom. "I'm not gonna get out of here any time soon, want to try for tomorrow?"

"I wondered. Yeah. Why not? Hope nobody out there has the plague, the air must be full of little beastules."

"Your concern for humanity is overwhelming." Blake pushed his dark bangs back out of his face. He really needed to find time for a haircut. "Dr. Schweitzer, please feel free to lend a hand!" Gayle gestured toward the waiting room for the mock offer.

"No, thanks. I wouldn't know how to deal with anything that had a brain large enough to question my brilliance. Sweet of you to offer though."

Tom removed his gloves. The building was too hot for him. Gayle let out a breath. He was actually quite tired now that he had stopped moving for a while. "Well, the wilderness will still be there tomorrow."

"You bet. It's getting kind of cloudy. Don't think we'll get snow, but there are definitely some raindrops overhead. I'll meet you at your place in the morning, take it slow, Blake."

"Don't think I have a choice. I'd better say hello to Mr. Caffeine." Dr. Gayle laughed half-heartedly and waved to Tom as he stepped out into the hall.

"Want me to close this?" Tannahill gestured to the office door made of a light-colored wood.

"No, I have three patients waiting in tiny exam rooms. I'll see ya, Tom." Blake closed the folder on his desk and stood up, grabbing his stethoscope as he stepped around the desk. "God I hate the flu!"

Tom Tannahill zipped up his blue parka as he went down the carpeted hallway. He tossed out a comment on how dogs don't get the flu as he headed for the clinic entrance. The clouds didn't wait long to begin drowning the town of Hagar, prompting Tom to pull the hood of his coat up over his head. His tan corduroy pants darkened with raindrops as Tannahill jogged through the parking lot. The windows in his Ford truck began to fog up as he searched his box of tapes for, *The Mama's and Papa's Greatest Hits*. When he found the tape he popped it into the cassette player, started the ignition and pushed the knob on the heater to defrost. Tannahill lived a few miles east past the Gayle's property and would pass it on the way home. He felt sorry for Blake as the guy had little time for just goofing off, and he was more excited about the land than Tom had ever seen him.

By the time Tannahill's truck rolled down the highway, Tom could hardly see the white lines on the road through the downpour. Despite the fact that the scenery was blurred by the rain, the veterinarian smiled as Blake's new land came into view. He and Blake were like two little boys with new ball gloves who couldn't wait for it to stop raining so that they could play.

The access road was just ahead and Tannahill decided to pull in when the rain pounding the roof of the truck drowned out

Cass Elliot. There was an iron gate barring the old road to the property, which was supposed to lead to a house that had not been occupied in at least sixty years. Tom had never seen it nor had anyone he knew, but he doubted the place would be standing now.

The coffee from his thermos was still hot as Tannahill took small sips. Visibility was limited to about fifty yards into the trees as the woods were thick in the area and a fog hung close to the ground. A short bridge held the truck over a deep ditch below that was already running with rainwater. Then he heard a noise. Tom sat up straight at what he thought was a scream. The rain had slackened enough to see the trees more clearly and Tannahill cracked the window to aid his hearing. It wasn't screaming, really, but he couldn't be sure. Was someone being tortured on Blake's newly acquired territory?

Tom was no hunter, as he preferred to heal animals, not kill them, so he had no rifle in the truck. A lug wrench firmly in hand, Tannahill climbed over the gate and slowly made his way down the abandoned road. His view was marred by the raindrops hitting his glasses, but Tom couldn't see without them. There were several voices that came through the trees to the left and they had a crazy edge to them. He should return to town and call the sheriff, that's what he needed to do, but something made him stop.

The trees were connected together in a weird sort of foggy weave and something rose up out of that gray mist. Beings with horns and antlers danced on two legs, howling and shrieking until they saw him. Tom's lips dropped to a frown as he said, "What the hell?"

Chapter Three

Harry sat at this desk at the forensic center finishing up paperwork before he took his vacation in June. The center had the look and feel of a hospital or a research facility with its antiseptic environment and people running around in lab coats. You never knew what would happen from one day to the next when working for the medical examiner. Dolan loved the unexpected and every case was different, except for the fact that someone was dead.

It could get exhausting, especially since his boss, Carol Whitechapel, was a workhorse and expected everyone else to be as well. She wasn't without a sense of humor though.

When Dolan remarked about how funny it was that someone with the last name of Whitechapel was a medical examiner she replied, "I'll have you know that the Whitechapel section of London is a very posh neighborhood now!" Harry had responded with the observation that Jack the Ripper was British royalty and would be even more at home in Whitechapel now.

The last week of his vacation Harry planned to spend with Blake exploring what he called his "virgin" forest. Dolan didn't believe that in all those years no one at all had stepped onto the Simmons land, posted or not. At the very least, teenagers had wandered through the forest simply because it was posted with no trespassing signs. Without a doubt, poachers had also found the area appealing since the owners had no interest in hanging around and there could even be old traps still buried under the brush. Before he did any traipsing about the woods, Harry wanted to spend some time planting flowers and painting Civil War battle scenes, as doing those things relaxed him the most. When he finished typing his report, Dolan hit the print button and leaned back in the office chair. A headache had begun right behind his eyes and he closed them against the fluorescent lights.

The phone ringing jolted him upright and he rolled the chair over to the right side of his desk. "Dolan," he said into the phone.

"Harry? It's Laura Gayle."

"Yeah, Laura, what's up?" Harry couldn't remember a time when Laura had been the one to call him. What couldn't wait two weeks?

"I know you were planning to come up here the last week of your vacation, but is there anyway you could change things around? If you can't, you just can't."

"Laura, what's wrong?"

"Something has happened to Blake's friend, Tom. He's just vanished…something isn't right here, Harry." Dolan found himself focused entirely on Laura's words. She was about the most unshakable woman that he knew, aside from Sr. Marcella, the nun Harry had encountered while in South America. It took a great deal to upset Laura who panicked over nothing.

The last time Harry had heard that kind of strain in her voice, Blake had been exposed to the Marburg virus while in Zaire. Somehow, Dolan didn't think it was hemorrhagic fever that bothered Laura now. "What happened with Tom?" Blake had mentioned a vet named Tom Tannahill, but little else about him.

"We don't know, Harry. Blake saw him last Friday afternoon in the office. They made plans to meet the next day at our house then Tom left. No one had seen or heard from him in a week, but his truck was parked at his house."

"What do the police say?" "The cops aren't too concerned and I don't understand why. They gave us the usual bullshit about how he's a grown man that doesn't have to tell anybody his plans, but Blake went up to Tom's house when he didn't show up that morning. There was no sign that he'd been home at all...he's very neat and clean, he wouldn't wear the same clothes two days in a row, but his suitcase is still in the bedroom closet along with all of his clothes. The ones Tom wore that Friday are not in the hamper or washer. Harry, he's the only vet here. He wouldn't just take off, not without calling Blake and canceling their plans."

"How's Blake holding up?" Dolan had a feeling that the blank canvas in the attic was going to remain blank.

"Tom was his only real friend here. He's really upset, but trying not to let on. Neither of us has a good feeling about this. I don't know why I called you, or what you could do."

Harry thought back over the years to that shy, gentle doctor who had put in long, stressful hours in a chaotic field hospital. Drenched in blood, tears and death, Dr. Gayle managed to make time to talk to his wounded patients and never spoke a harsh word. Blake smiled brightly at every picture given to him of wives, girlfriends and children and listened to stories of back home even when he could barely keep his eyes open. Dr. Gayle went out of his way for the injured soldiers, Dolan included among them. If Blake needed help then Harry would be there.

"I may not be able to help at all, but I can come up sooner. I'll drive so I can bring Orphan."

"I really appreciate this, Harry. Please be careful driving. There are some real idiots on the road anymore." Laura's voice sounded better.

"I've seen some of the worst shit holes on the planet, tracked some of the meanest SOBs in the world and you're worried about me on America's highways!" Dolan laughed.

"Just watch out, Mr. Bond. Call us when you get ready to leave, okay?"

"I'll do that. Talk to ya soon, Bye now." Harry would get Mrs. Murphy, who lived a half mile down the road, to watch the house while he was gone. She was a retired school teacher that missed very little that went on around her. So much for gardening and painting this vacation!

Chapter Four

The room was dark except for the flickering candles that lit up the preacher's eyes as he paced back and forth before the group of men who sat in metal folding chairs, their attention owned by the man with the narrow mustache.

"We have to be strong in these days. We are God's chosen ones. The Apocalypse is waiting for us gentlemen! God is relying on us to give this planet back to the white race. The time is running out. I want all of you to paint the Aryan symbol on the roof of your houses. It has to be seen when Marduk returns for us. I'm telling you that there is no time to waste in this endeavor. If you want to be rescued and rule this world from above, get that symbol on your property and then get it on yourselves. Some of you have yet to do that, do you want to be left behind with the mud people?" The men suddenly came to life when one man replied, "Shit, no!"

Shouts of Rahowa (short for, racial holy war) synchronized into a chant. The struggle was one to be taken very seriously by the white people of earth, but only a few of them realized the importance of Aryan superiority. It would be up to the wolf warriors to restore Anglo-Saxon rule to Christ's kingdom on earth since most white people had hopped on the equal rights band wagon. It was enough to make decent men sick.

"We will strain the impurities from this world with no mercy. Those that mix their gift of Aryan blood with that of Hell bound Jews or other types of mud people will be the first to go!"

The leader of the Elder Church of the New Order wiped the beads of sweat from his forehead that his stringy, black bangs did not soak up. He cut the hair over his lip to resemble Adolph Hitler's mustache. Hansel Berge believed Hitler to be a great warrior in the fight against the evil of Chaos, of which the Jews were servants. Chaos is the oldest evil of all, the origin of the Satan tales. Hitler was a great watcher who had been struck down by the watered down Christians of the modern world.

The idiots did not understand the enormous burden of the white race to keep the earth pure for the return of Jesus Christ. Berge's followers were a step above the other Aryan groups, such as the Aryan Brotherhood, which had a compound nearby at Hayden Lake. The Elder Church represented the Sons of Marduk, the God that first knocked evil into the dark abyss of Hell. Marduk, Jesus and Hitler had all been temporarily stricken by the filth of the mud people. It was up to the true believers, like the Sons of Marduk to save what was left of the white race.

"We have a problem, men. We lost the most holy of places to an outsider. A man who will treat any nigger, kike or spick that walks through his door, not that we have many of those around here." Berge chuckled. The crowd laughed in agreement and Berge continued. "Now, he is a white man and a healer, so he has some merit, but spring is coming soon and we cannot have our rites screwed up by some college boy out there pissing all over the woods marking his territory. Hansel took a sip of water from a glass smudged with dirty fingerprints. "I have a nonviolent solution." He let the idea hang in the air until someone asked about it. "We don't have much money individually, but together we own enough property of get a loan to buy our land back from Gayle. We can form our own corporation or better yet, our own religion and be tax free!"

The members of the Elder Church swallowed beer, rubbed unshaven chins, mumbled and belched through the thought process. They had never really been all that organized in the past. While most believed that there was a racial holy war to be waged and won for all Anglo-Saxons, the belief had never cost much before.

"I don't know, Hans, if I lost my house over this I'd have my own holy war at home!" Jim Brentlinger took slaps on the shoulders from those in the same situation.

Berge's face suddenly darkened, his twinkling eyes fastened on Brentlinger. "So, you think this is some kind of social club, do you? A fart-off place to get away from your old lady! Well, you little pussy whipped moron...go join the Goddamned National Guard or the fucking Elks if that's what you're looking for!" Berge's chest heaved with each breath. He clenched and unclenched his fists as he paced like a wolf surveying sheep, his head shook back and forth in total amazement.

"God save us all! We expect to overcome the Zionist Occupational Government and its nigger police with a bunch of rednecks that think this is all about beer and barbecue! Holy shit! I may as well just go out to Detroit and recruit me some skinheads, at least, by God, they've got dedication and balls!" Hans stormed across the room to put on his coat.

"Don't go, Hans! He's sorry. It's just that..." Mike Rogers tried to explain the situation, but was interrupted by the preacher.

"If we don't win this war, people, it won't matter what kind of financial trouble you're in. Don't you all get it? I've preached and tried to teach the true Gospel and I get this kind of crap in return. I wonder if Butler had this sort of grief?"

Robert Butler was a minister for the Church of Jesus Christ Christian. His group, The Aryan Nations, had their own compound at Hayden Lake. Butler, like his ordainee, Mark Thomas, of Allentown, could whip his followers into a frenzy; an unquestioning fury and hate for all non-whites. Hansel Berge was hurt and disappointed in the lack of enthusiasm by his own followers. Berg could see his own group falling apart like Butler's two years earlier. The great leader had died recently with his dreams in the toilet.

"Just what do you people think we've been doing in those woods? You think that it is a game when we summon the Watcher? Sweet Jesus! If we aren't strong mentally and emotionally, this whole mess can be turned back on us. Anyone that does not believe in the Elders, the Ancients and Chaos can just hit the door now!" Berge licked his thin lips and placed his bony hands on even bonier hips. "You dick brains better think long and hard about what we've done in those woods...very long and hard"

Chapter Five

"Things I do for my friends!" Harry grumbled to himself and the Basset hound that peered forlornly out the passenger side of the Suburban. The trip had been long and the weather a challenge from Denver to Idaho. "You know, I should have just left you home and flown up here." Dolan announced to the dog. Orphan let out a groan as if insulted.

The town of Hagar wasn't all that impressive to Harry. It had the typical main street of any village in the middle of a state highway. The gas stations and convenience stores were locally owned with none of the flash of the national chains. There was no McDonald's, no twenty-four hour stores and no large discount store such as Wal-Mart or Target. He couldn't imagine why the Gayles would want to live in a place like Hager. Snow still clung stubbornly to the curbs and rooftops, but had melted considerably in the yards and sidewalks of the residents. Dolan did not get a warm feeling from the town, but maybe it was better when spring was in full force.

Harry had been to visit Blake when he was stationed in Virginia and Panama, but this was his first trip to Idaho. Laura had said to follow the highway signs east through town for eight miles, then watch for a mailbox shaped like an ambulance. It was kind of hokey, but the novelty mailbox made a good landmark.

The woods were dense and dark past the first few feet from the road. It reminded Dolan of the Franklin Woods close to Machais, Maine where the trees linked together high above the highway and darkened the route. Sometimes it was necessary to turn on the headlights during the day if it was cloudy. Along the road to the east was a lake and near the water lay an enormous flat rock. Local stories had it that every year a mangled body would be found placed on the rock, but Dolan never knew the validity of the tales. He hoped Hagar didn't have the same sort of legend.

The Gayle house was probably eighty yards from the highway and could not be seen from the road. It was a good thing that Blake got funny with the mailbox. Harry pulled up next to a green Explorer about the same time that a woman appeared at the front door. The storm door was clear from the top to bottom to show off the ornate wood door behind it. Laura smiled and waved then motioned for him to come in.

The architecture was wonderfully suited to the forest environment around it. The house with its natural wood siding blended in with the pine trees and the windows were paned glass. Hunter Green drapes adorned the large living room windows with white, lacy panels. Laura opened the door for Harry who stamping his feet to knock off the snow of the treads.

"So, how was the trip?" she asked while watching the dog yellow the snow near her vehicle

"You owe me big…Orphan! She's got the whole damned forest and picks the driver's side of your car to pee on, go figure." Dolan feigned confusion.

"She house broke?" Laura asked as the Basset ran past her to the fireplace.

"Of course! You should know by now that I wouldn't allow dog turds in the house."

She rolled her eyes. "You want the spare room upstairs or the on down here?" Laura took Harry's coat.

The living room was huge with dark brown beams supporting a vaulted ceiling. The fireplace was in the center of the south wall with a bedroom to right of it.

"I'll take the one downstairs. Sometimes I can't sleep and I just get up and read. You wouldn't have any coffee made?" Dolan eased down into an overstuffed chair. "When's Blake coming home?" he asked loudly enough for Laura to hear him in the kitchen. Laura poked her head out the kitchen door.

"You're asking for coffee?" Harry usually only drank cold liquids. "He should be here in an hour or so, I don't think he plans on being late tonight. It seems like everybody has been getting this flu around here." She poured two cups of coffee and returned to the front room.

"This is real coffee, right? Not that cappa-whatever."

"It's just plain old black coffee, Mr.Nineties. I wouldn't think of wasting my fancy stuff on you!" She gave Harry his cup then sat on a couch that matched Dolan's chair which was a dark green and burgundy plaid.

"How's work going, not in anymore trouble I presume?" Laura referred to Dolan being suspended for obstruction of justice on the Wilkerson case.

"I've been very good, but speaking of trouble, you really think Tom has met foul play and is just not off frolicking somewhere?" Harry took a sip of the coffee then tried not to choke when the liquid burned its way down his esophagus. He had requested something hot to drink as earlier in the day Dolan had chilled and couldn't seem to warm up. Laura stirred the cream into her coffee while watching the color turn from dark brown to a light tan.

"He wasn't exactly a favorite with the locals, even though Tom grew up here. He changed a lot when he went to college in California and some of his liberal attitudes didn't play well with his former pals. Plus, he was just as excited about exploring the property as Blake…Harry, there just isn't any way that Tom walked off without telling anyone, including his employees at the animal clinic."

Dolan took a coaster from the end table next to his chair and placed his hot cup on it. The coasters were made to look like a stack of logs cut crossways.

"They didn't find any footprints around his truck or house. The ground was still pretty hard when Tom disappeared, so I don't think there would have been any." She let out a deep sigh.

"So what's really wrong?" Harry leaned forward with his elbows on his knees.

"Oh, I shouldn't have prodded Blake to come here…I don't remember things being this way when I was a kid. Of course we lived in Washington and maybe Idaho was full of these Hitlerites then too."

Dolan recalled the days he had spent at Fort Lewis, which were few as he was always being sent somewhere to ply his trade. He had heard the stories of trip wire vets roaming the Idaho wilderness, but knew little of the right wing groups in the area.

"You mentioned the SS fan club. You think they have something to do with Tom vanishing?"

"I don't really know, but I thought of them first. I don't know if Tom actually had any confrontations with them, but the Neo-Nazi groups came to mind first." Laura finished her coffee and placed the cup on her own mini cross section of logs.

"It's really beautiful here; don't blame yourself for misjudging the population. Surely not everyone is on the Hitler bandwagon?"

"Well, you have to watch what you say, how you say it and whom you say it to…it can get stressful."

"I have to admit that my first impression of Hagar wasn't that great, but I thought it was just my suspicious mind." Dolan tested his coffee again. "Jesus, Laura. Do you always boil your coffee?"

"Coffee has to be very hot to bring out its full flavor." She adopted a lecture-like tone.

"If it melts your taste buds, it won't matter how damn good it tastes."

The sound of Blake's car engine struggling to shut down preceded the front door opening. Gayle had been in a bad mood since Tannahill failed to meet him that morning. He had wondered about every male patient that day perched on an exam table. Had those ears heard Tom last or did those eyes see his last moments on earth?

"Harry! See you brought your fleabag." Blake nodded toward the dog snoring near the fireplace.

"Think I wore her out, which is easy considering her favorite activity is napping."

"Honey, need some coffee?" Laura asked as she stood up.

"Actually, I'd rather have a beer." Gayle laid his coat across the back of the couch.

"Good choice, your wife's coffee could make the enemy surrender." Harry blew on the steaming liquid.

"Didn't think you drank coffee, Harry? So, solved any good murders lately?" Blake took a bottle of oatmeal stout from Laura then sat beside her.

"Nothing interesting. Sounds like you've got more mysteries up here."

"We've got something all right. I just don't know what. The cops took a report, which was amazing as I didn't know any of those clowns could write, but they still think he's just screwing off somewhere." Blake kicked off his shoes and pointed his feet toward the fireplace. Tom didn't just take off!"

"Well, why don't we go out to his place and see if there is anything at all to go on?" Harry suggested as he sipped the now drinkable coffee.

"Yeah, it's a starting point anyway. I have a key, but the cops didn't show any interest in looking around." Gayle ran a hand through his hair which remained staying upright. "I just don't think he ever made it home."

"Maybe not, but if the cops didn't take his disappearance seriously, then we need to check things over, it's a place to start, Blake." Dolan tried to instill some hope into his old friend, but lost the battle with the laugh building in his throat.

"What?" Gayle asked and looked surprised when Laura began to chuckle and looked toward the top of his head.

"Not all of us have that, 'I can ride with the top down', kind of hair!" Blake pretended to be insulted.

"That's the first time you've shown any humor in days." Laura remarked. "Why don't you guys just hang out tonight and get any early start in the morning?"

"You're right. Yeah, Harry, let's do it."

"Okay, but I tolerate no interruptions when *Law and Order* is on, not even for a visit from ET," Dolan joked.

"Now that's the Harry I know." Blake commented while pointing the remote at the thirty-five-inch Magnavox. "Should check out the weather situation, but I don't think it's supposed to do anything."

In the loft overhead, Stark Gayle, the teenage son of the couple, crouched against the wall. He had been listening to the adults below discuss the disappearance of Tom Tannahill. The whole scene scared the shit out of him. Since they had first discovered that Tom was gone, Stark had run twice as many miles and climbed the bleachers with such ferocity that if it were not for the fencing at the top, he would have run right off the edge. He was a nervous wreck. His white Nikes creaked as he rocked back and forth on them, wondering how long it would take for his turn to come around and for everyone else to figure it all out.

Chapter Six

Jim Brentlinger winced in pain as his shoulder scraped against the door of his twenty-year-old pickup truck. He didn't know much about medicine or infection control, but the condition of Captain Squid's tattoo shop left much to be desired and it wasn't that Jim didn't like the man or his old lady, Hoover, as they were nice people, but it wouldn't kill them to clean up once in a while! The couple were both bikers that lived in the apartment over the shop and would lend a hand to anyone that needed one.

Brentlinger didn't have the balls to ask Hoover how she got her nickname, but he wondered about it now and then. The symbols etched into his skin were required by the Elder Church. On the left biceps was a five-pointed star and on the right a triangle with its apex extending outward and ending in two circles: symbols of the Aryan race and both oozed with infection.

Hansel Berge was sitting at a grungy desk adding up receipts from his auto repair shop when the front door swung open and banged the wall.

A blast of frigid air sailed over the desktop. Jesus! Get that door shut!" Berge rubbed his greasy hands together. The cow bell attached to the door clanged loudly as it shut.

"You picked a funny place to live for a guy that can't take the cold."

Berge grunted. "Fortunately for us, neither can the niggers. I can bear it. Aryans have a nack for adapting to any situation."

"I hope my arms adapt to that Goddamned ink! Ain't natural to carve pictures into your body." Brentlinger slipped off his coat to relieve some of the pressure on his wounds.

"None of the other boys has said anything about having troubles with theirs and mine didn't hurt, sure you ain't just a wuss?" A crooked grin made one side of Berge's Hitler mustache creep upward.

"Fuck you, mine's infected. I might have to get some antibiotics or something', it's gross. Shit, it's been two weeks and I still got puss draining all over the place…"

Berge choked on his hot toddy. "Thanks for sharing, dickhead. You didn't get yours at the compound, did ya?" He referred to the Aryan Nations headquarters at Hayden Lake.

"Nah, remember I had to work when you guys went up there, so I went to that biker, you know? The one off the highway? The place was a pig sty."

"Jesus Jim! Why did ya let him do it then?" Hans asked in amazement.

"Cause you said it had to be done now, remember? We'll be left behind with the kikes and niggers if we don't have them on us. Son-of-a-bitch, you think I'd have these things on me otherwise?" Brentlinger had an attitude now.

Berge stood up and leaned menacingly over the desk. "Use your head, boy, they ain't gonna want ya if you're sick. Go get some pills for that, you jerk." Hans sat back down in the old office chair.

Brentlinger looked at the dressing that was caked with blood and pus again and nodded in agreement. "Yeah, I will."

"Got them symbols painted on your roof yet?" The adding machine rattled on as Hans totaled sums.

"No, old lady has got me fixing shit around the place, told her I was gonna paint the barn next though, so I'll do it then." Jim was getting irritated with Berge's bossiness.

"You gettin' worked up about Saturday? Man, I love them rituals."

Berge looked up at Brentlinger. "Brings ya right in touch with nature, don't it?"

Jim agreed while thinking of the raw, primitive, animalistic feelings the rituals brought in him. "Yeah, it does do somethin' for me, but it's hard to explain."

"Most modern men can't even begin to appreciate what it means to be a man, the top of the food chain...they're so damned busy with their computers and their designer colognes and being sensitive to their pussy, that's it's a wonder that their balls don't just suck up into their bellies and become ovaries!" Berge's face reddened.

Brentlinger stifled a laugh. Berge had a way of saying the funniest things and not mean to be funny. You did not laugh at Hans when he didn't mean to be funny. "Know what ya mean."

"Now, my old lady knows who wears the pants in our house. She wouldn't dream of telling me what to do or not do."

Jim just nodded. He didn't quite buy into Berge's theory that women must completely obey their husbands. Sometimes Brentlinger relied on his wife to say no to his stupid ideas, especially when it came to finances. She understood that at times he just needed to talk about a scheme and not really do it. Hell, if he had a wife like Louise Berge they would have lost the house years ago. Berge was right though, the woman wouldn't think of having an original opinion must less argue with her husband.

"Think them woods is safe now they belong to that doctor?" Jim was wild about being caught.

"Well, he don't strike me as the woodsy type anyway, especially with his buddy doing a disappearing act, but eventually, Gayle will be a problem. Course, that's why I suggested we buy it back from him." Berge blew his nose with the strength of a foghorn then shoved the hanky into the upper pocket of his coveralls.

"Wonder if he won't sell? I don't think he's gonna want to do that."

"Guess we'll have to persuade him that it's in his own best interest to do so."

"Hans, I don't want to go killin' somebody else...I...." Berge sprang out the chair, sending it bouncing off the wall behind him.

"Shut up! Shut the fuck up! You ever say that word again and you'll join him...I make myself very clear?"

A shudder rippled down Jim's spine. There were times when he wished that he could just keep his mouth closed. He definitely was not the smartest owl in the tree.

"So, get yourself to the yuppie doc over there and get yourself healed up. If you're sick when the time comes for Rahowa, then you won't be no better off than the Jews and mud people. Go on now." Berge's voice softened as he walked toward the garage area. "Go on."

Berge's breath hung in the air as he walked across the cement floor to watch Brentlinger climb into his truck from the garage door windows. A fine film of frost coated the glass which blurred the images outside. He pulled a pack of Marlboro's from his shirt pocket beneath the stained coveralls and took a cigarette from it. The sound of Hans tapping the end of the cigarette against a metal lighter filled the garage for several seconds. It was a habit left over from the pre-filter days of smoking when Berge found it necessary to pack the tobacco firmly before lighting up. As Brentlinger drove off, Hans wondered how trustworthy the asshole really was and if the mission was safe with his kind around. Jim Brentlinger tried to be macho, tried to believe in what the Bible said about women being made for men, but he didn't quite cut the mustard.

The Bible should only be interpreted by men such as Hansel Berge, who understood what God was saying. When the Word commanded that a man should leave his parents and cleave to his wife, that's exactly what it meant. The wife and kids became his family and parents no longer had a place or a say in anything, even God hated a mother-in-law.

Once a woman was isolated from bad influences she was much easier to control and God understood that fact. Berge thought that Jim had entirely too much respect for his wife, her mother and their opinions. There were many things tolerated in this modern world that should only be spit upon. Fags, coons, spics, Hebs and blanket-asses all interfered with the full potential of the planet Earth. A very hard line was needed to please God now and keep Him from destroying everything out of very justified anger and the Reverend Berge had volunteered for the task. The planet needed one giant enema!

Chapter Seven

The inspection of Tannahill's house was postponed by the unshaven, unwashed man who perched on the exam table before Dr. Gayle.

"Let's get your temp and blood pressure out of the way, Mr. Brentlinger." Blake explained as stuck a thermometer into the patient's left ear. "102.7…Why don't you take your shirt off and let me see what we've got here?"

Jim slowly removed the plaid flannel shirt. "I should have come sooner, Doc, but I thought a little alcohol would clear it up."

There were bandages on both of Brentlinger's upper arms which were soaked through from drainage. Gayle gingerly removed the one on the right arm first then used a saline solution to clean the wound which was red and swollen around a star shape. The extent of infection was obvious in the yellow drainage and the pockets of pus that made the man's arm look like a piece of bubble wrap.

"You need to be careful about where you get a tattoo, Jim. I'll need to get some blood for the lab and we should do an AIDS test as well, just to be sure."

Brentlinger snapped to attention. "AIDS? Oh, God!" He just couldn't have that fag disease.

"It's just a precaution." Gayle lifted the other bandage to reveal a strange triangle type design. "Where did you get the artwork?"

"Uh, Captain Squid's, you know? It's off the highway south of town?" Brentlinger was dumbfounded.

"They need to be shut down. I don't have anything against tattoo art, but it has to be done responsibly. This kind of thing really makes me mad, Jim." Blake was disgusted by the infected flesh.

Jim hung his head and studied the hairs that lined his beer belly. He had never considered the possibility of AIDS. The boys won't understand getting that homo disease. They'll think he polished some guy's knob with his asshole. Sweet Jesus, he just could not have that. Not that!

"Okay, I guess you better test me. I got a wife."

"You most likely don't have it. But with the amount of infection you've got we have to assume a lack of infection control. Let's just be safe." Gayle rubbed a topical antibiotic into the wounds. "Keep these uncovered at night so they can air out."

"How soon will we know?" Brentlinger asked as sweat beaded on his forehead.

"The lab work will be sent to California, so it takes about two weeks, but don't dwell on it. Come back Monday so I can see how these are healing."

Blake wrote out a prescription. "Get this filled as soon as possible."

Jim carefully pulled his shirt on in silence. He felt sick and didn't know how to tell his wife.

"I suggest you take it easy for a couple of days, stay inside and don't get chilled. Just come on in Monday, you don't need an appointment... be sure you get that filled and get started on it." Blake pointed to the script in Jim's hand.

"Okay, Doc." Brentlinger was sullen. He should never have let Berge talk him into this crap.

"I'll unlock the door for you, Bye now." Blake was anxious to get going and he was uncomfortable with people that ran with Hansel Berge. Gayle didn't know that much about Berge, but what he did know he didn't like and the man's personal appearance was sleazy.

Stark rode with Harry to unlock Tannahill's house. He really liked Dolan, the true macho man. The man had nothing to prove because he was the real thing and enjoyed it. For Harry Dolan it had been easy to be Lt. Colonel Henry Dolan, Army Ranger and a graduate of the Royal Marines Sniper School. He was a combat veteran and now a medical investigator that helped answer questions about death. Nobody would think it strange that Harry wasn't married. A wife and kids would slow him down. But for Stark, life was a struggle, a daily battle in which he tried to remember the role he had assigned himself.

It wasn't easy trying to be the school jock, the big man on campus whose father was a doctor. He was a guy nearly every girl in town wanted to date either because of his looks and status or his father's money. Stark longed for the day when he would take off for college in California. The act could go then and for once in his short life Stark Gayle could relax. He would have no one at all to talk to if Tom was found dead, and Stark was sure the man was dead.

"What are we looking for Harry?" Stark scanned the living room, which was neat and Early American in style.

"Anything out of character or unusual that you didn't know about. We'll just start from the inside out. The guy didn't just disappear for no reason." Harry walked through the living room to the dining room.

"Dad doesn't think he made it home at all. We didn't find his dirty clothes, nothing in the trash from dinner, no dishes in the drainer, nothing." Stark felt his throat tighten.

"Well, his truck made it home somehow without him and that isn't kosher. If we take things slow and be observant, something will jump out at us." Dolan replied, while opening a door in a large, ornate china cabinet. Inside the bottom of the hutch was a pair of candlesticks, and what appeared to be an oversized chalice. Next to the chalice was a large knife with elaborate carvings in the handle. "So, did Tom like to entertain?"

"Here? No. He was more of a wine and cheese kind of guy, not beer and hot wings." Stark peered into the cabinet. "Must be stuff he picked up at auctions? I've never seen it before."

The rest of the dining room revealed nothing of interest, so Dolan strolled down a hallway peeking into rooms until he found a den with a huge mahogany desk at the center. Harry eased down into the swivel chair and opened the middle drawer which contained the usual desk items. He went through each of five drawers without finding anything out of the ordinary. In the bottom left hand drawer there was a pile of canceled checks and a locked metal box that Dolan picked with a paper clip. Inside were some five star medallions and a rosary with the crucifix hanging upside down.

"What the Hell is that?" Stark gawked at the shiny black beads as his uncle held them up to the window.

"Hell is correct. It seems like Tom had another side to him. Blake didn't know about this?"

"Dad? You must be kidding? He doesn't have a sense of humor about this kind of stuff. Nothing against his church."

Harry watched the inverted cross as it twirled around, gleaming in the sunlight. He hadn't expected this sort of thing in Redneck Land, especially from a friend of Blake's. Dolan wasn't sure if the discovery was relevant or not. "I know a woman at the university that teaches comparative religion, maybe this time of year has some sort of significance." Harry spoke of Abby Issac who specialized in pagan religions.

"You think this Satan stuff has something to do with his being gone?" Stark seemed somewhat relieved.

"Who knows? But it wasn't something that I expected to find, so it's a lead worth following." Harry caught what sounded like excitement in the young man's voice.

"So what's going on?" Blake Gayle leaned into the room.

"This!" Harry turned the distorted rosary toward him. Blake squinted.

"Where did you get that?"

"From the desk. A little creepy isn't it?" Harry handed the beads to Gayle who acted as though they would scald his hand.

"It's appalling…I don't understand this." Blake's face appeared pained as he searched the room for answers.

"Tom must have been a real bad boy and we didn't have a clue!" Stark chuckled.

"This isn't funny!" Gayle snapped.

"Blake, we'll figure this out. He may be something he tried a long time ago. It doesn't mean he was a card-carrying Satanist." Dolan stood up and guided Blake to the desk chair.

In truth, Dolan didn't know what to think. He'd heard al the bullshit about satanic ritual abuse with the human sacrifices and how it was supposed to be happening from coast to coast, but Harry had a hard time taking any of the stories seriously. One of the predictions was that Satan would take over the planet in June of 1999, but that date had come and gone without everyone having a 666 burned into their foreheads.

"I thought we were friends…thought we talked about everything."

Gayle mumbled in disbelief.

"We can't really know everything about people, Dad," Stark comforted his father. There were indeed things that his father didn't know about Tom Tannahill.

Chapter Eight

They had gone too close to the road, but the men were swept along with the waves of passion that only a few modern humans knew or could handle. Even those brain deprived Skinheads who etched *Berserker* into their foreheads had no concept of the term. The label had been placed on the wolf warriors of ancient times, the Vikings, by other Europeans. The Berserkers scared the living shit out of the more civilized populations when they would come howling out of the mist wearing wolf skins and leather caps with antlers attached to bring terror to the weak. Berge ran and danced through the woods letting his brain slosh back and forth its pan as he became one with nature. It was a fact that only the strong survived and no accident that God was dog spelled backwards.

It was also a fact totally lost on the bleeding heart Christians of the modern world. Those lily-livered pacifists would one day let the sandniggers shove Allah up every decent white man's ass. Europeans should have let Vlad the Impaler finish the job, but sympathy was the curse of the weak.

The others were just as caught up in the ritual as Berge with the effect of the wine and mushrooms enhancing the illusion of becoming wolves. It was then that they saw him, that nosey bastard. There was no privacy at all anymore, not even in a rain storm in the woods! If they just hadn't strayed so close to the highway it would never have happened. How noble of him to protect his rich doctor friend's land! What was in it for Tannahill? Had Gayle told him that for his loyalty the land from here to the sea was his? Berge doubted it. A knight to the rescue! How droll.

The Sons of Marduk shoved a used snot rag into Tom's mouth and carried him deep into the forest to a spot that overlooked the lake. Berge sent two men in the group back to get rid of the vet's truck while it was still raining and distorting the mud tracks. The rest of them dropped their prisoner onto the ground while they removed the brush that covered the entrance to the bunker. Hans had discovered the old underground room while poaching years ago. It must have been something the military had built or had do with mining, but either way it was quite a find for the Elder Church's leader.

Berge was not sure what to do with Tannahill, so they shackled him in a device that Brentlinger called a "Black Box. It was a hell of a contraption that consisted of handcuffs, a metal box that fit over them, leg shackles attached to the box and a chain that wrapped around the body to hold the whole mess together. Apparently, Brentlinger had stolen it when working as a prison guard. Why he had taken it, Berge had not cared to guess.

The veterinarian was left in the bunker under an old mattress after being knocked unconscious with a large rock. When they returned a day later, Tannahill was still secured, and had a nasty scrape on his forehead from falling while attempting to escape.

Tom was terrified for his life. He tried to scoot away from the men whose dogs he had vaccinated and patched up for one reason or another. The taste of the dirty rag still made Tannahill want to vomit and his joints ached from lying on the cold cement for hours. The night had been long in the dark forest as Tom lay dreading the outcome of his predicament.

"How did you like our accommodations?" Hansel Berge titled his head and clasped his hands over his stomach as if he were a butler asking about the dinner wine. Tannahill used his legs to push away from Berge. "Wasn't satisfactory?

"Looks like he busted his head last night. What are gonna do with him?" Wilbur Wakes turned his bald head toward Berge. Wakes owned the only coin laundry in Hagar. He had been a member of the Aryan Brotherhood, but found them too liberal for his taste.

"Good question, what are we to do with you Mr. Tannahill?" Berge took a few steps toward Tom who had scrunched himself into a corner.

"You know, Hans, I remember when Tom here was a regular guy that looked and acted like the rest of us. Now look at him! He wears Dockers and them suede shoes and he don't hang with us anymore. I think California turned him into a fag." Brentlinger shook his head like a disappointed schoolmarm.

"Yuppie turd rag," Eddie Herman growled. A machinist in nearby Grangeville, Eddie was nearly as educated as Jed Clampett, but didn't have as much common sense.

"Mr. Tannahill ain't what you think he is, boys. Are ya?" Berge crouched down to face Tom who eyes reflected fear and concentration. "Think real hard where you seen me before?"

The shackled man stared at the black eyes and a vision came back to him. Berge used to be heavier and had long hair and a thick beard that nearly covered the pentacle he used to wear around his neck. While in college, Tom had dabbled in Satanism, which he had found to be basically harmless. Then he ran into a Satanic High Priest who called himself, Nicholas, in North Hollywood. Satanism is a religion based on human desires and ambitions and sometimes involves sexual orgies.

Tannahill didn't mind the orgies, it was the sadistic nature of the priest Nicholas that had made him sick. Watching women gulp down the priest's urine and then allow him to cut them and lap up the blood with his tongue was nauseating enough, but

Nicholas made the women of the group copulate with dogs. When they were through with the dog, Nicholas would have the congregation hold the animal down as he plunged a large butcher knife into its chest. Tannahill had only needed to see that ritual once before shelving everything he owned for celebrating the Black Mass. Now he realized that Berge was Nicholas.

"You ain't the typical Yuppie, are ya Tom? Think anybody would bring their pets to you if they were to know what kind of shit you're into?" Berge leaned in close to his captive and almost whispered.

There were no expressions of sympathy from the dozen or so men who stood behind Berge. They were acting crazy like they had the afternoon Tom caught them dancing around in some insane ritual. He suspected the men were on something, though rednecks tended to choose alcohol as their drug of choice.

"Tom, we probably shouldn't have kidnapped you and all, but we can't turn back time. So, we got a problem." Hans stood up and motioned the others to follow him outside.

In a panic, Tannahill struggled to push himself to a standing position by using the wall as support. Berge turned around and told him to get back on the ground and a horrified Tom obeyed. Once satisfied that the vet wasn't going to be any trouble, Hans met his church members near a huge, flat stump several yards from the bunker. There were in fact, twelve Sons of Marduk, not including Berge, who waited to hear the fate of Tom Tannahill. Most figured that they would beat holy hell out of him then let him go with a dark threat, but Hansel Berge had decided that the Elder Church needed to cross a new threshold.

"Get your robes and put them on." Berge referred to the black robes used for worship services. He slipped his own on as the others grabbed theirs from the box near the bunker. "The time has come to show God the how serious we take our mission here on Earth. Until now we have not put ourselves on the line, today that will change. Jesus Christ cannot return to a place where His own followers will not take a stand! "Berge began to get that look in his eyes, the one that Charles Manson liked to flash to the cameras. "Raise your hands, raise them up to nature and all her glory! Now put on your hats and feel the surge of raw courage these animals possessed." Berge referred to the helmets made of deer and dog skulls.

It was too difficult to obtain heads of cougars, bears and wolves, but Aryans had long ago learned to compromise. He began to dance around the stump howling like the Rottweiler on his head could no longer. The other men, wearing their respective animal heads, also danced behind Berge and picked up the tempo with each pass around the large stump. Human imitations of wild animals filled the chilly air as the Sons of Marduk worked themselves into a frenzy. Tannahill, still bound and gagged could see the men outside through the door as he lay on his side, the cold cement numbing his cheek. In a way that only the most primitive part of the human mind can grasp, Tom knew he would die that day. Nicholas had graduated to a new level of depravity, or would after he murdered the terrified veterinarian, who waited with a heart bordering on tachycardia. He thought of the many shaking, shivering little dogs with wide eyes who had stood on his exam table awaiting their fates and he imagined that they felt fully vindicated now.

Berge came to a slow halt and the others followed suit. Hans filled the doorway with a look most other humans attained only with the aid of Angel Dust. Tom was carried out to the stump and lay on his back. The box was opened by Brentlinger and his limbs were freed from the shackles only to be held down by two men on each appendage. Berge retrieved a black case from his gym bag against the bunker and flipped it open where Tannahill could see. He took a large, white-handled knife engraved with the Celestial Script from the case then held the knife like it was Excaliber up to the sky.

"Like Marduk, Jesus and Hitler before us, O Lord, we offer thee this token of our devotion." Hans reached with his left hand

and ripped the buttons from Tom's shirt. The fear in the man's eyes was sweet to Berge as was the way his chest heaved with anxiety. His muscles were taunt with stress and sweat, not sweat from heat, but the perspiration generated by the fight or flight response.   Tom's cheeks puffed out against the duct tape as he struggled to speak. Berge could feel his penis begin to harden under the robe in anticipation of the kill. He plunged the blade deep into Tannahill's sternum. A few of the Sons of Marduk lost the vomit battle and dumped various delicacies on the forest floor. Hans grinned as he made eye contact with the man whose brain wrapped itself around the dagger protruding from the middle of his life force. The muscles in Tom's neck slowly relaxed and urine flooded his pants as Tannahill's last breath escaped with a kind of whimper.

A look of pure satisfaction covered Berge's face as he ejaculated in harmony with the man's demise. There was little blood due to the fact that Tannahill's heart function was abruptly stopped. Steam rose from the open wound as reality presented itself to Berge.

"We have crossed a threshold that has no exit door and we have summoned forces that will be difficult to manage…"

"That a nice way of sayin' we're fucked?" George Chaney asked. He owned a local bait shop.

"Don't lose it now, people. This ain't a game, it never was a game." Berge's voice had a hard edge to it as he observed the faces of his followers.

"The rest of the world ain't gonna give a shit about our racial holy war or about us being the Sons of Marduk!" Brentlinger stated to Hans who still studied his handywork.

Berge looked up. "Don't any of you puss out on me now! Every damned one of you is as guilty as me! Or as honored in the eyes of the Lord, remember what we are all about."

"The world thinks this is a crime, Hans." Someone under a deer's skull remarked.

"I know that! And you remember that God barks, boys. He does not whine and whimper like I'm hearing you do. Be proud that we went the distance, we are for real, not like those swastika toting numbnuts jack booting their way through Skokie!"

"What the hell are we gonna do with him? The ground's still too hard to dig." Brentlinger shivered as sweat ran down his back.

"You're the dog catcher, ain't ya? We'll chop him and burn him. Case closed." Berge smiled a tight little smile under his Hitler mustache.

"Yeah, yeah, that would work." Brentlinger rubbed his chin and the men nodded in relief at the suggestion.

Chapter Nine

The afternoon temperature had increased to the mid-forties and the snow was melting on the roads. The frozen snow shielded by the towering trees, however, remained deep and crusty. Harry and Stark had no trouble plowing through the terrain, but Blake panted and lagged yards behind his son and Dolan.

"Maybe we ought to wait for Dad?" Stark turned to grin at his father.

"Blake, sorry man." Harry stopped to let Gayle catch up. He hadn't considered that the other man might not be in great shape.

"Yeah, well, you know Dad wasn't exactly a Delta."

Blake approached the other two. "I can see your college fund dwindling by the minute. Oh shit! And to think me and Tom couldn't wait to get out here! He worked out about as much as me. Gayle was embarrassed at being so out of breath.

"Don't worry about it, Hell, give me another year and I'll be the same way." Dolan slowed his pace.

"Right, Rambo." Blake's chest ached in the cold air.

"No, I mean it...not about getting flabby, but cutting the Rambo stuff. I think I've finally had my fill of that kind of excitement." Dolan's voice carried a serious tone.

"You had a close call the last time?" Blake now walked shoulder to shoulder with Harry.

"Yeah, it was close, but that's not why I want to quit. I found myself really enjoying working with those nuns and the job almost became secondary, you know? I can't have that kind of assignment be second in mind. "Dolan looked at Gayle.

"You mean you liked working for the good of mankind? Gayle quipped.

"Well, I was doing that when I took out drug lords, but I kind of liked treating the wounded again, helping the poor, you know? Something meaningful."

"But you help the cops solve crimes don't ya? That's good." Stark asked.

"I meant that I liked seeing some results with the living." Harry squinted at the lake just visible over a snow-packed hill.

"God, that's beautiful and it's all mine!" Blake rubbed his hands together in imitation of a miser.

The small lake reflected the snowy hills and pines that surrounded it. The scene was unblemished except for an odd looking brownish disturbance in the distance. Dolan began taking the ground in strides, forgetting the poorly winded doctor in the thrill of the moment.

"Harry! What do you think it is?" Stark jogged in the space between Dolan and his father.

"Can't tell from here." Dolan shouted. A circle of trampled snow and mud spiraled out from around a large, flat stump.

"Looks like somebody had a party." Stark casually commented.

"In this weather?" Harry shivered.

"Why not? Booze will keep you warm and so will girlfriends." Stark nodded toward a brick building sunk half way into the ground.

"Something is just funny…"Dolan studied the snow.

"What?" Gayle wondered aloud. "The snow, it's not just trampled down. Some of it's missing, like when you build a snow fort, but I don't see anything made out of snow anywhere." Dolan's eyes followed some slight depressions in the snow that went toward the lake. Harry chased what appeared to be footprints rounded off by the melting snow down toward the rocky bank. He turned suddenly as Gayle let out a string of curses. Blake had slipped and lay chin deep in crusty snow.

"Jesus, Doc. You and Mother Nature sure have a shitty relationship! Can't believe a tomboy like Laura married such a greenhorn." Harry laughed.

Gayle pushed up his glasses with his middle finger. "So, Miss Fletcher, what do you think happened here?"

"Might be some kind of spring pagan ritual. Abby hasn't got back to me yet, so I don't know." Dolan felt the cold wind that blew over the water and pulled his collar up.

"You're not serious, that kind of shit out here in Redneck land? The only thing they worship in this place is Monday Night Football and the Bible, when they want to beat somebody over the head with it." Stark picked up a large rock and pitched onto the frozen lake.

Blake arched an eyebrow at his son. "You have some other explanation?"

"How about some assholes poached a deer and dressed it out here?" Stark answered.

"Maybe. The satanic stuff may mean nothing at all, but it is a direction to go. There should have been more blood, but who knows, maybe they cleaned it up." Dolan knew that the locals would be aware of the capabilities of the National Fish and Wildlife Forensic Lab in Ashland.

"Why would anyone clean up deer blood? Can they find poachers like regular criminals?" Stark studied the melted tracks then looked back toward the stump.

"They investigate animal deaths just like human homicides at the lab in Oregon. It's really fascinating." Dolan admired the lake and could understand why Gayle wanted to buy the land.

"Why the hell would they go to that much trouble for deer murders?" Blake rubbed his chin which was red from the snow.

"Comes in handy for stopping illegal trades like elephant tusks and the killing of endangered species." Harry grinned at Stark who was laughing. "What's so funny? You don't think Bambi would like to know who murdered his mother?"

"Next we'll have *Law and Order: The Wildlife Forensics Unit*" Stark became somber. "You think Tom is dead?"

Dolan could see Blake anxiously awaiting his response. "I have to tell you it doesn't look good, but with the amount of fruitcakes holding prisoners these days, who knows." Harry let out a chest full of air. "I wish I could stay longer, but a week in June is all they would give me. Everybody wants their vacation in June. I could come back in some month like October when nobody else will want off. Let me get some people I know to check out where the cops are here. Who owns the land next to yours?" Dolan asked while peering at the far edge of the forest.

"Some guy from Seattle, a corporate type, why?" Dr. Gayle stomped his feet to ward off the chill.

"Just curious to know if he's had trouble with trespassers or poachers."

"He isn't here enough to know. Think he plans to build a vacation house, but I've only seen him once." Blake shivered.

"Yeah, it's pretty cold when you're not moving," Stark commented.

"Okay, guys, let's go on back and get warmed up."

———

The evening was spent around the fire as Stark pulled war stories out of Harry. Dolan didn't spend much time talking or thinking about his combat experiences while in the military, but Stark liked to hear them, so Harry obliged. Dolan was wounded twice while in Vietnam. The first time he took a bullet in the shoulder, which was for the most part, patched up in the field.

The shrapnel that ripped through his left thigh was serious enough that Harry was flown to the 65th EVAC hospital. It was there that Dolan met Dr. Blake Gayle who was of the opinion that young Lt. Dolan should be sent home. As much as Harry would have loved an early escape from Nam, he didn't feel right leaving the other guys behind. It was one thing to finish your tour and go home and another to leave like a whipped dog. Harry just couldn't do it. After three weeks of jaw boning Captain Gayle, Dolan received his pass back to the war.

"So, Harry, what did you guys do for fun?" Stark stretched out on the floor in front of the fireplace.

"None of your business!" Blake teased. Wounds were not the only need for doctors in a war zone. Gayle treated a good deal of venereal disease as well.

"Not all of us were horn dogs, I like to play cards and I had several women who wrote me and I sketched pictures."Dolan shook a finger at Gayle.

"So, you never went into the village for some action?" Stark smiled at his father.

"Son, I had enough horizontal action in the bush without courting syphilis and gonorrhea. Don't get me wrong, I like sex as much as the next guy, but I could wait until I got back home and I did." Harry took a swallow of oatmeal stout.

"And you never did drugs? It seems like everybody did that in Vietnam."

"There were plenty who did, but the media focused on everything that was done wrong. I did not shoot children or blow pot...nobody would order me to shoot children. I would have gone to Leavenworth first." Dolan recalled how he was treated when he arrived home in 1970, which drew his lips into a frown.

"Yeah, it was a bad time." Gayle stared at the coffee table before him.

"How did you get wounded, Harry?" Stark rolled up on his side and rested his head on one hand. He looked much more like

Laura than Blake with his dark hair and deep brown eyes. Gayle had sandy hair and blue eyes. "We were near the Cambodian border, in the Renegade Woods, when several hundred NVA ambushed us. Jesus, I thought that was the end of us. They were dug in and blasted us from every direction for nine very long hours. I was just a young kid then, you know? It scares me to death sometimes to think that other people depended on me to lead them. I didn't know anything about life then, how can you at nineteen?" Dolan shook his head back and forth, his bottle of stout grasped firmly in his hands.

"We were all young then, Harry. I was patching up horrible messes that had once been fit young men when most of those I went to medical school with were removing gall bladders and doing hysterectomies. I had nothing in common with them when I came back to the states and that's part of why I stayed in the service for ten years."

"You had a lot of trauma experience, Blake, but you never worked as a trauma surgeon." Dolan looked to Gayle. He had aged much since they first met, but his eyes still held that kindness a young Harry had noticed so long ago.

"I know, Laura thought I was wasting that skill and maybe I did, but I just could not look at another butchered human being. I had plenty of offers, all that paid very well, but I guess I just had enough of the trauma and I burned out early."

Gayle finished his beer and stood up. He reached for Dolan's empty bottle and asked if he wanted another. "Yeah, why not?"

"How about me Dad? I'm almost eighteen…" Stark sat up.

Blake thought for a minute. "Okay, but just one. Your mother will kill me if you wake up with a hangover."

The teenager rubbed his hands together. "All right! Hey, Dad, bring back some chips!"

The phone rang while Blake was in the kitchen and he answered the dark blue wall phone next to the refrigerator. "Hey Harry! It's your sister, Sarah."

Dolan felt a sourness form in his stomach. If she was calling him out here, there was more trouble. Everything had gone to Hell in a hand basket since the death of his mother, Lucy Blue. Blake brought Dolan the wireless handset along with his beer.

"Hey, what's going on?"

"Sorry to bother you up there, but life is turning to shit here."

Sarah's voice was strained. Her health was not good and had deteriorated drastically in the past year. Sarah was now a double amputee, on dialysis and her circulation was shot. Since the untimely demise of Al Blue, Sarah had been living in their mother's house with the idea that she would die there just as Lucy had from cancer.

"What's happening?" Harry waited for the bad news.

"Alex and his old lady are trying to throw me out of the house, now they're saying that Dad wanted to sell it. They want me to move into those apartments down by the river. Harry, those damn places are almost five hundred bucks a month! I only get six hundred from social security. I wish I hadn't written that letter for him, he isn't trying to help me at all."

Dolan had also written a letter for Alex who sought a Hardship Discharge from the army to supposedly care for Sarah and divide the estate between the four children. Al had favored Alex in the will, but Dolan's baby brother insisted from the start that he would be fair and split everything four ways. A bad feeling had been hanging over Harry for some time now as Alex's behavior had been increasingly strange and cruel.

"So what's the hurry in selling the house? He knows you don't have that long left, his wife tired of paying rent? Too bad. You know that he told Aunt Pat that Mom beat us and never cooked dinner?" Harry scowled.

"You're shittin' me? Mom never cooked? Yeah right, where did Alex grow up? He's really been playing down what the Cheeze did to us, like good old Al didn't do anything that bad. Guess Alex thinks his asshole was worth a lot more than ours." Sarah chuckled.

"Guess Alex was the call girl and we where just street whores!" Dolan laughed out loud. They often joked about the abuse they suffered as children, but the fact that their own brother was turning against Harry and Sarah was anything but funny. "When does he want you out?"

"He keeps leaving me these chickenshit notes and won't talk to me face to face. The last time Alex said anything to my face was when he accused me of stealing the Cheeze's credit cards. *He's* the one who is helping himself to Al's credit cards. The Pentagon Credit Union called here wanting to know if the card was stolen because it's been used out of state and the signature is different. I should have told them it was stolen." Sarah was getting really angry. "Who the Hell does Alex think he is? He hasn't done anything except treat me like shit since he's been back here!"

"We'll take care of things. Wish I had known he was going to be such a backstabbing shit and I would have contested the will right after the Cheeze was killed." Harry smiled slightly as he remembered Al Blue hanging off those monkey bars with his own dick in his mouth. How Alex could even think of defending their father was beyond comprehension, but money could change weak personalities. Dolan just didn't realize who Alex really was and he wished that he didn't know now.

"I'll be back the day after tomorrow, I'm going to come back here sometime in the fall and finish my vacation."

"Any luck finding that Tom guy?" Sarah sounded tired.

"No, but none of us really believe he's still alive. I'll see you soon." Dolan heard Sarah tell him to take care then the dial tone.

"Sounds like you got your own set of worries." Blake wore a concerned expression.

"I'm really embarrassed about Alex's behavior. Mom didn't raise us this way…HE did, but I never dreamed that my baby brother would turn out to be just like Al. You know, I found a card that he wrote to the Cheeze…he said that he was glad that Al was his father and that he was just like him and pleased with himself. How could anyone say that to a sadistic pedophile? The son of a bitch doesn't have enough money for me to ever kiss his ass that way or any way at all!" Harry's chest felt heavy.

"He said that kind of stuff to that maggot? Alex must be a real asshole." Stark hopped up from the floor and sat next to Harry.

"I don't know what to say about it. Maybe I just never really knew him. I left when he was a kid and he was already in the army when I moved back home. I always thought that Alex was a really good, honest guy, how could I have been so wrong?"

"Maybe he was always that way and you just didn't want to see it." Gayle leaned forward on his knees.

"Mom was so proud of him, she went to every one of those candlelight vigils when Alex was in Desert Storm, and then she would sleep on the couch with CNN on in case she might hear his name or see his face on TV. Now he's telling people that Mom never did anything for him, nor did she praise him for anything. Never thought I would want to pound the shit out of baby brother, but he's asking for it." Harry's jaw muscles tensed. "He's so two-faced. All this time he's acted like he accepted Sarah's sexuality and my religion, but it's been nothing but an act. He hates both of us and probably always has. I don't know if Alex has ever spoken the truth to me."

"Sounds like Alex wouldn't know the truth if it jumped up and bit him in the ass." Stark sipped his beer while giving Harry a sympathetic look.

"Sorry, you guys don't want to hear any of this."

"Everybody has to unload some time, Harry." Laura emerged at the top of the stairs. She had been sewing in her craft room.

"You heard all that?" Dolan titled his head at the attractive woman who peered down at him. She wore a pink shirt under a white sleeveless pullover and blue jeans.

"You've sure had more than your share of problems." She descended the stairs and stopped near the couch where Laura placed a hand on Dolan's shoulder.

"I'm just so disgusted and ashamed of his behavior. I know Sarah can be a real pain, but she's dying. Why would anyone crap on a sick sister? I feel bad for Mom too, and she can't defend herself."

"Your mother was a good person and her reputation is solid in Golding. Anyone who believes what he is saying isn't worth their weight in manure." She squeezed his shoulder then headed for the kitchen.

Stark laughed. "All right, Mom!"

"She can have a way with words." Gayle looked toward the kitchen where his wife filled a glass with ice.

"We went from war stories to my family." Dolan put his empty bottle on an end table.

"Wasn't that much of a leap." Stark belched.

"Stark! That wasn't nice."

Gayle chastised his son, though Harry wasn't sure if it was for the burp or his remark. "Think I'm going to call it a night, guys. I'm going to wander around Hagar tomorrow and feel out the locals."

That night Dolan dreamed that he was back in the 50th Rangers. He was huddled in the jungle with a buddy who turned out to be Charlie when Harry lifted his helmet to see his face. He woke feeling hurt and confused.

Chapter Ten

The Wild Goose already had a fair crowd by three o'clock in the afternoon. The bar was located in the cluster of buildings that constituted downtown Hagar. It was the same sort of main drag that ran through countless other small towns across the country, just one more little nondescript little bulge in the highway. The customers were working class, flannel shirted men whose images were barely discernible through the cigarette smoke. They huddled around round tables downing beer from quart sized mugs emblazoned with, 'Red Simons.' When Paul Dice bought the bar from old Chris Simon he saw no need to stop using the large, heavy mugs or change the name of the place.

Simon had been a huge bear of a man who served his beer in mugs to match his size and the bar was a long-standing tradition in Hagar. Dice had no desire to tread on toes or ruffle feathers, so he left the sign bearing a large lumberjack with flaming red hair over the entrance and kept the mugs.

Harry Dolan switched from the blue parka he usually wore to the old olive-drab field jacket he had left from the war. Laura's description of the natives led him to believe that he would fit in better as an old warrior. It wasn't something that Dolan did very often as he didn't understand those that clung to the Nam like little girls cling to favorite dolls. Those guys were like battered wives who continually let an abusive husband into their lives again and again to inflict pain and misery. The Vietnam War was a mutation in Harry's memory and he refused to let it color his life in cancer-tinted hues.

The walls of the bar were dingy and covered with pictures of men bearing trophy fish and game. Stuffed bass hung behind the bar between shelves of hard liqueur and clean mugs. Dice leaned against the wooden bar and read a magazine. He straightened and rubbed his hands together when Harry slid up on a red leather stool.

"What can I get ya?" Dice's smile ended in deep dimples.

"How 'bout the house favorite?"

"Bud it is." Dice retrieved a chilled mug from a chest freezer then stuck it under the spigot. Harry could see several of the men surveying him in the mirror behind the bar.

The bartender noticed Dolan watching them. "They haven't seen ya around here before."

"This is a tourist trap kind of place, isn't it? I wouldn't think that strangers would draw much interest."

"Well, some guys don't have much to do"

Harry smiled and nodded his head. Yeah, far be it that they should read a book or take a class. Let's just sit on our collective asses. "I see."

"I used to work for the post office so I worked all year round. Damn I hated the wintertime." Dice remarked while placing more mugs in the freezer.

"Bet you could freeze your ass off up here."

"I did too, but the real pain in the ass came when you got a rural route. You wouldn't believe how some of these people live up there in the hills, all tucked away in shacks that don't look any better than their beatup, rusty mail boxes, Jesus!"

He began to dry mugs out of the dishwasher.

"Guess that would have been a bitch, especially if you didn't know the area." Harry drank the beer slowly. He really wasn't a beer drinker.

"Hey, I did know it, but in the hills, in the snow and ice, it's hard to see…and there were people living up there that I didn't even know existed."

"Yeah, it was like that in Virginia and North Carolina. There were old ladies living like that with Model Ts in the garage right off the cherry tree! They all seemed to own shotguns too." Harry laughed as he remembered how he and Sarah almost had their rear ends loaded with buckshot in Virginia.

A guy with dark, greasy hair, wearing coveralls just as greasy, pushed his chair back from a table in the far corner. With a half full mug in one hand he strolled over to the bar and took a stool one over from Dolan. The man needed a shave and plastic surgery to remove the weasel appearance from his features. He sprouted a small, cheesy mustache above a weak mouth and it dipped into his beer with every gulp. He finished up the bottle then set it down hard on the bar and belched. "Give me another one, Pauly."

"Berge, I told you not to call me that."

Hansel Berge made no apology. "Wait, give me one of them Kanuks." He immediately took a long drink of the Moose Head beer that Dice opened for him.

Dolan cold see the skinny little man study the Ranger patch then move his dark eyes to the red and gold Tropic Lightening patch on Harry's jacket. Why did it always attract the assholes?

They seemed to suck up to it like a magnet. Dolan continued to sip his beer while ignoring the admirer next to him.

"So, you're a military man?" Berge looked Harry up and down like he was a dancer at a topless bar.

Dolan instantly disliked the stranger. "Was, the war's over."

"That particular battle, maybe, but the war is still raging on."

Harry glanced at the man then looked away. "Not for me."

"We all have to fight the fight, brother." Berge placed a hand on Dolan's biceps.

Harry pulled his arm out of Berge's grip. "And what fight is that?"

"The only one that matters, and we are running out of time!"

"The man doesn't want to hear your brand of bullshit, Hans." Dice waved a hand in a gesture of dismissal.

"Think you're wrong, Dice. I know the look of a battle weary man and this man ain't tired yet. Am I right?"

Dolan gazed at the yellowed ceiling. "I'm weary all right, I came here to relax, not listen to you."

"Sorry, sorry, guess I was wrong." Berge grinned into the bottle he held close to his lips.

Harry Dolan lifted the now defrosted mug to his mouth and let the cool liquid run down his throat. He watched himself in the mirror behind Dice. The low light made him appear much more handsome than the unforgiving rays of the sun. Somewhere down the road, when he wasn't looking, middle age had crept up on him and Harry was surprised by the graying man looking back at him. He could see a grin cross Berge's face. "You know so much about soldiers, what unit were you in?" Dolan asked.

"Got bad knees, wouldn't take me. But I would have been hell on wheels, tell you that!" Berge turned to face Dolan.

"Right." Harry had a feeling the guy was full of shit.

"There's other kinds of war, friend. And basically the goals are all the same, are they not?" Dice let out a laugh.

"Berge, how do you keep from boring yourself to death?"

"Up yours, you old fool." Berge snapped.

The owner feigned being insulted which made Harry laugh too.

"Just wait, Dice. When we have to save your ass from the hordes...we just may not!"

Berge slammed money to cover the beers down on the bar. "Hope you're not as dim-witted," he said to Dolan on the way out the front door.

"Oh Jesus! That guy cracks me up!" Dice grabbed himself a mug and filled it with cold beer.

"He's a flake, what the hell was he talking about?"

"Oh, you know? The white race thing." Dice cleared his throat. "Some of their ideas ain't so bad, but the whole Nazi thing is further than I want to go."

"Yeah, I didn't see much color around here." Harry glanced out the large window where the sun turned the snow blue as it sank below the trees.

"People here are okay, if you know how to approach them. Not everyone is a racist, but the loud mouths tend to draw most of the attention."

Dice took a good swig of the draft. "You didn't come to Hagar for the sightseeing? Now don't sell this quaint little hamlet short, it has its good points…the scenery is nice." Dice waited for the stranger to offer a name or a reason for his trip, but none was forthcoming. "Berge is an odd duck, maybe even a little psychotic. I try to avoid him outside of here."

"He's not exactly best friend material is he?" Dolan chuckled. "I heard something about a man disappearing around here, a veterinarian?"

"Only one we got here too. His mother is a wreck, poor lady…it's hard not knowing anything."

"His mother lives here?" Harry hadn't heard Blake mention Tom's parents.

"Lives over on Berry Street. Husband died a couple of years ago. You know Tom?" Dice asked.

"No, he was a friend of an army buddy, Dr. Gayle."

"You're a friend of the doc's, nice to meet ya, Paul Dice." He extended a hand to Dolan.

Harry shook the hand offered him. "Harry Dolan. You've got a nice place here."

"Thanks for lying. It's a dump, but beats the hell out of freezing my ass off outside. I'll leave mail delivery to the younger generation."

"What kind of a guy was Tom?" Dolan wanted an opinion outside of the Gayle family.

"He seemed a good sort to me. He let people pay out their bills, never badmouthed anybody that I know of. I did hear that there was some friction between him and his parents."

Dolan shook his head and finished off the beer. "That's not unusual. Guess I better get going."

"Hey, drop by again. I'll keep my ears open and let ya know if I hear anything." Dice offered as Harry hopped off the stool and walked out the door, his boots landing heavy on the bare wood floor.

Chapter Eleven

Edna Finkel was a short, plump woman of nearly eighty who was either baking something or cleaning her neat, two bedroom house. The house perched on a hillside over the city dog pound and Edna had a nice view of the rooftops of Hagar from her garden. She talked to the birds with a German accent that the decades had not managed to wear completely out of her speech. She was Catholic, but married Toby Finkelstein in 1937 against her parent's wishes. The Bruners were terrified of the fate that could await their only daughter for marrying a Jew, but Toby was only Jewish by birth and not a religious man. He converted to his wife's religion, Catholicism then dropped the Stein from his name when it became obvious that life would be unhealthy as a Jew in Germany.

Just when it appeared that the couple would make it through the war without being deported, a neighborhood child denounced them to the Gestapo because Toby had made the boy mad. The Finkels were sent to Auschwitz, but survived the few weeks until the camp was liberated. Edna would never forget the chaos and the intense sense of urgency in the camp as the Nazis rushed to gas and burn the remaining inmates. The air had been thick with fear and pure evil and stench of death. The smell of human bodies being incinerated remained forever etched into her brain. It was never any joy when the wind shifted and sent the smoke from the dog pound incinerator through her backyard. Yet, there was something different about the fumes that hung in the air a few days ago. The windows in her bedroom needed insulated again, and so did little to seal out the fleshy odor as she laid reading in bed. The first whiff made her lower the book and concentrate on the familiarity of it.

It couldn't be though, not here in America! Toby had not believed in anyone or anything after the war and had no such trust in Americans. He was a cynic that had no doubt that the same sort of hate that fueled the Nazis could easily occur in the United States, so he had never taken back his Jewish surname. He would not be hunted twice. Toby had died fifteen years ago before the rise of these neo-Nazi type groups. Edna was afraid of the militant attitudes of Hagar, but she was too old and poor to start over again somewhere else. She had learned to ignore them until that odor had invaded her sanctity. Now she sat in her recliner and thought about strange coincidences like the mysterious disappearance of Tom Tannahill and the sickening smell. Could they be related? Edna chastised herself for being a suspicious, paranoid old woman. She decided to bake some brownies to put in her mailbox for young Stark Gayle as he came running past her house. He was a good looking young man and often stopped to chat with her or fix things that needed mending and the boy loved to eat. It at least gave Edna something to do with her time besides thinking up wild stories.

Chapter Twelve

Dolan walked into the house of his parents and wondered about the powerful smell of urine that permeated the kitchen. Maybe Sarah was incontinent and didn't want anyone to know or she just couldn't get out of the wheelchair to the toilet fast enough. He found her in the living room watching the Discovery channel and asked about the smell.

"You tell me? I've sprayed Lysol around, I washed the bathroom rugs, I don't know what it is, but it's strong in the kitchen." She began to wheel herself into the large, carpeted kitchen.

The white carpet was filthy as Al Blue had taken up the plastic runners the day after his wife died and tracked grease from the garage into the house. Harry had considered renting a rug cleaner as Lucy would never have let her house look this way, but Alex had accused him of stealing things from the house, so he didn't feel inclined to do much work in there. He had developed a real God complex since becoming the executor of Al's estate and Harry didn't care to deal with Alex at all anymore. Dolan followed his nose to the large, trashcan near the back door and pulled the plastic bag out of it. There was around an inch of urine in the bottom. "What the Hell?" Harry had a strange look on his face.

"What is it?" Sarah glided over and stopped in front of the washer and dryer.

"Somebody took a piss in the trash can! Who would do that?"

"He's getting really weird, man. The door was open when I got home from dialysis today and he left a note that I could have $300 a month to help with rent when I get out of here."

"He left the door open? Why?" Harry set the trash can out on the carport to wash out later. "Three hundred bucks, huh? That's big of him since it belongs to all of us anyway."

"I ain't counting on anything from him. Every time he opens his hole, nothing but crap comes out. He's such a liar." Sarah's voice mixed anger and pain.

"He's a pompous little bastard. I'll say that. Glad Mom never knew what he was really like...wish I didn't know." Harry studied the note Alex had written with a magic marker. "Says to give him a call and he'll help you find a place, yeah, and his old lady will pick out another place you can't afford." Dolan sat on a wooden chair that went with his mother's dining room set, which he had left for Sarah to use. Harry didn't trust Alex so he had removed the furniture in the kitchen before Alex could give it to some member of his old lady's family.

"I called and left a message, but he won't call back. This generosity is all for show and he's full of shit. He pimped his kids out for our inheritance then goes down the to the Church of the Poisoned Mind and sucks up to Jesus three time a week. What the hell happened to him?" Sarah stuck her finger to run a blood sugar test.

"This is a bad time to be selling a house. The market stinks and this place needs some TLC. The Cheeze didn't do anything after Mom died. The gutters were crammed full when I checked them out, but I'm not going to do anything else as Alex either takes credit for what I do or says that I tore something up." Dolan could feel his temper rise. "Who the Hell does he think he is? He uses us to get a discharge then stabs us in the back when he gets it. I'll be surprised if we get anything at all except for some used furniture and nick knacks…Al took my inheritance out of my ass before Alex was even born and now he waltzes back here acting like we are the ones in the wrong and poor old Al got a bad rap. It's too much to bear."

"He has no more right to this house than the rest of us, and I think he's got Dana brainwashed too. I just want to die here and I'm sorry that it's taking too long for them!" Sarah injected herself in the arm with a little more force than usual. "I can't afford to live anywhere on my disability check." Her voice began to choke as tears welled up.

"I'll figure something out and…" Dolan heard a car door and went to the kitchen window. Alex was talking to the cop next door who had stopped in the middle of the street to chat with him. "Alex is still driving the Cheeze's truck and he's talking to Officer Weasel next door."

"Yeah, I forgot to tell ya. Alex came flying over here the day before yesterday and threatened to get a restraining order against you. Since you're one of my caregivers, he can forget it." Sarah turned her wheelchair to face the back door. "I had to throw that cop's kid outta here again yesterday. Says he wants his candy and cookies. Guess we know how Al made him pay for it."

Alex Blue opened the screen door and came into the house as though there was no friction at all between them. He wore a goatee since joining the civilian world, which amused Harry because Alex stood for everything any self respecting beatnik would abhor. Dolan braced himself for whatever face Alex would wear that afternoon.

"How's it going?" Alex sat down as Sarah wheeled herself into the bedroom. She couldn't handle any more of her younger brother. Harry leaned against the sink, not happy to be left alone with Alex.

"All right, I guess. So we having a sale or what? Can Sarah still have the frig, stove and washer and dryer? She can't afford to find a place and buy everything to set up again." Dolan wanted to slap his baby brother as he knew that the kid would tell him whatever he wanted to hear then do as he pleased.

"Oh yeah, whatever she needs. I thought we could all go through once more to decide what we want, could Aunt Pat come this weekend you think?"

"I don't know. I'll ask her. Mom would want it that way; you know she was a totally selfless person." Dolan's jaw muscles tensed as he thought of the insults hurdled at the deceased Lucy by Alex and his wife.

"I know it. Sometimes I go out to her grave and just talk to her." Alex put on his best concerned son face.

Harry looked at his brother without responding for a few seconds. *What a load of crap,* he thought. "Yeah, I do too." *It's funny how I never see you there.* "I think I have a place for Sarah to go, but it won't be ready until April first."

"Not a problem, but if the people that bought the house could get in a week early to lay carpet that would be great." Alex stood up, his allotted few minutes with his family members fulfilled.

"I'll try, but I can't guarantee anything. It's a shame though, this carpet isn't very old, and it should clean up." *And Lucy paid for it with her own sweat, you little punk, not Al.*

"And I think I'll take the cat down and put her to sleep for Dad." Alex said while going out the door.

For Dad? Dolan eyebrows arched. Nuisance was Dana's cat, not the Cheeze's. The Cheeze was a nickname the four siblings had decided fit their father, Al Blue. Dana said he reminded her of the crusty stuff that accumulates in the crack of your butt. "Yeah, she's getting pretty old and looks miserable."

As Alex Blue climbed into Al's royal blue truck, Sarah returned to the kitchen. "Was he talking with both sets of lips or what?"

"Jesus, he acts like he hasn't done a damned thing. I'm beginning to wonder if that Gulf War Syndrome isn't for real. I have a feeling that he's going to pull something, like change the locks on the doors while you're at dialysis. There's a little oil field house across town that I can pick up cheap, but it needs a lot of work. I can't close on it and remodel it before the end of the month though." Harry sighed as he looked around his mother's house. Her personality still lingered everywhere.

"Hey, that would be great; I just want to get the hell out of here." Sarah looked around the room. "You better get the stuff you want now or he'll give to his old lady's family."

"I'm never going to forgive that little shit for making us feel like we don't belong in our mother's house. Al bought her the cheapest dump he could find, then jerry-rigged everything in the place. God, he's still causing misery even when's he's barbecued!"

Sarah laughed. "Wish I could have seen that bastard fry!" Dolan smiled broadly, as he recalled the look on Al's face as that arrow slammed through his back and pierced his chest. He would never hurt another child or old lady again, thanks to his oldest son. There hadn't been enough of Al to waste on a coffin, so Harry had taken his ashes out to the lagoon of a feedlot so they could float amongst the cow shit. Sarah would love to know that it was Harry who tortured and killed Albert Blue, but Dolan had told no one and didn't wish to make Sarah an accomplice. Not that Harry had any intention of being caught for taking trophies on his "Chicken Hunts" as he called his wet works for justice.

"Well, try not to worry about things. I'll see you later. He won't bother you anymore. We don't merit two visits in one day."

Chapter Thirteen

Every time that Harry Dolan thought he could relax, something would happen to invade that peacefulness. The medical examiner that he worked under, Carol Whitechapel, was being pressured by the bureaucrats to not take so long on autopsies and to stop storing evidence for longer than five years. The forensic center was Whitechapel's baby. There would be no regional forensic lab in the area if it was not for her, but Dolan had a feeling Carol was on her way out. They were doing forensic exams for Sedgwick County and many others who did not have medical examiners and, yes, they were behind.

Whitechapel had seen many cases ruined in the past due to mistakes made by medical examiners or evidence that no longer existed because it had been destroyed, so she was extra diligent in her work. She could be a real bitch who spent eighteen hours on an autopsy and Dolan had filled in several times for autopsy technicians who had quit due to her personality, but sometimes you had to take the good with the bad. The work atmosphere was tense and divided, as some employees liked Carol and others did not. The ones who did not like her were increasing in numbers. Harry would hate to see her go as she had done so much for the county, but he would just have to go with the flow as the pencil pushers couldn't care less what one medical investigator thought.

The home front was no better as Alex and Dana had teamed up against Harry and Sarah. Sometimes Dolan felt very alone. He knew that when Sarah was gone that no one would remember the days before Alex and Dana were born but him. Alex had begun to imply that poor Al didn't abuse anybody and Lucy was the bad parent. Only Harry and Sarah knew how terrible things had really been in Virginia and Okinawa, only those two had known Lucy when she was young. At least they had Aunt Pat who had no trouble recalling what an ass Al had been even before he joined the army. According to Alex, Lucy hadn't done much of anything for her children, but Harry didn't have the same memories of his mother at all. She was a den mother for Alex's troop, made Halloween costumes and always tried to make every holiday something special. What Alex was pulling was unforgivable and sickening. Anyone that would side with a sadistic pedophile against Lucy Blue had holes in his soul. Lucy never cooked? Alex must not have lived in the same household as Harry. Dolan was giving some serious thought to moving out of Kansas after Sarah died. It just was not home anymore. Harry had not seen his niece or nephews in months, so aside from his aunt and uncle, Dolan had no reason to stay in Kansas.

The oil field house Dolan bought was gutted now and the electricians had just finished with the wiring. His Uncle Jack was going to help with the paneling so Harry didn't have it all to do himself. It was Friday night and Dolan had just got home from work and put his feet up when the phone rang.

It was Sarah. Alex, his wife and a niece of Al's had met Sarah at the house when the bus brought her home from dialysis. They had packed her stuff and called the cops for a sidewalk eviction. They were demanding that Harry come and get his sister.

"Harry, the place is a mess, they've tore up everything and they're talking real loud and saying bad things about you "Sarah was crying. "They want you over here."

"They think I was born yesterday? What the hell is Becky doing up here? Alex promised her a new house? He already gave her the Cheeze's car." Dolan knew what Alex had planned. Cousin Becky was obnoxious, as was Alex's wife, Alice, and they hoped that by screaming lies in front of the cops they would get either Harry or Sarah arrested that night.

About that time a police officer showed up at Dolan's place. He told Sarah to hang on. Harry opened the screen door. "How can I help you, officer?"

"Your brother Alex says that he made arrangements for Sarah to come live with you. I need permission to bring her and her stuff here." The cop was young, stocky and obviously did not like his present task.

"I bought a house for my sister to live in, it isn't ready yet and Alex knows that. He has made no arrangements for Sarah at all, and my house is not wheelchair accessible. They need to provide shelter for her." Dolan was about ready to explode.

"Yes, sir, that's all I needed to hear. I'll tell Mr. Blue that he needs to get a motel room for Sarah." The officer returned to his patrol car.

"You still there?" Harry picked up the portable phone. She sobbed into the receiver. "Okay, we're going to turn the tables on that little bastard and the women who do his fighting for him. He told the cops that he had talked to me about you living with me and to bring you here, and I said no. It's not that I don't want you here, but I'm not going to let him use me to make himself look good. The cops are going to make Alex get you a motel room and tell him that he cannot leave you on the street. I'll call Aunt Pat and tell her what's he is doing and people at your church. They need to see that what we've been saying about Alex is true."

"You're damned right! The cops are really nice. I don't think they want to be here. I'll let you know what motel I end up in." Sarah hung up the phone. Becky and Alice were straining the decibels with scathing remarks about Harry and how he had victimized his poor daddy. He and Sarah were also just after poor Al's money and cared nothing for his memory. Alex was in serious need of a shrink. Dolan called the minister at Sarah's church and talked to the youth minister instead, as Reverend Croft was out of town. Steve Oxford tried to tell Harry that he was mistaken about Alex Blue, as he was a good guy.

"That so? Well, Saint Alex is at this moment throwing his dying sibling in the street. Hey, I thought he was a good guy too, but reality isn't always what we think it is." There was a pause on the other end of the line.

"Family should be taking care of this..." Oxford didn't believe that Alex was doing any such thing.

"Family is doing this, pal! I can't go over there as I know my father's cousin and my sister-in-law too well. The plan is for me to spend the weekend in jail and I would lose my job over the crap they are making up about me." Harry was losing patience with those who had no trouble believing the worst about him and Sarah, but who basked in the glowing, angelic glory of Alex Blue.

"I'll do a drive by. I'm sure this is a mistake."

"I made the mistake when I helped that little bastard get out of the army." Dolan hung up the phone before his language could descend any further toward the netherworld. He then called a couple who had been taking Sarah to church and explained the situation to them. They said they would go right over to lend support. He had to remind himself not to be so upset over people being fooled by Alex Blue as Harry had been at the top of the list.

Well, so much for the four of them sticking together. Thanks to Alex; Al's legacy would live on, not Lucy's. Alex had to spring for two nights in the motel and after dumping Sarah off with her wheelchair, he went to Golden Corral to celebrate his manly feat. In an afterthought, Becky and her husband Charley dropped Sarah's heart medicine and insulin at the motel before they crossed the street to partake in the Viking-like tribute to their enemy's defeat. When they arrived, Aunt Pat and Uncle

Jack were there with Sarah. Charley had the nerve to ask everyone, "How's it going?" Jack replied. "Better than for some." *What a henpecked jerk,* he thought. But then again, Alex had already given them Al's Cadillac, so more than likely their pockets had been considerably lined. Buying friends isn't that hard.

"Becky told me that Jesus doesn't listen to my prayers." Sarah slumped in her wheelchair in the stuffy room.

"What? Don't you believe anything they say! They know nothing about Jesus." Aunt Pat was having a difficult time holding back the anger as Becky's mouth was running non-stop. She was disturbingly similar to an agitated Porky the Pig.

"We told her to get out. She was told." The chubby woman's several chins quivered with agitation.

"You don't have anything to say about it and we have notes from Alex that Sarah had until the end of this month." Pat bristled every time Becky's face hovered hear hers.

"No, huh uh. That's not true." The woman was as round as she was tall and her sweater clung to every fleshy roll.

"We have the notes." Pat had never wanted to hit someone so much in her whole life. *Who the hell was Becky to decide what happens to her sister's house?*

"No, that's not the way it happened." Becky defended Alex who brushed passed his aunt without comment.

"You better get to a church fast, Alex." Pat stated to her nephew and she didn't mean that Nazi palace where Alex pretended to be righteous. He made no response. She fumed with disgust while remembering how proud Lucy had been of him. Their brother Jeff had been correct when years ago he had remarked, "I don't trust that sneaky little bastard."

At eleven at night Alex dropped off two boxes of perishable food to spoil in Sarah's hot motel room. Sarah didn't want to call and bother anyone about picking the boxes up that late. She was the ultimate in picky eaters which meant that about one-hundred dollars worth of seafood went into the trash.

Harry wasn't sure what bothered him the most, Alex's betrayal or Dana's. Neither of them had ever hesitated to ask for his help or advice and now the two of them decided that they were superior to their two oldest siblings. He had done nothing wrong to either of them, but when he asked for financial statements, Harry became the anti-Christ. If Alex and Alice were not stealing from the rest of them, why get upset when asked for an accounting? He should have known something was up when all of a sudden Dana was allowing her son to attend Alex's church. She had the same opinion of those uptight, hatemongers as Harry, but now it seemed that she had no problem with the Church of the Poisoned Mind. Money truly could buy anything and damned near everybody.

Chapter Fourteen

The AIDS test came back positive. Brentlinger sat on the old couch in his living room of tan, green and orange hues and let the feelings of doom sink in. He hadn't even bothered grabbing a beer from the fridge Jim was so devastated by the news. Car doors slammed shut in the garage which meant his wife and kids were home from the grocery store. The two youngest were sweet children and Brentlinger didn't want to take out his frustration them. His wife, Joan, was always bright with a positive attitude. She didn't approve of Berge or his beliefs.

Jim didn't know what he was going to do. He had made such a fucking mess out of a wonderful life. He wanted to bawl when he saw Joan with both arms full of brown Lane's Foodbarn sacks. Sally and Eric were still in grade school and shouted something about some new type of candy. He pretended to be excited for them.

"Dad, you lift up its tail and candy comes out!" Sally was seven and was amused by most anything around her. The bright green dinosaur "pooped" out pastel colored candy into her hand. "Yum, yum!" Jim popped one into his mouth. He cringed as he realized that he was now a bio hazard to his family. "I got a T Rex."

Eric wore his ball cap backward, his brown hair sticking out every which way. "Did ya get one for me?" Brentlinger teased.

"Dad!" The boy made his dinosaur attack Sally's then ran off to his room.

"Don't eat all of that! Dinner will be ready soon." Joan put the bag on the kitchen table. "Jim, you want a beer while I'm in here?" He could hear the bustle of groceries being put away.

"No, think I'll go feed the dogs before it gets any colder, grab one on the way back in." Brentlinger needed some space. He couldn't let them see him cry, but he had to have a release of some sort. Jim was going to die.

The pen was twenty by thirty with an opening into a tool shed that now served as a doghouse. When the three big lab mix dogs heard someone approach they grew excited. The animals were supposed to be the responsibility of his three kids, but Jim usually ended up doing the watering and feeding. He unlocked the building and stepped inside. The dog food was stored in a fifty-gallon drum with a lid to keep the dogs out. Brentlinger chastised himself for being such a stupid man as he snapped open the barrel. Not just stupid, but very stupid! Why did he ever get involved with Hansel Berge? He loosed the ring that held the lid tight and stared at the brown chunks as if they were runes. He just could not believe it. He had AIDS. How could he have let that happen? Berge had told him to get that crap tattooed on his arms? Jesus, his own bigotry had killed him. Brentlinger had a good life and now it was gone. How could he tell Joan? Gee, honey, I'm a proud member of the Sons of Marduk and out of my devotion I got these things carved into my arms. The price of this dedication is a slow, agonizing death, but hey, you don't mind wiping my asa while you raise the kids by yourself, do you? You'd do that for the glory of the white race, wouldn't you? The dogs sat quietly while waiting for their master to fill the empty bowls. They seemed to sense that the man was in pain.

"I should be eating out here with you…well, which isn't fair, you guys haven't done anything." He wiped away tears with his sleeve. Brentlinger heard his oldest son's car pull in.

The dogs eagerly ran out into the pen to check on the newest human arrival. The first thing out of Jason's mouth was an obscenity yelled at the dogs. He obviously did not know anyone was in the shed. The kid wasn't bright. He was the product of Brentlinger's first marriage and his mother had run off right after he was born. Jim was in no mood for Jason's brand of bullshit today.

"That the way you talk when you think nobody's around?" Jim asked calmly as he as he shut the shed door behind him. It gave a high pitch, woody groan as it closed. Jason's mouth hung open for a second. No decent lie would surface so he just shook his auburn haired head. "So, you think your little sister's dog is a fucking nigger?" Brentlinger was trying to control the rage that was brewing within him. Deep down, Jim really didn't like Jason and hoped that he wasn't his kid.

"Black's black, ain't it?" Jason thought the remark clever and to the point. Brentlinger back handed the boy across the face.

"You get your act straightened up, boy, or you won't be living here. I am clear?" Jim knew the attitude was his doing, but couldn't stop himself.

"What the hell did I do?" Jason's face beamed red with his father's hand print.

"Just get to your room. We're gonna have a long discussion later, but don't even think about copping an attitude, cause I've had all I'm gonna take." Jim suddenly felt hot all over like he had a fever.

Joan appeared at the kitchen door. "What's going on?" She could see the tension as her stepson turned his face away.

"I slipped on the gravel and smacked my face on the car." Jason replied after determining that he hadn't seen that kind of look on his father's face before.

"We better get some ice on that. You okay?" Joan asked sensing an undercurrent of some sort between the two.

"Yeah, why don't you go inside and wash up. I'll be in shortly." Jim tried to sound friendlier for Joan's sake.

"Dinner's ready, so don't be long." She commented while touching the mark on Jason's cheek as he passed her. He shrugged her off. "I'm putting it on the table now."

Brentlinger smiled and nodded, then got in his truck. He was going to find Berge and break the son-of-a-bitch's face!

Chapter Fifteen

Hansel Berge had a problem. Louise had decided to get a wild hair up her ass and turn him down for sex. When he forced her, she told him that she'd had four abortions in the last decade. Four? Berge could have had little versions of himself running around and she murdered them! Hans nearly beat the life out of her. Louise lay in their bedroom all curled up like a whipped pup and had not said a word for the last twelve hours. She had head wounds that leaked onto the pillow. Berge was afraid she was going to die this time. She should have obeyed him like God wanted her to do, her only purpose on this earth was to serve him and make babies. Louise had failing grades in both.

The last time Hans tried to check on her, the woman had given him a cold blank stare that he had never seen before in anyone living. Louise was a very neat, clean little lady, but she made no effort to get up to change her dress or shower. He had plucked some cord this time that played an eerie tune. Berge was actually scared. He did not like being scared. "I'm going to the garage and I expect you to be up, showered and have dinner cooked when I come back." There was no answer, but Hans hoped shear fear would get the woman to drag her ass out of bed.

Louise lay listening to the sounds of the back door slamming and the truck's engine turning over. She bled from her nose and left ear. The fluids matted her hair and Louise stuck to the pillow when she tried to sit up. Her body ached from what seemed like hundreds of punches and kicks, but she would get up.

Hans had taken the keys to the old Impala thinking that she would be trapped. Louise had once belonged to St. Patrick's Catholic Church in Hagar before her husband decided that all other churches, save his own, were wrong. She hoped that Laura Gayle would remember her. She struggled to stand. Her rib cage burned with each step toward the phone in the hall. The left ear was numb so Louise placed the receiver on the other ear. She prayed that Laura would answer the phone. The doctor's wife used to counsel battered women at the YWCA. She would understand.

"Gayle residence, how can I help you?" Laura sounded pleasant to the battered woman.

"Laura, this is Louise Berge. I used to attend the same church." Her throat was sore from being choked.

"Louise, oh yes! I haven't seen you for some time." Laura hardly recalled the woman, but did remember that she was quiet and sweet. "What can I do for you, Louise?"

"I know that this is a very large thing to ask, but could you come pick me up? I need to go to the bus station; right now...I really need help, now." Louise's voice quivered with fear that Berge would return unexpectedly.

Instinct told Laura that the woman was not overacting.

"Of course, I'll leave right now. You're at home?" The poor lady must not have any friends if she had to call someone she hardly knew.

Louise watched the drive through white lace curtains. It would have been better to clean up first, but he could show up at any minute to work her over some more. She would just have to swallow the humiliation provided by her appearance. "Yes, I'm here at the house. Thank you, thank you so much. Please hurry."

Laura did her best not to gawk in horror at the bloodied and bruised woman who opened the back door. The house was surrounded by five acres of land and several outbuildings. One bore a sign stating that it was the Elder Church. She had heard that Hansel Berge was a flake, but Laura didn't know the half of it. Louise had packed a small bag and was ready to go.

"Do you have enough stuff? That's not a very big bag."

"I'm going to my sister's in Texas. " Louise stifled a sob. "They always say, get out, get away from an abuser, but they don't realize that you're leaving behind your whole life, not just him. Many of these things were my mother's." She looked around the living room one last time. "We better go."

Once they were in Laura's Explorer Louise slid down in the seat. *What kind of a monster is this guy?* Laura thought as she pulled into the street. As if she read Laura's mind, Louise explained herself.

"I don't want him or any of his cohorts to see me with you. I don't want anything to come back on you for helping me."

Laura had to talk Louise into coming back home with her to shower and change. The battered lady had been ready to jump on a bus looking like she'd been in a five-car pileup. The way Louise grimaced at every bump in the road, Laura expected broken ribs or worse. More than likely, Blake would want her to stay a few days to heal before any long bus ride.

"Is anyone else at home at your house? I think I would like to clean up before anyone sees me." She had begun to calm down and the reflection of her tortured face in the side mirror shocked even Louise.

"It's all right. We'll be alone for a few hours." Laura smiled sympathetically.

Blake was at the clinic and Stark was out in his car somewhere. There would be plenty of time for Louise to bathe since she had refused to file charges against Berge. The abused wife just wanted to get far away from Hansel Berge. Louise didn't want to play the legal game or let his defense lawyer make out that she brought the violence on herself. She did give into Laura's request to take a few pictures just in case.

Chapter Sixteen

It took twelve days to remodel the house efficient enough to move Sarah in. Thanks to the Grace Lutheran Church and the First Baptist Church, Sarah at least had a motel room for shelter while Harry, Uncle Jack and Aunt Pat worked during the day then remodeled at night. It was ready by March 15, one of the several deadlines that Alex had used to threaten his dying sister. Of course, he was now denying that he gave her any time at all.

Apparently Alex didn't think that Harry kept the notes he had left on the table while Sarah was out. For six weeks Sarah's health deteriorated. It began with the night Alex tossed his sister and her wheelchair into the street. That night she had her first heart attack and spent a few days in the hospital before she could even spend one day in the house. She was terrified that Alex would break into her house while she was being drained and strained at dialysis and steal her computer and TV. Harry wasn't sure just how much of a mental bran muffin Alex really was, but didn't discount Sarah's fear for her things or her own safely. Anyone who would piss in a trash can to scare his crippled sister had at least one busted light bulb.

Alex sent his mother-in-law on a drive by to check out where Sarah was living, and after Dolan saw Alex speed by the house in the Cheese's truck, Sarah bought a knife big enough to gut a bear. Alex and Dana completely wrote off Harry and Sarah, yet just had to keep tabs on them. They were getting all the money, what was the problem? Sarah had three more heart attacks then qualified for Hospice care. Dolan was relieved to have some outside help. His sister was the third family member to die with the aid of Hospice in two years and six months. This time there were only Pat and Jack to give support. Harry had sighed as he watched the van from Hospice bring equipment into Sarah's little house and wondered how much more he was going to be able to take without cracking.

A couple from Sarah's church went to offer support when she was being evicted. The woman was a survivor of the Holocaust and told Sarah that she remembered when the Germans did the same thing to her family. They threw them into the street and took their house and things for themselves. Alex truly was a little Nazi. It really hurt to have Alex and Dana treat Harry and Sarah just like Al did; like they were two pieces of dog excrement that got stuck on their shoes.

Harry knew he was hated because he asked too many questions. Dana had a problem with Sarah because her boyfriend went through Sarah's wallet and she told him that she would break his goddamned legs for doing it. Apparently Willy couldn't stand the daily fear of an amputee woman stomping his ass at any given time, so Dana disowned her sister and even forbid her to attend her son's birthday party. Harry hoped that the two of them enjoyed the Cheese's money, as it was now the only thing they had. There were times when Sarah would call Dolan, weeping that she had messed herself and the bus was coming for dialysis soon. He would run over there and help her change, not having any words of wisdom for her.

A part of him seemed to wither every time he had to watch someone slowly die, except for Al, and his death gave Harry nothing but pleasure. As Sarah tried to clean herself and fight embarrassment, Harry fought tears. She had such a sad life, yet clung to every day of it, just like Lucy Blue. When Sarah died, Harry was out of town on an investigation. She had gone to the hospital after telling Aunt Pat she didn't feel very well.

The cardiologist determined that Sarah had a mild heart attack and kept her for eight days. That Sunday morning on May the seventh Sarah ate a good breakfast, then screamed that she was hurting all over. The doctor was on the floor, but by the time she came into the room Sarah Blue was gone.

It took Harry more than two hours to drive back and he had the hospital hold her body until he got there. As Sarah was going to be cremated Dolan wanted to see her first before letting her go. His aunt and uncle were there when he arrived. His sister lay dead, and her eyes half closed with a strange, pleased look frozen on her features. She was a pathetic figure with her legs and finger missing as she patiently awaited the funeral home attendant. Dolan sobbed for a few minutes while his surrogate parents gave him comfort. If he'd had any idea that Sarah would never go home again, Harry would not have left the area. He was starting to envy those that got to go first and somehow it felt obscene to always be a survivor.

Sarah wanted to be cremated and did not want Harry to spend money on a fancy service. She only wished for him to play Led Zeppelin and scatter some of her ashes over their mother's grave. The rest of Sarah would blow over St. George's Island via a friend's grieving hand. She did not want Alex or Dana listed as survivors, nor did Sarah want their father listed as preceding her in death. Since their mother Lucy did not get her wishes due to Al's lizard soul, Harry was determined that no one would interfere with Sarah's requests. As usual, there was a complication. He should have known. When the obituary came out in the Golding Times, Alex and Dana dragged their kids down to the funeral home to manipulate the old lady into changing the way the obituary was written. They wanted to be acknowledged as siblings and they wanted their father's name mentioned. Dolan was furious at the hypocrisy and the wheelbarrel full of balls it took to demand recognition now. They want to honor poor old Al too? Christ on a crutch!

Of course, nothing would be corrected or added to the obituary that Sarah had written herself. Alex just thought that he would throw his weight around at the mortuary and get his way like he seemed to do everywhere else. Then, the truth for the visit surfaced like a corn-filled turd in a still creek. They asked about the insurance policy. Al had called the insurance company in Oklahoma while Sarah was at dialysis and made himself the beneficiary of her burial policy, voiding the friend who was also her power of attorney. The two youngest siblings thought Al was still the beneficiary and they could just collect a check for anything left over.

Fortunately, Sarah's friend was sharp as a tack and noticed when the beneficiary was changed. If Al had tried that trick twice, he would have gone to jail. There would be no mad money for Alex and Dana at Sarah's expense. Harry had heard that his two remaining siblings as well as Alex's in-laws were pissed at him. As Dolan recalled, none of them helped him fix the house up nor did they ever come by for a visit even though they knew Sarah did not have long left to live. Sarah had seen Dana's son, but only because her Aunt Pat brought him over. It was a joy for her, but Sarah cried afterward that the little boy would not remember his grandmother and Sarah would be recalled later in his life as the weird aunt with no legs.

Dolan didn't recall Alex's in-laws doing much of anything for the Blue family, or coming around when Lucy was dying. Social humiliation must be the Achilles Heel of right-wing Bible thumpers who had no explanation they could retell of why Sarah omitted her two youngest siblings. They were not ashamed of how they treated Sarah, only at how it looked. Harry began to seriously entertain thoughts of moving to Colorado, maybe Leadville. Golding just was not home any longer.

Chapter Seventeen

The Sons of Marduk worked diligently until they produced an offer the good doctor couldn't refuse. Dr. Gayle wasn't going to refuse. He just didn't know it yet. The group had begun to get excited about actually owning the land they had been using for several years. It felt as though it were theirs; land homesteaded by pioneers who cared for the land and nurtured it by merely enjoying its beauty.

"How should we present it or where?" Mike Rogers was one of the more sophisticated of the Elder Church and the only one to wear suits on the job. He sold insurance.

"Well, I've given it some thought. We catch him when he is the most relaxed and clearheaded. We'll go to his house where his old lady can aid in persuading him to sell." Berge had a confident grin.

"Think she'll want to do that?" Brentlinger asked, snidely. His attempt to dissociate with the Sons of Marduk had bought him a busted nose and a threat of worse injury. He had also been reminded that he was an accomplice to murder.

"She will. Women cannot resist large sums of money and what use is the wilderness to her? What was she gonna do? Grab a rifle and hunt Bambi?" Berge thought of women only as beings in heels and aprons. The shame of having his wife run off was an emotion he spared himself by not allowing the other men to know about it.

"My wife has hunted with me, and before that with her father. Hell, sometimes Joan can shoot better'n me!" Brentlinger laughed along with a few of the others.

"Because you're pussy whipped, Jimmy and your wife is a dyke. If my wife ever tried acting like that with me, she'd be sneezing blood for a week." Hansel's eyes threw darts of disdain at the pudgy man in the blue flannel shirt who didn't enforce the chain of command at home. "She don't get ideas like that because I don't let her hang out with the other hens and generate stupid notions such as her equality with me!" Berge slapped the table hard with is open hand. The same one he used to silence Louise.

Brentlinger was tired of Berge and his insults as well as his attitude that no one else was entitled to an opinion. "It's my business how I treat my wife and mine alone!"

"If you can't understand the need for total loyalty in our cause, then maybe you should have left when you still could." Berge's tone was chilling. The twelve members of the Elder Church of the New Order fell silent.

It was no longer a trivial thing to be a Son of Marduk and no longer voluntary. The fact was spewed into the air by Berge and now slowly absorbed into the skin of the church members like a chemical agent. There wasn't anything to say or dispute. They were in fact bound forever unless prison was to be considered a viable alternative. Berge was pleased with the reaction. "We'll go Thursday night. He should be home and tired from a week's work. He'll be better open for suggestion." Berge heard his stomach growl. "Now get home and make sure those little ladies are rattling pots and pans for their hungry men."

The church building was an old shop on Berge's property. It was far enough from the house that there would have been no excuse for Louise to snoop. Hans had built a makeshift steeple, but had yet to find a bell to fill it. He watched as his followers put on jackets and hats for the long trip down the drive to their cars. There was a storm coming and the wind slammed against the ancient windows as dark clouds rolled overhead.

"Meet back here Thursday afternoon and we'll all go out to Gayle's place together. Rogers, we'll use that big van of yours and Smith...bring that station wagon." Hans barked orders as he studied the threatening weather. He warmed himself by the wood stove in the center of the building. Rogers nodded as his slipped a Stetson on his bald head.

Ansel Smith thought his wife would probably need the wagon for her Girl Scout troop, but he wasn't about to argue with Berge. He would just make sure that he had the car in time for the meeting. Smith gave an affirmative wave as he opened the door to the heavy raindrops that darkened the ground. Alone in the church, Berge listened to the sounds of men running as the rain fell faster. He accidentally touched his hand to the scalding metal of the stove which made him jump and swear.

At age seven his father had held his little hand on such a stove unit it blistered, a reminder that hunger was to be ignored in the Berge household and food eaten only when Edmund Berge said it was allowed. The chunk of cheese had cost Hansel a burned hand and the additional chores of his two brothers. Barbara Berge had a lesson that day also when her husband beat her black and blue for defending her son. It wasn't fair, she had argued, the boys were not allowed to eat until full so what did Edmund expect? They did hard farm labor and needed to eat well. She had defied him in front of his sons, so what choice did Edmund have?

Hansel could see the logic in his father's actions now as he had a wife of his own to handle, or did have. Edmund Berge had made his boys hard and strong heads of their households. Hans had nieces and nephews, but his brothers were yet to become uncles by Hans. Louise had seen to that bit of shame. All this time he thought that Louise could not conceive due to a beating which led to a miscarriage some ten years earlier. He had suspected that it was her tense, frigid behavior during sex that caused her infertility. Berge felt a stirring in his genitals that indicated that it was time to try again to extend the family blood line. But where was Louise?

———◦—•—◦———

It was amazing, the amount of losers who hung out in the twilight hours drinking, bullshitting and generally screwing off in dives across the country. They contribute nothing to society except add drunks to the welfare rolls and unwanted brats. Berge sipped a draft while watching a bar fly go from one customer to another at the bar attempting to procure some business. Her hair was too dirty a blonde, the skirt way too short and the make up too thick. She looked like the bad side of a run over possum.

It was then she noticed him sitting at a small round table in the back and walked seductively back to him. Outside she appeared even worse. The sunlight flushed out every wrinkle and made her face appear pasty. The whore was cheap and trashy, even for a whore. She stood by the car just looking at Berge as he opened the driver side door. "Get in." He tried to sound friendly.

"This a date? I got expenses." The hooker really didn't like the looks of the guy, but she needed some stuff in a bad way and business hadn't been the best.

"Of course, we all do." He unlocked the passenger door and patted the seat next to him. The car belonged to one of his customers and was much nicer than his old truck for attracting prostitutes. Sonja Kelly hoped the asshole didn't want much. She was going to get out of the life soon. It was wearing her down. If she just didn't need to shoot up once in a while, Kelly could get a regular job. Places like McDonald's didn't pay shit and at minimum wage a girl would have to work twenty four hours a day to make ends meet. Sonja lowered herself into the expensive looking car. At least the interior was clean with a fresh, new car scent the john probably got from a bottle. "Got a place around here?" Sonja asked, noting that the man took much better care of his car then his person. God, just let him want something simple.

"Motel room okay? I'm from out of town." Berge could feel his disgust rising by the minute. No wonder God made man the dominant sex, just look at her! Trashy bitch made her entire living by tempting married men. Of course, women mainly had one purpose in life and that was bearing children, so Berge guessed they couldn't help but search out males. He had no motel room and Hans could not understand men who wasted money so that whores could lie on comfortable beds, not to mention the fact that someone might recognize them at a later date. The usual ploy should work. The old, 'I have a cabin in the hills I'd like to show you' plan. She responded by slowly nodding her head.

"Hope you don't mind, but I like to take a drive before I get, you know, intimate with a woman. I need to connect with you first. I bought an old cabin not far from here, it's not fit to live in yet, but there is a couch there."

Kelly had heard this one before; the cheap bastard didn't have a room anywhere, but what the hell? He looked like a five minute job. "Okay, but I get paid up front. Fifty for the works or twenty for a blow." She held out her hand.

"Fair enough." Berge dug out his wallet and pulled out two twenties and a ten.

"All right then. Let's go see your cabin." *Shit*, Sonja thought. *Another backseat fuck. She was getting too old for this kind of crap.*

The maroon Buick headed west on interstate 12 toward the Lower Granite Lake. Traffic was light as the sun began to set. Hans glanced at the hooker as she watched the scenery fly past and for a second, she was almost human. The turnoff was void of tire tracks as Berge knew it would be. There was an old house several hundred yards up in the trees that was used for storage by some yuppie turd with too much money to spare.

The car came to a slow stop before the ancient two story house. No one had been out to check on the place for some time as there were no tire tracks in the mud in spite of the recent torrents. "Backseat?" Kelly asked unnecessarily.

"You mind? I don't think I can wait," he replied in an attempt to flatter her and gain confidence.

"It's okay. It's nice and warm in here."

Sonja smiled. *Right, you jerk off.* She knew the type, old limp dick at home. They slipped off their coats then tossed them to the front seat.

Berge loosened the shirt and tie he wore for these occasions. "I like to do from behind. The wife won't go for it." Berge acted embarrassed as he dropped his pants and pulled a condom from the pocket of his dress shirt.

"That's fine, honey, however you want it." *Christ! Why did they always have to mention what the old lady won't do? Most of the time they complained that their spouses refused to partake of a little dick sickle.* The first five minutes were better than Kelly expected. The weasel was huge and not half bad. He had a way of hitting the right spots the right way. She found herself getting really wet. This didn't happen very often when she was working. Sonja rarely ever enjoyed sex with a john or climaxed, but she was going to this time. The first warm wave poured over her and forced a smile then suddenly she could not breathe.

Berge looped the necktie around Kelly's neck and pulled tight. He kept pounding her as her body finished its orgasm. He could see her scarlet face, the eyeballs bulging and the rigid veins stand out in her neck. Berge slammed the woman harder, exploding inside her as Sonja's life ran out of her. He leaned back away from her, allowing his penis to flop down into its natural position. Hans smacked her bare ass. "Jesus! Was it good for you too?"

The nice thing about strangling people was that it was clean. He didn't always kill that way, but it was the best method with no mess. Berge dragged the body around to the trunk. The general public didn't realize how much of a chore hauling a dead weight could be, then to heave it up into the trunk of a car. Murder really took a great deal of effort. No one ever missed whores or drug addicts in this world, which made them the perfect targets. Their families had thrown them away and the cops didn't give a damn. The ones Berge met were mostly yuppie brats who thought their computer, and compact disc player lives weren't fulfilling enough. Shit! The problem with society was the lack of discipline and respect for the pecking order as laid out in the Bible by God.

If every family were led by a strong man, then there would not be the dysfunctions that presently rotted American society. There wouldn't be the drug abuse or unwed mothers and there damned well wouldn't be that bullshit label, domestic violence! That sort of crap was dreamed up by dykes with mustaches and limp-wristed fags who were freaks with no place to fit in, so they sought to destroy the sacred union between men and women.

The heavy, lifeless body of the old whore strained the muscles in Berge's back, but it was an unwritten rule that one did not dispose of bodies close to the place of sacrifice. The murder had been an offer; a blood sacrifice for the good of mankind. Such trash served only to deteriorate the structure of society and at least now the woman now had some purpose for her existence. It was nearly midnight. Berge needed to get home to see if Louise had come crawling back. He would get her for murdering white babies no matter where she had run. The thought of her made him want to slap that whimpering look off her face.

The absolute stupidity of his followers made Berge snicker and shake his head often. They really had no idea that the bodies of many faceless women and one fag whore who tried to pass himself off as a woman lay on the hill over Gayle's lake.

An old mining road jutted deep into the forest from the land that adjoined the doctor's and Berge had used it often. Amidst the thick trees the mouth of an abandoned mine opened wide for the tasty morsels that Hans threw down its throat. Humans were so incredibly gullible.

Chapter Eighteen

It was October by the time Harry Dolan was able to take the second half of his vacation. The job he had such a passion for was becoming a depressing ordeal for him. He was sick of illness and death and cruelty, and longed for the woods of Idaho where he could immerse himself in peaceful solitude. The last case he worked was a ten-year-old girl who had been beaten to death by her mother's boyfriend. The scumbag only got five years. The frustration and stress of losing half his family and spending forty hours a week staring at dead people were taking its toll on Dolan.

There was still no new information on the disappearance of Tom Tannahill, and though Harry had no desire to spend his free time investigating anything, he couldn't ignore the agitation of his friend Blake either. Dolan was also curious about the fear displayed by Stark. Why would a high school kid be so disturbed by a missing adult friend of his father's?

Except for the landscape, there was nothing redeeming about the town of Hagar. It had not improved any since Harry was there in the spring, if anything the cold made it worse. His Basset hound, Orphan, was flopped on the back seat totally unimpressed by the surroundings. She whined and her legs jerked as Orphan ran in her canine dreams. *It wouldn't be all that bad to be a dog*, Dolan thought. What did you have to worry about? Dogs had no knowledge of death, Heaven, Hell or sociopaths, and they had no bills. The Suburban hit a bump and the animal passed gas. "Jesus, dog!" Harry made a face at the sudden obnoxious odor, but Orphan couldn't have cared less.

Several Idaho County Sheriffs' cars sped past Dolan going out of town. Just outside the town of White Bird he had seen a congregation of law enforcement agencies near an old logging road. Someone had called for more backup, so the situation wasn't good. "Glad I don't work here," Harry said aloud. He noticed that one of the deputies responding was a woman in her twenties who wore a solemn expression as she guided her patrol car down the highway. Youth had its own brand of enthusiasm and the woman made Dolan feel old. Large snow flakes began to fall as the Suburban rolled past the, 'Hagar City Limits', sign.

There were only a few cars in the parking lot of a café called, Mom's Kitchen. It was mid-afternoon so the small diner was quiet until the dinner rush. Dolan's stomach grumbled and he gave into the urge before going to Blake's house. The place was clean, with black and white tiled floors and red and white checked tablecloths. A fifty's style theme included old records on the walls and a counter top with stools. As soon as Harry slid into a red upholstered booth, a waitress was right there with water and a menu. *Well, they have good marks so far*, thought Dolan.

"Could I get you some coffee?" The waitress was forty plus with her hair attractively pulled back.

"Ice tea, please, not much of a coffee drinker. Any specials today?" Harry smiled at the woman.

"Just on the weekends, but we make a mean chicken fried steak. Comes with mashed potatoes, gravy and the day's vegetable, which is corn."

"Okay, I'll take that." Dolan noticed that her name tag said Mary in bright red letters.

"I'll be right back with that ice tea." She was off in the crisp, swift motion of a waitress with many miles under her belt. She was not nosy either which pleased Harry.

The chicken fry was about half eaten when the deputy that passed Dolan a short while before yanked the door open letting in a blast of frigid air. She appeared irritated as she took a stool at the counter. The baseball style cap bearing the logo, Idaho County Sheriff, was tossed on the stool beside her. Her cheeks were slightly pink from the cold and the deputy's short brown hair remained neatly in place in spite of the way she jerked the hat off. The waitress, Mary, set a cup of steaming coffee before the woman without being asked.

"Bad day?" Mary asked in a motherly fashion. Harry figured the deputy must be a regular at the diner.

"I might as well come in here and wait tables for all the good they think I am!" The officer pulled off the flight jacket style coat and laid it over the cap. The name plate bore the name, Keefe.

"Now, Libby, it takes time to earn your wings in any job, and you've got egos to deal with out there." Mary filled a pitcher with ice tea and made her way around the counter toward Dolan who held his glass up for a refill. "No offense meant about the ego thing."

"None taken. Just because I'm a guy doesn't mean that I don't have to contend with egos too." Dolan took a long drink of tea.

"What kind of problems could a guy like you have?" Libby spun the stool around to face him. She noticed the man was fairly tall, stocky but not fat. He wasn't that bad looking for an older guy and he had a commanding manner about him.

"The same as you. It took me forever to finally get the job I wanted, and then sometimes I still get treated like some old fart who needs put out to pasture. I was an army Ranger for years, yet the young guys didn't believe I still had anything to offer." Harry studied the trim young woman and suddenly felt his belly struggling against his belt. He pushed the plate away.

"A Ranger, huh? I would think that would help you. I mean the experience and all." Deputy Keefe seemed impressed.

"It depends. Some people are respectful of my Vietnam experience and others look at me and wonder if I might go berserk at any time. It can go either way. If you really like that job, you don't let them chase you away. Name's Harry."

"I'm Libby Keefe, short for Liberty. My parents are into the whole patriotic thing." She walked over in shiny boots and shook Dolan's hand.

"So, what did they leave you out of back there?" Dolan nodded toward the town of White Bird.

"Just one of the most exciting things that could happen here. What kind of job do you have?" She slid into the booth across from him.

"I'm an investigator for a coroner back in Kansas. The doctor here was an army buddy of mine years ago and invited me up here." The woman's youthful face made Dolan feel more like a father figure than anything else. So much for fantasies.

"Dr. Gayle is a nice guy and a good doctor," Mary remarked from behind the counter as she put clean glasses away. There were no other customers.

"Yes, he is. I'm here on vacation. Hope to explore the land he bought awhile back." Dolan finished his dinner having decided that a father figure was expected to have a little paunch.

"They wouldn't let me stay and guard the scene, the bastards. I could do that!" Keefe's mouth pulled into a straight, thin line. "My shift was up so they let Peters take over."

"You didn't get close to the crime scene then?" Harry asked.

"No, damn it. Don't tell anybody, but they found a woman's body about a quarter mile down the old mine road. Man, how am I supposed to get experience when they won't let me do anything?"

"They will, just be patient. I saw something going on driving up here, figured it must be something hot." Dolan noticed that

Mary was intently watching two men across the street through the snow.

They were standing in front of Red Simon's. The shorter one wore the dark suit and collar of a minister and looked very much like the jerk that pestered Dolan the last time he was at the bar. The other man was big, with blond hair cut in a buzz and a rock solid jaw.

"Hope the hell they don't come in here." Mary appeared disgusted.

"Is that Berge wearing the priest suit? Thought he was a grease monkey." Dolan pulled out a twenty to pay for the meal as he wandered over to the counter next to the cash register.

"Oh yeah. That's him and if he's a preacher then I'm a nuclear physicist. Got himself a new friend to join his fanatics, the guy scares me." The waitress took the bill and made change.

"Who is the other one? Look likes a poster boy for the SS."

"Close, name is Dylan Clever and he used to live at the Aryan Nation compound, but they weren't radical enough for him. Ever since Berge's wife took a hike, Hans has gotten weirder and weirder. He moved Clever into his house." Libby stood next to Harry in a parade rest position as she narrated.

Dolan smiled at her crisp uniform and military stance. She really was enthusiastic about police work. "Blake said something about Berge's wife leaving. Guess he used to beat her." Harry dropped the change into his jeans pocket as he watched Berge's hands wave around in some animated conversation.

"Never called the cops though, she was terrified of him. We used to see her in the grocery store several days after a good pounding when the bruises were turning yellow. Poor lady." Mary shook her head.

"I hate wife beaters, they're chickenshits." Keefe hung her thumbs on the utility belt around her waist. She studied the men in the distance with blue eyes.

"I've seen the end results of domestic violence, and it isn't nice." Dolan pulled on his blue parka. "Thanks for lunch, tell Mom the food was great. Maybe I'll see you two around."

"Come back any time and I'll tell Art you like his cooking. Yeah, 'Mom' is an old fat guy named Art Munson." Mary grabbed some menus for the customers just walking in and showed them a table.

The snow fell fast and heavy on Dolan and Keefe as they stood on the sidewalk near the diner. Everything was covered in bright white frosting and their breath hung in the air a frozen mist. The young officer pulled the radio from her belt and told the dispatcher she was now ten-seven, or out of service. "Well it was nice meeting you, Harry." Libby extended her right hand. "Maybe I'll see ya around?"

"It's possible, watch yourself now." Dolan brushed off the snow on the door handle of the Suburban as Keefe backed out of the parking space. She drove slowly past Berge and Clever, making eye contact as the tires marred the fresh snow.

Dolan monitored the situation through his passenger mirror as the back window was blocked by a layer of snow. Keefe had the possibility of being a good cop, if she lived long enough. Berge seemed to be taken by most residents of Hagar as just a sneaky wife beater, but Harry had a bad feeling about him. It seems that Mary, the waitress, did as well, but Keefe was challenging the man which could only lead to trouble.

Laura was shoveling the walk when Dolan drove up. She wore a red and white waist length coat that stood out dramatically against the green of the pines and the twirling snowflakes. Harry shut off the engine then went around to the rear of the vehicle to fetch a snow shovel that he kept in the back in case he should get stuck in the boonies somewhere. He began with the far end close to the Suburban. She laughed, not expecting the gesture.

"I'll do one half. You do the other," Harry shouted through the frigid air in a singsong type of voice.

"And I'll get to Scotland before ye!" Laura sang, her dark eyes twinkling like a child's. She loved Dolan's spontaneity.

"Hey, what do you know about Hansel Berge?" Harry continued to scoop snow.

"More than I ever wanted to…he came here with his brood and tried to get Blake to sell the land to them. Of course he was told no, but they came back again and they were nastier about it. Blake told him to go to Hell."

"Anything happen after that?"

"The son-of-bitch watches us every now and then, especially me or Stark. We'll come out of the grocery store and there he'll be, just sitting in his truck, glaring at us." She finished up the sidewalk, which was rapidly turning white again, but Laura liked to stay ahead of it.

"Wonder why he wants it so bad?" Dolan leaned on his shovel and asked the heavy clouds over head.

Chapter Nineteen

The more Berge thought of the sons he could have had now, the angrier he became. He remembered the numerous times he had humped that old cow just to impregnate her and it had all been for nothing. Louise would just lay there as if nothing more exciting than Hans taking a leak was occurring. He laughed at the thought of the timid little woman frantically trying to keep his dinner warm and tasty without knowing when he would be home. She would be back. Louise couldn't make it without a man. Berge's old pickup slid to a halt at the stop sign. Damn!

He hated this kind of shit, but it was a small price to pay to be among the white race. He wiped the windshield clear with a gloved hand. The heater took a long time to acquire a decent temperature. Berge might have to look into a newer truck. Too Goddamned bad that Tannahill's truck couldn't have been confiscated for the cause! What a waste. The familiar form of Brentlinger's Ford F-250 came into view. The man was stupid and could not keep his wife under control. He was a weak link in the chain, but also privy to information Berge didn't want out. Hans honked at Jim who flipped him off as the Ford cruised by. Berge watched the truck roll by with an open mouth and his heart quickened with anxiety. This was not a good time to be losing control over people.

The house was dark, quiet and certainly never smelled of recently cooked food since Louise had run off. Hans thought back to a few months before when he had come home after that last beating. The house had been quiet and dark then too. He had nearly panicked at the thought of a stiffening Louise Berge still on their queen-sized bed. She always did as she was told so she had to be dead. He had taken a deep breath and bellowed her name. He called out a second time, still nothing.

What alarmed him as much as Louise's absence was the fact that she had not cleaned the sheets and pillow cases. She would never do that. Berge had pulled open his wife's dresser to find her bras and panties gone. A check of the closet found many of her clothes missing along with her old suitcase. Hans had then run to the living room to check for her purse, which she kept next to her recliner. It too was gone. She had actually left him.

Clever lived in the spare bedroom, but spent most of his time outside the house. The man was rock hard both physically and emotionally. His eyes were an icy blue, void of any need for frivolous conversations. Clever was an ex-Green Beret who had tired of the government, fags, coons, and after the Gulf War, sandniggers. He too was sick of federal interference in people's lives. Dylan spent most of his time either in the church or the workshop out back and most of the time Berge left him alone as instinct told him to do. Hans was sipping a beer in the living room when Clever's form appeared in the door to the kitchen. His dark-blue tee shirt was stretched tight over broad shoulders and bulging biceps and he was carrying a rifle and cleaning kit which he placed on the couch. He asked if there was another beer, then went to retrieve it from the refrigerator when Berge nodded to the affirmative.

Dylan sat on the edge of the sofa and opened the kit. The De Lisle carbine was a gift from a British friend and his pride and joy. Originally designed for commando raids during WWII it was a favorite of Special Forces for sentry removal. The weapon was completely silent with a velvet-lined cavity to collect shells. The barrel was vented with a system of plates, which silenced the bullets passing through it. The De Lisle was perfect for head shots at one hundred meters.

"What do we do about the doctor and his land now?" Dylan rubbed the rifle like it was a sensual woman. He did not look at Hans.

"I'll give him one more chance to let it go." Berge frowned as he recalled the last effort made by the group to procure their sacred land.

The doctor's old lady had told him to fuck off and never come back again. Laura Gayle needed some of Louise's medicine to knock her back into her place. The first time they had asked about buying the property, she hadn't been so rude. For whatever reason, the woman was now a problem.

"What if that doesn't work?" Dylan's icy blue eyes drifted up to Hans.

"I have a plan that he can't ignore." Berge tried to calm the hairs that stood on the back of his neck. Clever was a scary guy.

"That doctors' friend, what do you know about him?" Dylan finally unscrewed the lid off the bottle of Canadian beer.

"He wore an old field jacket last time he was up here. Had a patch with lightening on a red background and a small patch that said, Ranger. Mean anything to you?" Berge's cheeks blew out as he stifled a burp.

"Tropic Lightening, 75th Rangers. He's seen some action and he could be a problem." Clever looked to Hans like he expected a detailed plan. He actually believed that Berge had a calling from God to save the white man and had suggested that Hans start to dress like a minister.

"I don't know, he didn't seem real into fights of any kind, but he does think we're full of shit."

Dylan cleaned the rifle in silence for a few minutes. "I think he's up to something. He was wearing that jacket for a purpose."

"He's not wearing it now." Berge shrugged. He didn't see how what the man was wearing was relevant.

"So what if he is, he's just one guy." Clever studied the De Lisle. "This plan you have, it will have to be drastic."

Berge snickered. "You could say that about it all right."

Chapter Twenty

It really felt good to give Berge the finger. Jim Brentlinger drove around some after stopping at the hardware store to grab a bag of Ice Melt. He had to keep his head clear to handle the hurdles that faced him. Hurdle one was telling Joan about his involvement with the Sons of Marduk and the fact that he put their home up for collateral so that the Sons could buy the land. The second hurdle was telling Joan that he was HIV positive as he had not been able to get the words out. It was all so insane. She would want a divorce, unless she was an idiot, and Joan was not.

The family had begun eating by the time Brentlinger slipped through the kitchen door to the dining room. Joan smiled, but it was a put on for the kids. He could tell that she knew things were not right, but she would let her suspicions cook on the back burner until it was time to serve them up. Jim took his place at the table, then requested that Jason pass the fried chicken platter. The boy did what he was told with a steely reserve. Jason had little respect for Jim Brentlinger, who claimed to subscribe to the philosophy of white superiority, but was pathetically lukewarm about it. He didn't even hate fags anymore. What the Hell was that all about? His father wasn't nearly intense enough to be a patriot and had even jumped Jason for calling a dog a nigger. Jim Brentlinger no longer had the stuff to be a true member of the Elder Church or a warrior for the holy racial war to come. The uncomfortable silence was interrupted by the telephone ringing. Jim told Jason to answer it.

"Yeah, he's here. What?" The boy seemed excited, nodding his head to the voice on the phone. "Okay then, yeah. You wanna talk to Dad?" He handed the receiver to Jim.

"Who is it?" He asked with a mouthful of mashed potatoes.

"The Reverend Berge." Jason whispered. Brentlinger swung his head back and forth.

"No." His voice was muffled.

"Dad's in the bathroom, he'll call you back." Jason smiled into the receiver.

"Just what was he saying to you?" Jim's tone was accusatory. Jason sat back down in front of his plate.

"He wants me to join his church. I can't believe he asked me!" The kid had his appetite back.

"No, that's all I'm going to say about it." He pointed a fork as his son. The two youngest children thought the situation was funny and snickered at their half brother.

"I didn't know he was a minister. I really don't care for the guy." Joan looked to her husband.

"You just don't really understand him or his cause! He wouldn't bust my ass for calling a dog a nigger!" The boy's pasty skin reddened to match his hair.

"Excuse me?" Joan didn't appreciate this conversation at the dinner table.

Jim stood up, crumbs from the chicken tumbled off his shirt. "Oh, I don't. Well, let me tell you one thing about Hansel Berge and his ideas…"

"Man, you don't have to tell me anything about it. You are the one who doesn't understand."

"That so! You just try calling any canine a nigger in front of him and see what happens to you! You want to be a Son of Marduk? You better get used to one thing!"

Jason rose up from the table. "And what is that?"

"God barks, boy! And His bark is nothing compared to His bite."

Jim's bearded face was inches from the smooth skin of his son.

"What is going on here?" Joan demanded to know.

"We need to talk. The sooner the better." Her husband's tone took a sad turn.

"You two can talk, I'm out of here." Jason grabbed his coat from the closet doorknob.

"You stay away from Berge, am I clear?" He took a handful of the boy's green parka. The red hair and the green coat made the kid look like a giant carrot. The younger Brentlinger jerked away.

"Or what?"

"I'll knock the piss and fire right out of you!"

Berge snuggled down deep into his easy chair in the dark front room of his house. He had finished off the better half of a quart of Jack Daniels and was letting the alcohol saturate his brain while recalling past rituals. It was necessary to bind with nature in order to communicate with God. That was a fact completely ignored by mainstream Christianity and its polyester-suited Sunday morning preachers. The Baptists with their vacation Bible schools, the Methodist bake sales and the Lutheran picnics all made Berge want to vomit. What a load of shit!

Every one of them set out to take the physical reality of sex from human existence and deny the raw animal instinct. Not one of those pus bags would be prepared for Jesus when he returned or be able to fight the battle to pave the way for him. He needed to change his recruiting strategies. Older, married men were too set in their ways to be very useful. Sure, they got off on weekend outings to the land as they liked the club type atmosphere of the group, but they had limits, too many limits.

Berge had seen the faces of his followers when Tannahill was sacrificed. There had been far too much horror and regret. Hitler had the right idea to start with the youth of society. Youth were like green ware; molded to a basic shape and ready to be painted however, one wished, then fired to a finish.

Jason Brentlinger had all the earmarks of a simpleton that would believe whatever one chose to tell him. He was a misfit at school, homely and destined to be blue collar just like his father. The difference would be that Berge would get him before his was forty, worn out and looking to find himself during a mid-life crisis. It would also be a good way to keep Jim Brentlinger's balls in a vise. Hans wasn't about to let that pot-bellied, civil service geek ruin all of his hard work by ratting them out.

The snow in the drive groaned with the weight of a vehicle as it rolled toward the house. Berge was jolted out of his slumber. Christ! Was it the cops? A nervous hand parted the lacy curtains near his chair. It was an old orange colored Firebird. The driver's door opened to reveal a lanky, redheaded kid. It was Brentlinger's boy. Hell, Berge was in no mood to start the lessons now.

"Jason, how can I help ya?" Hans hung out the back door, the icy air decreasing some of the fog in his skull.

"I'm with ya! I want to join the fight and work for the white race." Jason proclaimed like someone responding to a Billy Graham crusade. "My father's an asshole, he doesn't believe in the cause any more."

"He doesn't? Well, come in and tell me about it." Berge stepped aside to allow the kid to pass.

Clever emerged from his room at the sound of voices. He said nothing as he looked Jason up and down.

"Hi, I'm Jason." The goofy looking teenager extended his hand to the large stranger.

"Clever, Dylan Clever." He took the kid's hand, which felt cold and weak.

After an hour of listening to Jason Brentlinger lament his life's miseries Clever's expression was stony. Hans was encouraging the conversation though, and nodded in empathy to the kid's complaints. The ex-Green Beret didn't have the patience for this sort of maneuver and had less use for whining. He knew that Berge was working the boy, but Clever wasn't sure the kid would be of much use in a tense situation.

"He is too worried about what Mom will think about The Elder Church. She doesn't like words like, nigger. Dad won't even try to convert her or explain how important the holy war is...and I'm surrounded by faggots at school. We have to do something about what's happening."

Berge smiled. The kid swallowed the bait, hook and all. "Yes, we do and that is why the Sons of Marduk must remain strong in spite of so many who don't understand or have the fortitude to carry on the fight."

"Things could get very ugly before the victory. People will die. You understand that, don't you?" Dylan had seen many a gung-ho teenager turn to mush in the jungle and strongly suspected Jason would do so as well.

"Yes, sir. I hope to get some niggers and faggots myself."

"Fine. Let's drink to Rohowa." Berge retrieved three shot glasses from a china cabinet near the dining room table that had belonged to his mother-in-law. It would be a cold day in Hell when Louise would ever get it back.

They clinked their glasses together, then downed the whiskey. Clever and Berge grinned as Brentlinger tried to stifle a gag with watery eyes.

Chapter Twenty-one

The locker room reeked of the usual smells that accompanied physically stressed teenaged male bodies. The coach was a grizzly old fart that made them run even in single digit temperatures. He ran with them and seemed to be the happiest when the outing became miserable. Ice would form on his stubble and the sub-zero wind would chap their faces raw, but Deegan was fueled by the slow freezing of his flesh.

Jesus, Stark mumbled to himself as he felt his skin start to thaw out. *He simply had to get out of Hagar and Idaho!* It wasn't that Stark Gayle didn't enjoy sports, as he did get some pleasure out of them, but the practices and games gave him a distraction from the yearnings that plagued him. It was also a good cover to ward off the girls who saw Stark as husband material.

When you were strong and athletic, people tended to not hassle you about your social life. It was the general attitude of the other boys that made sports an unhappy experience for him. Many seem to see sports as a modern version of the hunt and that first touchdown the act of blooding. Every macho achievement was logged in personal files to impress the best girl. It was a human county fair, but Stark didn't have much choice.

Jason Brentlinger reached out and smacked the bare buttocks of a passing teammate, Kevin Blackburn, who responded with a resounding, "Faggot."

Brentlinger laughed and told Kevin only in his dreams. Stark listened without comment as Blackburn stood inches from him and retrieved his clothes from a locker. He rolled his eyes at Gayle. Jason was asshole who tended to be popular with a small group of loud, obnoxious types who could barely read. Kevin sat on the bench beside Stark to pull on his socks. He wasn't tall, but was well proportioned.

"Any word on your dad's friend?" Blackburn asked as he rubbed antiperspirant under his arms.

"Nah, nobody seems to give a shit. Cops aren't interested cause he's a grown man and could have just taken off." Gayle ran a comb through his dark hair while trying to view the process in a tiny mirror attached to the inside of his locker.

"Yeah, like the guy just up and said, to hell with my business and my nice house." Kevin stood up and tucked his tee shirt into well-worn Levi jeans.

"They just don't want to get of their fat asses. Hagar cops are worthless." Stark put on a black and white checked flannel shirt over a black tee shirt. He could see Brentlinger a few feet away wearing his usual shit-eating grin. Some people had the gift of being able to make the meekest person want to go nuts with a ball bat.

"What are you looking at Gayle? Sorry, but I got a date tonight. With something that has a pussy." Jason laughed. He was tall and thin with arms like an ape. The zits on his face seemed to always be threatening to explode at any given minute.

"You be sure to take it easy on that goat, Brentlinger, your mom might want to milk that sucker to make cheese." Stark answered with a straight face. It took several seconds for Jason to process the insult then he turned scarlet and called Gayle a tulip.

Blackburn looked at Stark then at Brentlinger. "Ya know, it seems to me that you are the only one grabbing guys asses around here. Who are kidding anyway? Any girl who lost a bet and had to kiss you would have to start antibiotics the week before!"

"You better not turn your backs on me, either one of you!" Jason pushed past Stark and Kevin as they snickered.

"Count on it! I wanna be a virgin when I get married," Kevin shouted as Brentlinger rushed out of the locker room.

Stark slapped Kevin's open hand. "See ya tomorrow, man."

The rest of the school day dragged on for Stark. Four years of busting his ass and putting on a show had worn him down. The lectures droned on, the games meant nothing and the girls that wanted him for his father's money or his looks had turned him cynical. At the end of sixth period, Stark Gayle nearly ran to the parking lot. The pavement was shiny from what Stark liked to call an 'ice burst'. There were cloudbursts the rest of the year, but ice bursts hit suddenly, and created numerous patches of black ice. Black ice was nature's booby trap. The city kept the lot plowed, which made things worst when the ice landed on the parking area. He stepped gingerly out to his car and found the lock frozen over. A few taps with the butt of his pocket knife allowed the key to enter the lock.

"Why don't you just blow on it, Gayle? You've had plenty of practice." Jason smiled, pleased at his own wit.

"For Christ's sake, Pepperoni Face, find a vat of Clearasil and fall into it!" Stark gripped the hood of the car near the windshield wiper for balance, unsure of where this conversation would lead.

"I'm real tired of your faggot ass, Gayle, and your mouth!" Brentlinger puffed his chest like a Bandy rooster, secure in the knowledge that the friends surrounding him would back him up.

"You're tired of me? Then why the hell are you up my ass everywhere I go? You some kind of butt tick?" Stark tensed up and tightened his grip on the car.

Jason's buddies giggled, which made Brentlinger's face flush. "That's it, Gayle! We don't want your kind here." He brought back a long leg to swing at Stark who caught it in mid air and yanked its owner to the frozen asphalt. Brentlinger's head smacked the ice hard.

"Fuck! Damn it to hell, you little bastard!" Jason nursed his bleeding occipital lobe.

Stark opened his car door, then turned back to the boys standing around the fallen Brentlinger. "So? You got somewhere to be or what?"

"This ain't the end of this, Stark." Jason's eyes were rimmed with tears.

"Yeah, this is it, asshole. It ends today." Stark took a handful of crusty snow from the roof of his car and threw it in Brentlinger's face. "Get a life, you prick!"

Brentlinger's friends studied Gayle for a few seconds then decided that making further trouble would be counterproductive. Stark packed some muscles from his various sports activities, which could inflict serious injury. They helped Jason up without comment.

Stark slammed the door as he plopped into the driver's seat. He revved the engine as the group moved carefully over the icy lot. They weren't much to look at. One was rather blubbery with a stubby beard and the other two were nondescript except for their heavy metal tee shirts. Stark watched them in the side view mirror, then left the school parking lot. The clouds were heavy with moisture as the blue Cutlass pulled onto the street. He decided to skip his afternoon run. Between that sadistic coach and the hillbilly boys, Stark was out of the mood to run in the cold. Mrs. Finkle would need rock salt spread on her sidewalk and porch, so Gayle steered the car toward her house.

The small white house with blue trim appeared homey with the lights on and smoke rolling out of the chimney. He parked the Cutlass in front and checked the mail box which perched on a post near the end of her sidewalk. Stark tried to install one closer so that she wouldn't fall, but Edna insisted that she needed whatever exercise she could get. The porch light came on and the front door opened. "Stark, no running today?" she asked, her German accent still peppering her speech.

"Nah, we have a monster for a gym coach who froze out this morning."

The teenager followed the old lady into the house. A dark, flowery border lined the white walls of the living room. A light-colored sofa lined one wall under the front windows where Stark liked to sit. There was a matching recliner and a wooden rocker where Mrs. Finkle sat. The room temperature was always too warm for Stark and he removed his flannel shirt.

"Some coffee with brownies? I just made both!" She tugged on a pink sweatshirt sporting a collar and a basket of flowers on the front.

"Yes, please." He leaned back on the couch. The warmth of the house made him yawn. As she went to the kitchen, Stark surveyed the walls of the living room again. Old pictures from Germany hung in one group and photos from the Finkles' early years in America surrounded a mirror made to look like a window. Stark really hadn't known a traditional grandmother, as his paternal grandparents had been killed in a car wreck before he was born, and Laura's mother is a corporate lawyer. Edna did everything a grandma was supposed to do. She grew flowers, baked, told stories, gave Stark little presents and cheered him up when he needed it.

"Doesn't he look important?" Edna beamed at the picture of Albert Finklestein in uniform. "He was so proud. Albert was ten years older than me, you know, so I was eight when that picture was taken. But he was a child as well. At eighteen you know nothing of life."

"I know plenty." Stark sipped the hot coffee. It was dark and strong.

"You had a bad day?" Edna peered at him over the rims of her glasses.

"Why do some jerks have to bother other people that don't want to be bothered? I just want to be left alone." He stirred the liquid slowly while resisting the urge to put his feet on the coffee table, which was decorated with lace work.

"That's why they bother you. You are content with yourself and have nothing to prove, so they feel left out of the secret." Edna shrugged her shoulders.

"I'll be glad when I start college and get out of here. Everybody is so ignorant." Stark pouted as he chewed a brownie.

"And the Nazis ruled Germany, but Germany was and is a beautiful country, and it is beautiful here. Don't let the evil of the world color everything for you, Stark. That's what they want, for you to be as miserable as they are! There will still be ignorant people at the university too, you know?" Edna looked to the sulking boy then jumped back from her cup after drinking. "Why didn't you tell me it was so hot?"

"I like it that way...it must have been horrible in the camps."

"Yes, yes. It is so hard to describe to anyone who was not there. Those neo-Nazi types are saying that it never happened. What a load of bullshit! I only wished it had not. Who would or could make up such a thing as Auschwitz? History is much more terrifying than these horror movies on television." She pulled the quilt on the back of the rocker around her shoulders at a sudden chill.

The street lights came through the window and reflected off her lenses. "Stark, could you pull those blinds behind you?" Stark grabbed a coaster then set his cup on the table. It was dark now and easy to see into the house. He closed the mini blinds and noticed that the curtains had a strange odor to them. He sniffed the blue panels again.

"They smell bad, or is curtain sniffing the new fad?" She smiled slightly.

"You should take your act on the road, Mrs. Finkle. Yeah, they smell really odd." The teenager sat back down.

She walked over to the side window and put the curtains to her nose. "I thought I was crazy…I didn't think about the smell staying in the cloth. It was months ago…." She seemed confused.

"What was months ago?" Gayle looked to his older friend who suddenly seemed old and frail.

"I've smelled such a thing before, not so much inside the camp as outside when the allies were coming. The smoke stacks roared as the Nazi tried to gas then burn all of us up before the Americans could stop them. Humans have a unique odor and even more unique when cooked, but it couldn't be, just couldn't be that. Must have been something other than a cat or dog, an elk maybe." She stared out the window toward the dog pound at the bottom of the hill.

"It's a gross smell. You smelled it months ago? When?" Stark felt his fears place an icy grip on his heart.

Edna returned to the rocker and placed her cross stitch project in her lap. "Oh, don't let an old woman upset you! I'm just being foolish."

"Wonder if you're not?" The boy was having visions of Tom Tannahill's body burned to ashes.

"What are you thinking, Stark?"

"It might have been Tom."

"What would make you think a thing like that?" Edna threaded a needle with bright red thread.

"Harry thinks he was killed on our land. There are things about Tom that most people don't know. Did you ever have something that you just couldn't tell anyone?"

"Everyone has secrets, Stark. Everyone has at least one skeleton they don't want found. Can't you tell Harry about your concerns? He seems to be open to most things."

"Can I tell him what you said about the smell? He might want to talk to you….I think it's something we should mention. Wouldn't that be a good way to dispose of a body?"

"Hitler certainly thought so! Yes, I'll talk with him, but I don't know how much help I'll be." She stuck her finger and cursed silently.

The boy swallowed hard. He hadn't really intended to share his suspicions with anyone and felt a little foolish. "I just don't think Tom went anywhere, he's dead. Those Nazi crackers around here would love to fry him."

"You need to say all of this to Harry, especially if your fears are founded in fact."

"There's something about Tom that's connected to me and nobody knows about."

"Whatever it is you must tell your parents, Stark. They will either accept it or not."

"You're kind of liberal for your age, Mrs. Finkle." He chuckled.

"My parents were pretty riled when I started dating a Jew, let me tell you! They had nothing against the Jews, but were very afraid of what I was getting myself into…they didn't think I could have much of a life with a Jewish man in Germany at that time. And, of course, they were right. When you are young and know what you want you also have the strength to take the consequences. You can't wait until half your life is over to be free." She sipped the coffee that had cooled to a pleasant temperature.

Stark was quiet as he digested the old woman's words. He wasn't sure that he had the same strength Edna Finkle described. Gayle was an only child whose mother looked forward to a wedding and grandchildren. How could he tell her that it wasn't going to happen? "I don't think I'm as brave as you."

She laughed lightly. "Stark, you are a young man and you can do anything you want to do. I know you can."

Chapter Twenty-two

The air was chilly and wet, but Stark drove down the highway with his window down. A cold, crisp breeze always helped to clear his mind of the ogres that dwelt there. The isolation he felt at being gay in Hagar, Idaho had been compounded after Tom vanished. There was no doubt that that those beer-bellied Nazi fucks of Hagar murdered him. The only person that knew about Stark's sexuality was Tom and he had figured it out on is own. No one knew about Tannahill except for Stark, yet somehow his private life had been discovered by the ignorant factions of the county. Why else would anyone want to kill Tom? His sexuality had to be at the heart of it.

A banged up pickup was parked in front of the Gayle house when Stark came up the drive. The rusty piece of junk was in the teenagers spot so he had to pull off to the side. Two men were confronting Harry who stood on the porch with Blake and Laura to either side. The yard light spread an eerie glow over the scene and Stark cast a deep shadow across the snow as he approached the two men who blocked the porch steps.

"We have been using that land for years! We won't be stopped now by the likes of you!" Berge glared at Dolan. A large vein popped out in his temple. "This country was founded by homesteaders, not by yuppie sons-of-bitches like you."

"It is not for sale, not now, not ever! You can leave now or go to jail. It's all the same to me." Harry stated calmly. Clever planted himself next to Berge in a rigid parade rest and bored into Dolan with his icy blue eyes.

"What a waste of a fine young man....son, you can join some real men if you have more balls than your old man!" Hans beckoned to Stark who leaned against Harry's Suburban.

"You stay away from our son! You can stick your phony church right up your ass!" Laura had pushed her way in front of Blake and braced herself on the porch railing. She fought to retain her stance even though the smoldering glare on Berge's face scared her.

"You made the choice. Just you remember that!" The first step groaned as Harry placed a boot on it to prompt the two Sons of Marduk to leave. Clever was making Dolan uncomfortable with his expressionless silence. This would not be the end of anything. The two men returned to their truck and sat for a few seconds before backing out.

"Is there some connection between Berge and Tom?" Harry asked as they watched Berge and Clever creep slowly down the drive.

"How could there be?" Blake looked stressed. Stark ran up the steps into the house past his father and Dolan.

Laura held the storm door open for him while announcing that dinner was probably cold by now. "Come on, guys. Don't let that scum ruin the evening."

The Gayle's retired early that night leaving Harry and Stark sitting before a fire that painted the room with contorting shadows. Dolan had a gut feeling that the kid knew something about the situation that he was keeping to himself.

"Harry...did you want to be in the army?" Stark watched the reddish orange flames dance in the large fireplace.

"Yes and no. I wanted away my father and there was no work in Golding, so the military seemed the only real option." Dolan squeezed a lemon slice into his glass of ice tea.

"Wasn't being in Vietnam scary? I mean how did you do it, day after day?"

The first stop in Nam in 1969 was the Southeast Asian American Airbase in Bien Hoa. That was also the first time Harry wished that he had joined another branch of the service. The Air Force side of the place was neat and organized for a continued stay, but the army part was shabby and appeared fly-by-night. It was there that Dolan signed up for the sniper course. He had orders for Tay Nihn, but had to spend three weeks in a Ranger school before shipping out. Even though Harry went through Ranger training at Fort Benning, there were things about Vietnam that couldn't be taught in Georgia. Of all the things Dolan hated about Nam, the damned heat was right at the top of the list. It made everything five hundred times worse than it had to be.

"Yeah, it was. I spent six months in a long range patrol, an LRRP, where we wandered through the jungle looking for signs of Charlie. We'd plant claymores around and set up an ambush sites. There were many missions where nothing at all happened and then one day all hell would break loose. I didn't have an R&R until I got shot."

Stark turned sideways on the long couch to face Harry who was beginning to enjoy recalling the past. "How did you deal with the pressure? Not knowing if there was a tomorrow or not?" The teenager bit his lip. He was the same age as Dolan when he went to boot camp at Fort Dix, New Jersey. Stark wore a Big Dog tee shirt Harry had sent for his birthday.

"When do you ever really know if there is a tomorrow? I don't know...we played cards, drank, told dirty stories, took R&Rs to Bangkok or Hawaii, some guys paid for hookers, that kind of thing. When I was released from the hospital I transferred to a Blue team in the Calvary. As a LRRP we didn't actively engage the enemy, we were recon units. As a Blue, we went on short patrols looking for trouble, acted as quick response teams and rescued downed choppers." Dolan took a long drink of tea. "Why do I get the feeling that you aren't just after a history lesson?"

Stark went into the kitchen for a soda. He walked back slowly, his baggy sweat pants hanging low on slim hips.

Instead of sitting on the couch he chose his mother's easy chair adjacent to Dolan. "So what's a blue team?"

"Okay...blue teams act as QRTs to LRRPs, do search and rescue for downed choppers and do the short missions I mentioned. Man, Rangers carry so much shit! There were times when the Blues wished they carried as much ammo as the LRRPs." Dolan laughed as recalled the heavy ruck sacks needed for a week in the jungle.

"Tom and Dad were pretty close...he hasn't wanted to do anything they used to do and he doesn't seem that interested in the land now." Stark studied the fire again as if the answers flickered in them somewhere.

"Grief is very individual and we don't know what happened to Tom, that makes it worse."

"How are we gonna find out what happened when the dumb ass cops around here don't give a shit?" The boy swung his head around suddenly expecting a solution.

"I think there's someone who will help us out. Libby Keefe is with the sheriff's department and more than eager to prove herself. I'll see if I can get her to run a check on Hansel Berge, and I have some connections of my own."

"You think Tom was killed out by the lake?"

"It was no deer. Know anything about Tom's parents?" Harry moved to the end of the couch and leaned close to Stark Gayle.

The kid straightened. "Why would I know that? He was dad's friend."

"Since he hung out here a lot I figured that he must have mentioned them. Blake never talked religion with him?"

Stark head swung slowly back and forth like a pendulum. "No way, no way...there's a lot dad doesn't know about Tom."

"But you do."

Dolan leaned even closer. "Like what?"

The boy's expression displayed his regret at running his mouth. "You don't understand how much trouble this could cause. Please Harry!" Stark lowered his voice.

"Should I go talk to Tom's mother? It would be easier if you would just tell me what's going on."

"My parents don't know, nobody but Tom knew. You can't tell them, Harry. You have to promise!"

Dolan hesitated at the request then nodded. "All right."

Chapter Twenty-three

Libby Keefer was flattered that Dolan asked her help in finding Tom Tannahill. Once in a while, when the dispatchers called in sick she still had to work the radio and was NCIC certified, which meant that Libby could run criminal background checks on Hansel Berge. When she ran the checks, Berge didn't seem to exist before 1982. No records of any kind turned up prior to July 1982 including a driver's license. Dolan then called Detective Martha Ringer in Wichita and sweet talked her into digging round. Martha could be a wizard when it came to tracking people down and she didn't fail Harry this time either.

In July of 1982 Nicholas Hatchen filed a name change in Los Angeles County to become Hansel Berge. As Hatchen, Berge had a nasty reputation in Hollywood for sadism and was involved in some off the wall religion based on Satan. The reason given for the name change was that he had become a born again Christian and wished to start anew. The name Hatchen was Old English for 'a small wasteland' and Hans felt that it did not reflect his dramatic make over when he accepted Jesus as his Savior. As Nicholas was not on the run from the law nor had any serious convictions against him, the judge granted the name change. Martha had snickered on the phone when repeating the explanation for the change. Apparently she didn't buy the old, "I saw the light" routine.

Dolan was somewhat surprised at Stark's admission of being gay, but not too shocked. He knew that it would be a blow to Blake, who simply had no idea and Laura who looked forward to her first grandchild. Stark was convinced that one of the local homophobes had killed Tannahill, but Harry wasn't so sure. There didn't appear to be any connection with Tom's sexuality and his disappearance. There had to be something else, something not so obvious.

The mutated rosary in Tannahill's desk and Berge's satanic past bothered Dolan enough to pay a visit to Tom's mother, Francis Tannahill. At first she didn't want to talk about her missing son with a stranger, but Dolan made a good case for himself while freezing on the front porch. Francis finally decided that Harry was safe enough after he told her that he was staying with Dr. Gayle. She was pleasant and engaging once she opened up. Tom's falling out with his parents began when he brought a young man back with him the summer prior to beginning veterinarian school. They were much more than friends, which threw the Tannahills into a shock, especially Tom's father Daniel. Their son had never given them any indication that he was gay at all. Tom dated girls and seemed to enjoy it. Francis took the news better than her husband, but thought Tom could have been less aggressive with his announcement. He wanted the young man to sleep in the same bed with him, which sent Daniel Tannahill through the roof.

It was like Tom thought he had to bring gay rights to Idaho all by himself. Daniel had a difficult time coming to grips with his son's sexuality. He read books and articles trying to understand why a man would want to be romantically involved with another man. Tom always thought his father was just being ignorant and stubborn and he didn't listen when Francis tried to tell him that his father really had made a major effort to understand. The fact that Dan Tannahill had read about gay men at all was an enormous display of love for his son, but Tom never saw it that way.

Francis felt that if her husband had been given just a little more time he would have eventually accepted Tom's partners. He died shortly after Tom graduated from veterinary school. Francis didn't know much about her son's religious activities in California, but she did know that he totally rejected Christianity and all of its hypocrisies. After working in California for a while, Tom decided to set up practice in Hagar. It was a move that surprised his mother, but Tom had matured, sown his wild oats and was ready to settle into his career. Hagar had no vet, so the decision was sound financially, if not socially as Hagar was not the best town for a gay man to be. He had some guilt about his youthful treatment of his parents and wished to be close for his mother as he had not been for his father.

Francis didn't think that anyone knew about Tom's homosexuality, including Blake Gayle. Dolan wasn't sure what Tannahill's various lifestyles had to do with his disappearance, if anything. He would have to get home soon to resume his own increasingly unsatisfactory life whether he found any answers in Hagar or not. There were no large withdrawals of money from Tom's accounts nor had there been any break-ins at the vet hospital or the house. It may be that Tom was just in the wrong place at the wrong time.

———————

When Dolan returned to the Gayle house his aunt called to say that the funeral home tried to reach him. They wanted to know if Harry knew why the insurance company was delaying payment. His jaw muscles grew taunt as he thought of Alex and Dana pulling that bullshit acts at the funeral home. They were concerned how that bill was being paid, right. It was all Harry could do to maintain his composure on the phone to Globe Life. Someone had tried to change the beneficiary on May 30, which held up the claims process even though Globe wasn't about to let someone change the beneficiary after Sarah died.

Harry sat in Laura's old easy chair and felt empty. How could anyone be so greedy and cruel? They push Sarah to her death and the son-of-a-bitches want paid for it? Holy shit! Harry cursed to himself and swore to never set foot in a church again. It was just too bad that God didn't look after his followers the way that Satan did. He truly wanted to hurt someone in a physical way and gave serious consideration to hiring out as a mercenary again.

"You have to go on, Harry. You cannot change your siblings or their personalities. They chose to imitate your father and not your mom and it is a decision they will one day deeply regret." Laura sat on the couch near Dolan.

"I would believe anything that Al would do, but Alex and Dana are making me sick. How long have they hated me and Sarah?" Harry took the beer that Blake offered him.

"They don't need you, Harry, they have the Cheese's money. When that runs out or their lives turn to shit, they'll look you up." Blake stirred the logs in the fireplace.

"The days of old reliable Harry are gone. It will give me great pleasure to slam the door in their faces." For some reason the beer actually tasted good that night and Dolan took another swallow. "I've found out some things about Tom. Did you know that he was gay?"

Blake turned around with the crispness of a palace guard. "What? No way! I would have known."

"How? If he didn't want anyone here to know they would not and apparently he didn't. Tom probably just didn't want you to act any differently toward him. Sarah wasn't a flag waver either." Dolan finished the beer and crushed the can. It disturbed him to talk about his sister in the past tense. She was only thirty-eight, for God's sake! Maybe the Cathars had it right. The material world was evil and God had no say on the activities of Rex Mundi, the King of the World.

"Suppose that had anything to do with him disappearing? As I can't think of any other reason. The guy was nice to everybody. He could have offered help to somebody that came to the house, somebody claiming to have car trouble. If that's the case we may never know what happened to him." Laura looked to her husband and Dolan.

"You remember that satanic rosary we found in his library? Well, it turns out that Tom rejected Christianity when he left here and Berge isn't who he claims to be. Hans is really a Nicholas Hatchen who had a reputation in Southern California as a sadistic bastard into whips and chains. He was into some church that worshiped Satan. Guess they did every depraved thing you could imagine of a sexual nature." Harry shared the information he got from Libby and Martha with his confused friends.

"It figures, the pompous ass. He parades around town like he's Jesus...don't it just figure." Blake snorted. He was also hurt by Tom's deception and wondered if their friendship they had been real at all.

"You think Tom knew who Berge was?" Laura had an uneasy feeling.

"That I'm not sure of that as Hans has lost a lot of weight since his Hatchen days, here, Martha faxed me a picture." Dolan pulled a small black and white photo from his tee shirt pocket. Nicholas had roughed up a sex partner a little more than she wanted which earned him a trip to the North Hollywood police station. The woman changed her mind and would not testify against him, but Nicholas still had a file with mug shots and prints.

"That's Berge?" Blake stared in amazement. The man had lost not just fat, but muscle as Hans was scrawny.

"Yeah, hard to believe isn't it, but he wanted to change his appearance." Dolan took the photo from Blake and passed it to Laura.

"Why couldn't the local cops find this out?" Laura studied the mug shot.

"Because it was too much work. These clowns couldn't find their balls with a compass!" Gayle poked at the fire and it roared up in response.

"I think there is a reason that the Sons of Marduk want your land so badly…it would not surprise me to find Tom buried in the woods somewhere around the lake."

"What are we going to do? Can we call the police, will they do anything?" Laura realized for the first time that they could all be in danger.

"My guess is nothing as Berge hasn't done anything except offer to buy the land. If he comes back again you could get him for trespassing. I want to search the area near the lake again, see what I can find." Harry stood up, his knees sore from sitting too long.

"I want to get any early start. I only have a few days left. A sheriff's officer is going with me, Libby Keefe. She has the day off and wants to help. What's Stark doing Saturday?" Laura shrugged her shoulder's. "I don't know, Stark!" She yelled toward the loft.

The bedroom door scraped across the carpet as he opened it. "Yeah?"

"You got plans for Saturday?" Dolan asked. When the boy shook his head Harry told him they were going to get some exercise. "Okay, fine with me."

Chapter Twenty-four

The Sons of Marduk filled the Elder Church while Berge had Jason Brentlinger stoking the covered grill outside. It was snowing lightly as the cast iron cooker sent wisps of smoke among the snowflakes. Berge told Jason to invite some of his friends to the meeting and he had brought Will Chester, Wayne Smith and Charlie Jones. All had fathers in the Elder Church. Berge's mood was dark. The meeting had been called to deal with the land situation as well as recruit new members. Hans wasn't happy with the half-assed attitudes of his followers who had left the Aryan Brotherhood because of their liberal notions toward women, yet still made no move without the old lady's approval.

The racial holy war was yet to come. Clever would whip the Sons into fighting shape and the enthusiasm of the young members would bring new life to the movement. It was time to make the doctor an offer he could not refuse. As they munched on burgers in a semi-circle around the wood stove, the Sons discussed the best way to strike at Blake Gayle. It was general consensus that Stark was the good doctor's Achilles Heel and after Jason whined about the younger Gayle being a fag they all felt justified in their decision. Clever had studied maps of the four hundred acres owned by Gayle and found two abandoned mines. One was on a cliff over looking the lake, but Berge quickly refused to use that one for reasons not disclosed to Dylan and the other was a quarter mile north of the bunker where Tannahill spent his last night.

Young Stark would be snatched on his afternoon run and kept in the dank, cold mine until his stupid father came to his senses. Berge was not going to take one more day of insolence from that damned doctor. He only wanted that property for his yuppie antics while the Sons of Marduk had a responsibility to the white race and Jesus Christ. No more games would be tolerated. Clever went to one corner of the church and retrieved a large box which he brought to the center of the room. With one quick swipe with his pocket knife he opened it and pulled out banners and tee shirts bearing Celtic crosses, Nazi flags and White Power emblems.

He pulled off his polo shirt to reveal a powerful chest and bulging biceps then picked a tee shirt bearing a Celtic cross and put it on. The other men took the cue and began to search for shirts in their size while some placed the banners around the church. Berge grabbed a black tee shirt bearing the word, Rahowa, and pulled it on over his flannel shirt.

"We're going to start looking and behaving like an army, gentlemen. The games are over. Judgement day is nearly upon us and we have accomplished nothing! We will prevail or people are going to die, anybody not have the stomach for this? Too bad...this is the point of no return. Jason, you get the headdresses from the closet and pick some out for your boys. Soon we will be able to worship in private in the forest as God wishes. Rahowa! Rahowa!" Hans had an odd gleam to his eyes as he shouted and thumped his chest with a fist then saluted the Nazi flag like a loyal storm trooper.

They danced in a circle wearing animal heads, a strange mixture of Christianity and paganism. Horned shadows played around the church accompanied by growls and shouts concerning the glory of the white man. Clever went outside to gather more wood for the stove. He stood with an armful of split logs watching the bizarre scene through the windows of the church. It was like witnessing something out of the fifth century and Dylan was glad that he dropped the group at Hayden Lake.

Berge understood more about what God wanted than the Aryan Brotherhood or any of the other so called white pride movements. There was nothing lukewarm about Hansel Berge and Clever knew that Berge was capable of killing if necessary. The worship service ended around nine in the evening.

Clever laid out several different maps of Idaho County on the kitchen table to study them. The town of Hagar was about ten miles from Gospel Peak with an elevation of over eight thousand feet and the doctor's land abutted the Gospel Hump Wilderness area. It was rough country with several uncharted mines that Clever had marked on his maps. He didn't expect the local law enforcement to be much of a threat. Dylan was actually hoping that the feds would be called in for the kidnapping of Stark Gayle and he could give the government some payback. He could identity with the treatment John Rambo received in the book First Blood and Clever had no use for cops of any kind.

The abandoned mine Clever chose was well concealed. A person would have to know that it was there to find it, as the entrance was overgrown with small trees and bushes. Several air shafts emerged several hundred feet away, but they were hidden as well. A week's worth of supplies had been placed in the mine in an area about fifty feet across. The ceiling was low, just barely high enough for Clever to stand, and the interior was pitch black. Rather than risk the noise of a generator for lights, Dylan purchased twenty of those round portable touch lights and strung them on a rope leading down the room where Stark would be kept. There he had several more lights, food that didn't need to be cooked or refrigerated, some blankets and water. Large quantities of batteries had been purchased in Lewiston to avoid attention. Radio contact would be minimal and made from another location as he didn't want the signal traced to the mine or any of the Sons of Marduk.

Clever had been drilling that bunch of soft morons and was quite pleased with the results of the training. With a little military discipline and motivation anyone could be made into a soldier. Between Dylan's military expertise and Berge's ability to bullshit anyone into anything, the Elder Church finally had some fiery passion to its existence. The only weak link was Brentlinger whose change in attitude was a mystery to Hans, but Clever had seen to it that Jimmy would toe the line or go up in smoke like Tannahill.

One of the Sons was a Hagar cop named, Dan Jones, whose boy had just joined the church. Jones was a typical redneck, small town cop with the brains of a piss ant, but he had managed to run a check on Harry Dolan. He was the only worry that Clever had with his Special Forces experience in Vietnam and time as a street cop. The sheriff's department had a total of thirty-seven personnel including support staff and several of the deputies had less than two years on the job. Berge was convinced that the Gayles would involve no police if the right threats were made, but Clever had considered all angles. Things did not always go as expected and that was the only thing to expect.

It was nearly eleven o'clock. Dylan was an early riser so he folded up is maps and bid Berge a goodnight. Hans replied that it had already been a good night as he shut off the lamp next to his chair in the living room. He yawned and nodded to Clever as he opened the door to his bedroom. A half hour later Berge emerged in the darkness, careful not to wake Dylan. The sound of the other man snoring gave Hans the clue that it was okay to leave the house.

The excitement of the meeting had Berge stirred up in other ways as well. He didn't have time to go very far, but he thought he could find a hooker in Lewiston easy enough. Where there was a military reservation there were always pawn shops, used car dealers and prostitutes. It was closer to home than he liked, however, Hans hadn't killed any whores from Lewiston so it wasn't that much of a risk. Regardless, Berge had an urge that could not be ignored.

Clever's icy blue eyes gleamed in the street light that shined through the blinds near his bed. He listened as the engine in Louise Berge's car turned over then watched as Hans guided the vehicle slowly down the drive. A frown formed on Clever's lips as he realized that his spiritual leader was hiding something from him.

Chapter Twenty-five

It was a clear October Friday afternoon in Frank Wilber's physiology class and Stark was in a good mood. The snow on the roads and well traveled areas had melted off with a temporary rise in the temperature and the ice coated trees glistened in the sunlight. Stark loved to run when it was cold and sunny outside. He had changed into his sweat pants before his last period so that he could just throw his backpack into the car and jog around town after school. Wilbur's class was interesting, but today Stark was anxious to get out and exercise. It was the best stress reliever and loosened his joints after sitting in class all day.

The teacher stopped talking for a moment and stared at Jason Brentlinger and Wayne Rogers who griped that his father had to pick him up after school. Apparently, Wayne's water pump had bit the dust, information that the physiology class did not need to know. The two hushed up after making faces at Stark who sat two rows of desks over. Stark Gayle smirked back at them and looked to the ceiling in disgust. Five minutes before class was over Stark put his note pad and text book in the backpack so that when the bell rang at three o'clock he sprang up to join the crowds migrating through the halls.

He felt invigorated as he stepped outside into the frigid air. Days like today made Stark feel like his life was just beginning and the future was his for the making. The drudgery of life in a hick town was soon to be over. In the reflection of his car windows Stark could see big fluffy white clouds against a deep blue sky and his own youthful image. He smiled and tossed the backpack into the seat.

A red van pulled up behind Stark's Cutlass. The side door slid open and two men grabbed the teenager before he could realize what was going on. Jason took Stark's keys from his hand and got into the Cutlass as the van drove off with Stark. George Chaney and Dylan Clever gagged and tied the boy up on the floor of Mike Roger's van. Roger's guided the van out of the parking lot in a normal speed and tossed his Stetson into the passenger's seat as he grimaced at the sound of flesh hitting flesh. Clever mumbled something about the doctor's brat being too strong for his own good then flipped the kid over on his stomach for easier handling.

Stark involuntarily took a deep breath with his nose buried in the shag carpet and gagged on the filth of it. This was how it was all going to end? His heart raced and his lunch threatened to return from whence it came with every bump in the road. The men who had captured him were men Stark had seen around, as two of them had children in high school, but the blonde with the buzz cut who punched him Gayle had not seen before. It was now clear to him why a grown man would call to his mother when he was dying as Stark felt like doing the same thing, not that he could through the blue bandana in his mouth.

The ride seemed to take forever with numerous turns down roads that felt more like mountain goat trails. Stark realized that he could be gone for hours before anyone would even think something was wrong. Friday night was Mrs. Finkle's quilting group and on nice days his parents knew he usually ran longer. It could be seven or eight o'clock in the evening before the Gayle's would start to worry about him. His view was limited to the back of the driver's seat, which was stained with some unknown liquid, probably ice cream? He didn't dare to turn on his side because of that big blond ape who sat behind the driver in a comfortable captain's chair.

The other man, Chaney, must have gone to the rear seat as he wasn't next to the blond. Stark wondered what the owner of a bait shop would want with him, and he didn't know the other two at all. Someone had come up behind him while he was being shoved toward the van and took his car keys, which meant that they were going to move his car to prolong suspicion. What did they want? A ransom, or were just going to kill him for the hell of it? The van slowed to a crawl as the road became rough either from deep ruts or lack of use, Stark couldn't tell. His head bounced off the carpet as the front left tire dropped into a hole and Stark cursed through the gag.

Clever laughed and messed the boy's hair up which made Stark mad enough to roll up on his side. "You're all full of piss and vinegar, aren't ya?" Dylan winked at his captive and enjoyed the glare in the kid's eyes. "We're almost there, son. Don't waste it." When the old van could go no further as the mining road had turned to forest, Rogers shut the engine off. Chaney came up from the back and slid the door open then hopped out.

The air felt good after being in the too hot interior of the vehicle. Clever climbed out then pulled Stark out by his feet. He fell to his knees.

"Come on, get up. You can rest soon enough." Dylan lifted the teenager up by grasping his elbows. "All right, I'll take it from here. You tell the preacher to avoid radio contact unless there's no other way. I'll see you all at the church in the morning."

Chaney acknowledged with a slight nod then closed the door to the van and latched it. Clever watched for a moment as the two men in the van backed down the overgrown road then took Stark by the arm and pulled him into the woods. Stark Gayle looked to the large man for some sign of humanity and could read none. The frigid air that had felt so good earlier now felt as if it rolled out of a crypt. The short walk came to a sudden halt before a wall of thick trees and rock. Stark knelt to the ground as he was told with the eerie notion that he was now going to be shot. Clever parted the brush enough to let the boy crawl into a gaping pitch black hole. He looked around the forest to make sure no one was snooping around then pushed the hesitant kid forward by placing a large hand on his butt.

Stark was petrified in the cold, dark place which had a dank, musty smell to it. The man shoved him into a hard surface that scraped his forehead then a small circle of light revealed the rocky walls of an old gold mine. Clever grinned at the kid whose face was combination of youthful defiance and terror amongst the shadows. "You do as I tell you and you'll make it to the prom, kid." Dylan's voice was deep and forceful even in a near whisper.

"You gonna ransom me?" Stark fought to keep his tone steady.

"Why, your daddy got that much money?" The blond man grunted while walking along the rope touching lights to make them come on.

"Not anymore. Not after buying into the clinic then getting this property." Gayle immediately regretted divulging any information. If they did want money, he just screwed himself.

"Not your problem, kid. Just keep following me." The mine widened into an open area with a low ceiling still braced by ancient wood beams.

Stark stood quietly, hands tied behind his back, waiting for the blond to call the shots. There were several blankets against one wall, bottles of water, sacks of junk food and magazines as well as more of those round lights that came on with a touch.

"If you promise not to be an asshole I'll tie your hands in front so you can read or drain the bladder, okay?" Clever had a way of asking questions without really offering choices.

Since he had no desire to spend any more time unable to use his hands, Stark shook his head in agreement. He wondered whose idea it had been to provide magazines to a hostage. "Can I sit down?"

"Yeah. We're gonna spend some time together, so let's be comfortable." Clever sat on an old crate as the boy settled onto the blankets. He hoped that it would not snow until the situation was solved as Dylan would not be able to leave without making tracks to follow. If it did snow, it needed to be a blizzard that would quickly fill in footprints. Though Clever believed in the Sons of Marduk, he wasn't so sure about Berge's method of obtaining the land. But it really didn't matter how things turned out because Dylan was going to take out some pigs if they got in his face and die for the cause one way or another.

Chapter Twenty-six

Harry Dolan sat on the bed in the guest room on the verge of a breakdown. Thirty minutes before he had called his answering machine at home to find another message from the funeral home. The insurance company was not settling the claim as they were considering whether to let Alex Blue change the beneficiary on Sarah's policy, *after* Globe had received her death certificate. The whole scene was unreal. Alex made his sister's miserable life even more miserable, threw her in the street and now wanted paid for shortening her life! Al Blue's legacy of hatred and depravity lived on in his youngest son, Alex. Both Axel and Dana had bought new houses and vehicles while Sarah Blue went to the Salvation Army for food.

Dolan had dreaded this day when he would be without Sarah, when no one would remember how bad Al really was and now that day was here. A deep, seething anger welled in his chest as he thought of Alex's self-righteous, pompous attitude. Who did he think he was, God? Saint Alex speaks and all must obey or get a board shoved up your ass! He had the gall to look down on Harry for being Jewish and Sarah for being gay when Alex pimped his own children out to Al Blue for a used truck! He wanted to cry, but Harry had no tears left. As a boy he felt as if

God wanted him to blow his head off as He just kept letting that maggot rape his children, humiliate their mother, lie about everything and everybody, beat them, scream and cuss at them and resent his wife and kids for needing to eat and wear clothes. Albert Blue was the devil incarnate.

Harry had spent most of his life trying to climb out of the hole Al dug for him and now Alex was trying to shove him back in it. Why couldn't Alex just let things go? When he tossed Sarah onto the curb to fend for herself that should have been the end of it. Now Harry was going to get revenge for Sarah and poor Lucy Blue whose sweet personality has being turned to shit by a two-faced, greedy brat. A knock on the door brought Dolan back to Idaho. "Yeah?"

"Harry, have you heard from Stark? I'm getting a little concerned." Laura's expression said she was more than just a little worried.

"Want me to drive around and see if he's running some place?" Harry stood up to button his black and white checked shirt and left the tail hanging out.

"If you wouldn't mind, he's been acting a different lately, down in the dumps. Has he said anything to you?" She leaned on the door knob, cocking her head slightly.

"You know? Young man problems, nothing criminal or life threatening. He'll tell you when he's ready." Dolan slipped past her, hoping she would drop the subject. "I'll drive around town and see if his car is still at the high school or Mrs. Finkle's. Anywhere else he might go?"

"He's mostly a loner, but he spends a lot of time with Kevin Blackburn. He lives over on Olegrande, two blocks up from the clinic. Stark might be there."

"Okay. I'm sure he'll turn up. Be back shortly."

The night was inky black, the air a wet cold. Thick clouds covered the moon as Dolan drove through the tall pine trees toward Hagar. It felt like there was a brick in his stomach as contemplated what might have happened to Stark Gayle. The kid's fears could be legitimate. The high school parking lot was vacant, so Stark must have at least returned from his run. A quick check of the Blackburn residence proved they had no visitors that owned a car, so Dolan headed the Suburban toward the Finkle place. He could see someone using a payphone in the parking lot of the diner and turned to cruise past them. It was that scumbag Hansel Berge. Harry stared at the man as he passed. *Why was Berge using a payphone? He forget to pay his phone bill?*

Edna Finkle had just returned from her quilting group when Dolan pulled up outside her house. He introduced himself and asked if she had seen Stark that night as his car was gone from the high school and his mother was upset because he had not come home.

"Check the mailbox. If the cookies are still in there then he hasn't been by here." Edna unlocked her front door and waited as Dolan peered inside the metal box. He walked back to the house shrugging his shoulders with chocolate chip cookies in his right hand. "He ever not pick up the goodies?" Harry stepped inside when the old lady motioned him in.

"No, as least not until today. He was upset about something that he was going to discuss with you, or said he was, did he? Stark was very concerned about Tom Tannahill. He was pretty certain the man is dead." Edna hung up her dark blue wool coat and stuffed her scarf into one of the pockets.

"It doesn't look good for Tom. He didn't mention doing anything special this Friday night?" Harry watched the woman as she hung up the coat in a closet in the living room.

"No, Stark really doesn't socialize much with the Hagar kids, he is looking forward to college so very much. He really is a special young man...not many kids now days want to spend time with an old lady. Oh, I hope he's all right."

"I'm sure he is, I didn't mean to worry you." Harry smiled and let himself out.

He stood under the streetlight for a moment noticing the way the light made the colors seem darker and surrealistic. His breath hung in miniature clouds in the damp air. The temperature didn't seem that cold unless you stood still for very long then it seeped into the bones. Where was that kid? After scouting Hagar two more times, Dolan went back to the Gayle's. As soon as he came through the door, Harry knew there was something wrong. Blake stood near the telephone, hands hanging at his sides, with a dazed look to his eyes. Still clad in his dress shirt, necktie and pleated pants the doctor seemed to have lost a patient.

Laura had been pacing the floor then ran up to Dolan before he could even take his coat off. "Jesus Harry, somebody has Stark…oh God, I feel sick." Laura placed a hand over her mouth and her husband snapped out of his trance.

"Honey, sit down." Blake put an arm around her shoulder and guided Laura to the couch.

"What do mean "somebody" has Stark?" Harry stopped, unzipping his parka midway.

"Hansel Berge called here. He said that if we don't sell them the land that Stark isn't coming back, ever. They also said no cops and they would know if we called them. We have until Monday at one o'clock to make up our minds…this is insane! We're supposed to meet them at the title office then and sign papers. It can't be done like that, can it?"

"Hell, I don't know. It always seems to take awhile for a closing….let me think a minute." Dolan let out a deep breath and removed the coat.

"I saw that son-of-a-bitch using a payphone, damn! I never dreamed he was talking to you."

"How dangerous are these people?" Laura's eyes were beginning to tear.

Dolan perched on the arm of Blake's leather recliner. "He's on a mission and they believe they are in the right. The Sons also appear to have at least one member well connected enough to know what's going on around town, so what is important is that *they* believe things can happen like they decide."

"Should we call the police? We were afraid to…what do you think?" Laura looked to Dolan as if he had all the answers.

Harry could see Blake's expression and it was intense with fatherly agitation.

"I have a feeling that Stark is being held somewhere on your property. The land Berge wants. I would rather do an extraction then call the cops to round up the Sons of Butthead. I'm sure that the kid is close by."

"Extraction? What's that?" Laura asked with a voice mixed with hope and dread.

"Blue team, think it will work?" Blake lowered himself down on the edge of the couch next to his wife.

"Berge has a guy that knows a lot of jungle tricks the local cops don't. I would rather take three or four people who will listen to orders than have local law enforcement hanging around fucking things up. I can find Stark and get him out of there before you have to meet that asshole anywhere." Dolan spoke with a contagious confidence.

"You really think you can? Who will you get to help you?" Laura squeezed Blake's hand.

"I've been making some friends lately, it won't be a problem. In fact I'll call Libby now. She has some friends who are level-headed and into hiking and marksmanship. I'll get them out here tonight." Blake handed the portable phone to Dolan who waved his hand at it.

"No, let's stick to the land line, I don't want to heard on some jerk off's AM radio."

Libby Keefe brought three young women with her to the Gayle house. All were athletic appearing and very sympathetic to the Gayle's situation. Introductions were made, then Dolan suggested they all sit at the large dining room table to make a plan of action. Laura brought a few sheets of printer paper that Harry ask for and put them on the dark wood table. The four women sat close to Dolan and the Gayle's at the far end. Ethel Steeple was twenty years old and named after her great grandmother, hence the old-fashioned name. She wore her dark brown hair short, gold colored frames with tinted lenses shaded brown eyes and her face was lean. A map of Idaho County lay before her and she studied it while Dolan began drawing on one of the blank sheets of paper. Ethel would apply to the Idaho State Police right after her twenty-first birthday.

Next to Ethel was Matty Vickers who was a forest ranger at nearby Nez Perce National Forest. She was twenty-five, a long distance runner and a championship marksman. Her father had been a sniper for the NYPD who instilled a love of guns in his daughter and son before being killed on duty. The need for adventure and a challenge brought her out on a cold Friday night. Matty too had dark hair, but clear gray eyes.

To Dolan's left was Julie Cato. At age twenty-nine she was a Marine veteran who taught physical education in Grangeville. She wore her blond hair pinned up under a red U.S. Marines baseball cap and her green eyes needed no corrective lenses. She had the quiet reserve of those that know what they are doing, but don't flaunt it. The paper was filled with a sketch of the four hundred acres that Gayle owned and the Sons of Marduk wanted.

Dolan had drawn the creek that branched off from the Clearwater River and emptied into the lake, the old mining roads that were grown over but could still be seen, the bunker and a mine he spotted with binoculars. Harry hadn't actually been in it, but thought it would be a prime place to hide a hostage. The old mine that was boarded up overlooked the lake would be one of the last places Dolan wanted to check. "This mission is what we called a recon and extraction in the army. We gather information on the area, locate Stark then get the hell out. There's five of us which is plenty for this task...we are not out to engage the Sons of Marduk. I don't know how crazy these bastards are, but we're not taking any chances. Okay, listen up."

Harry pointed to the county map. "Notice how the road that loops between Slate Creek and White Bird is shaped like a bird's head? We are going to enter the property just north of the old road with the gate, which is at the bird's beak; about a quarter of a mile in there is an old bunker of some sort. I want to check for recent activities, but I doubt there will be any. Berge has an ex-Green Beret working for him and he's going to be running this show. The second area we'll check is the mine over the lake which is between the top of the bird's head and Highway Fourteen. We will be constantly looking for anything out of place as we travel. There are many old mines that are not on maps, so be on the lookout."

"I brought a good compass for us to use, I use it when out hiking." Julie pulled the instrument out of her black BDU pants.

"Great! Now we have two in case we should get split up, but I don't want to see that happen. We'll go out just before dawn. If we do not find Stark by nightfall we will head for Highway Fourteen. Remember, I don't know for sure that he's here, but knowing the way these assholes think, I feel that he is. If it begins to snow, we're getting out. We can be tracked down too easily then. Okay, now let's practice some Long range patrol positions."

Dolan led the group into a family room where Stark had exercise equipment. Harry would pull point and he made Julie Cato his slacker. She would follow close behind him looking the opposite direction as Harry. The term used in Nam was "Ranger Eyes." The other three would form an oval with the woman parallel to Dolan watching the rear. They would move through the forest in a tight group.

"We need to lose light-colored clothes, especially that neon Jarhead shirt, Cato." Dolan threw her a crooked grin. She flipped him off with a smile.

"Seriously now, we need dark, patchy patterns that are hard to see in a wooded landscape and we'll make sure that our white faces don't stick out either. Blake, you have any shoe polish?" The doctor and his wife stood near a weight lifting devise with strips of metal that fanned out behind them like a Japanese fan. "Yeah, black and brown. Will that work?"

"Close enough. First does everyone have an old coat that we can sew branches onto?" Everyone did except Ethel.

"I still have a couple of field jackets from the service. You're welcome to use one." Julie looked to Steeple who accepted the offer.

"We'll take water and candy bars, but I don't want to leave any paper or crumbs behind. We won't eat unless we get stuck and have to spend the night. If it looks like that might happen, we'll start searching for some shelter. Laura, you have any sleeping bags?" Harry felt himself get excited over having a mission once again.

"We have six, but two are pretty old."

"All right. We'll carry the bags strapped to our backs just in case…we don't want to be unprepared for a freezing night."

"Harry, are you sure about not calling the cops? I'd hate to see anyone get hurt." Laura's face was drawn.

"That's why we leave the locals out until we get possession of Stark…I was a cop and I've worked with them. Too many cowboys out there with something to prove. This requires teamwork and people who will listen to me. That guy Clever is the one we have to worry about. He'll know how to make booby traps, and more than likely there will be some out there. I'd rather do things this way, Laura." Dolan's tone was gentle, but commanding.

By midnight the rescuers were bedded down at the Gayle house for a few hours sleep. Everything was set for the trek that would begin just before sunrise. He would take his Winchester 70, Julie brought a Henry pump action .22, Ethel borrowed Blake's twelve gauge, Libby had her Para-Ordnance .45 and

Matty Vickers owned a Wilson combat arm, the Millennium Protector, which made Harry drool. He lay there in the dark unable to sleep and he suspected neither could the four women in the family room. There was just something invigorating about planning and executing a mission.

He had good feelings about the endeavor and the people who would follow him. They were young, in good physical shape and eager to learn something new. Cato had been a drill instructor in the Marines, which made Dolan feel for her gym classes. He was impressed that Libby would have such mature, intelligent friends who cared about something other than themselves. Maybe there was hope for the younger generation after all?

Chapter Twenty-seven

Berge had to be cautious with the men he left to guard the prisoner. Brian Chester, George Chaney and Orval Wicker were placed strategically amidst the thick trees around the mine where Stark still lay with his hands tied. Chester had never been married, Chaney was divorced and Wicker was a widower, which meant that there were no women at home to nag and bitch about them being out all weekend. Orval was a crusty old fart with a weather-worn face, a shock of white hair, a white beard and a beer belly that would make Santa Claus envious. At sixty he was still challenging younger men to arm wrestle and often won. An avid hunter, Wicker was more than eager to relive the Korean War and kick some ass. As a construction laborer, Chester was well muscled and still tanned from the summer's work. He liked to play a number of sports and felt Hitler's pain at the 1936 Olympics every time a nigger outdid him on the field. The sheer virility of the rituals made Brian feel like a powerful Aryan and he was prepared to fight hard to claim the land of their spirituality. Owning a bait shop offered few opportunities for greatness and Chaney had little joy in life.

Being a Son of Marduk was a source of pride matched by no other aspect of his existence. He wasn't at all sure about the fate of the group, especially with the extreme attitudes about the subservience of women. The Aryan Nations believed that men and women should work as partners like the pioneers, but Berge saw women as a necessary evil to procreate. That's why there were thirteen regular members and four novices in the Elder Church and thousands of members of the Christian Identity. The other Sons gathered at Berge's place where they discussed their impending victory over Dr. Gayle and dined on beer and hot dogs.

Hans played music produced by Resistance Records while he lectured on the unappreciated brilliance of Adolph Hitler. The white shirt, black tie and greasy hair that dropped onto his forehead made Berge look eerily similar to Der Fuhrer. He got off his soapbox when the rousing beat of, "The Coon Shootin' Boogie" vibrated the floor. Hans danced around like some sort of banshee with three of the new members. Brentlinger and his kid were locked in a sort of argument about who was more devoted to the cause. Joan had banished Jim from the bedroom until he dropped, "this Nazi crap," as she called it. Jason clung to every word that came out of Berge's mouth, even the part about how his mother deserved no respect. The ungrateful brat was spending more time with Hans than at home, not that it was a great hardship for Jim Brentlinger.

The three men currently standing watch at the mine would be relieved in the morning by three others fresh from a night's sleep. Berge was positive that the yuppie parents would be insane with worry and desperate enough to do as requested, so energy was high. Clever would come into town after he was sure the three replacements wouldn't fuck anything up while he was gone.

Adam King, a disbarred lawyer, jumped around with his shirt unbuttoned and a dirty tee shirt pulled out of his polyester pants. A hairy gut jiggled to deep bass vibrations as he bumped bellies with Buddy Meacham who was an auto parts runner in Hagar. Charlie Jones, whose father was a Hagar cop, ran up and joined in with a beer in his hand that splashed all over Meacham. "Hey, butthead, watch it! I might have to kick your ass."

Buddy wore a buzz cut that revealed the fact that he had pimples on his skull. "I'll just have my dad arrest ya."

Jones wore glasses that refused to stay on an oily nose. "He'd have to find me first." Meachan snorted. "And your old man couldn't find his asshole with a search team!"

"My dad is a good cop, fuck face!" Charlie retorted as he used his middle finger to shove the frames back up his nose.

Jason Brentlinger overheard the conversation. "Good at napping and eating. He always has some kind of crumbs on that uniform shirt of his!"

As if on cue, Officer Dan Jones popped through the door with the remnants of a Snicker's bar in his left hand. Jones had weasel-like features that undermined his authority with the citizens. Coupled with grease stains on his tie, he was Hagar's version of Deputy Fife. He wanted to handle the kidnapping operation, but Cleaver put a stop to that. It was obvious that the brawny blond had little use for Officer Jones who fancied himself detective material or the commander of a SWAT team. Berge threw Jones a Nazi salute as he sang along with some song glorifying White National Socialism. The cop responded by slamming his boot heels together and snapping his right arm upward.

Someone suggested that they go out to the church and get the headdresses which sent the group out in a cluster to party the night away. Eddie Herman, the machinist from Grangeville, got into a fist fight with Jones over a Rottweiler head because neither wanted to wear the deer. Brentlinger, who as dog catcher had procured most of the animal heads, settled the conflict by grabbing the head for himself.

Jones pouted as he pulled a yellow Lab's laughing jaws over his skull like a baseball cap. "Dumb Fuck!" Jones mumbled.

"He thinks he's Jesus Himself, the asshole." Eddie shouted to the Rottweiler, whose ears bounced as Brentlinger retreated. Jim spun around. "Eat me!"

"Gentlemen, please!" Berge's voice rose above the chatter in the church. "We must focus on the cause for this celebration and remain united. Soon we will be able to run through the forest unmolested by prying eyes and federal fucks who want to force us into one tight little mold."

"Shit, Dad! Do you have to act like that?" Jason chastised Jim who gave the boy an incredulous look.

"When you get your ass out and get a job and YOU supply the headdresses, then you can tell me what to do, you pompous little bastard!" The Rottweiler threw the Collie a challenging snarl.

"People like you are fucking up the white race, why do you even show up here?" Jason shoved his father.

"I was in the fight before you were born...don't lecture me, boy." Jim's voice was sharp, but tired. "Don't push me again. You will treat me with respect!" The hair on Brentlinger's chest poked up through his tee shirt giving him a beastly appearance.

Jason sneered sideways at Will Chester who peered out from under the skull of a Heinz Fifty-Seven. "Try earning it...Dad. You can't even run your own household. I'm more of a man than you are right now!"

A second later Jim Brentlinger delivered a stinging slap to the left side of his son's face, knocking the Collie head to the floor. The boy's cheek was nearly as red as his coarse hair and tears formed in his watery blue eyes. The sound of the slap brought silence to the room. Jason avoided the other men's eyes as the humiliation turned his ears pink. In retaliation Jason reached out and tore his father's undershirt then stared at the purplish sores on exposed on his chest. "What the fuck?"

It took several seconds for the mediocre student to compare the lesions on his father's body to the ones in his health class textbook, but then the revelation spilled out of his mouth. "AIDS? Fucking AIDS? Christ, I knew you were a faggot!"

Jim stood in the middle of the church feeling like Hester Prine with her scarlet letter. The other Sons of Marduk glanced nervously around the room not knowing how to respond. Berge bit his lip and wandered over to Brentlinger who hung his head.

"Jim is not a faggot. Those sores could be anything and even if is AIDS he could have gotten it from that shitty tattoo artist down there off the highway. Right Jim?"

"You know what kind of trouble I had with that infection, son-of-a-bitch, damn it to Hell." Brentlinger surveyed the prying faces around him for some sign of sympathy. He could tell that they were not sure how he contracted the disease. There would always be doubt and he felt anger rise in him as all of a sudden his pizza-faced son was the man of the hour. What a great son to expose his fairy father!

"Turn the music back on and let's forget it about it. I've known Jim a long time and he is no ass pirate." The tail of Jones's uniform shirt hung nearly to his knees in order to get a size big enough to cover his stomach. He had to go to a three extra large. A beer stain trailed down the front of the blue nylon Hagar police shirt along with the remains of a devil's food cupcake that was smeared into the buttons.

"When we gonna get a chance to do some of the ass kicking?" Herman asked as he leaned into Berge's face.

"This isn't about "ass kicking" Eddie. If we can accomplish our goals without alerting the government to our presence then all the better!" Hans illustrated his point with wild movement of the hands.

"We thought that was the goddamned point, Hans! To make our presence known?"

Victor Marsh, who owned a plumbing business in White Bird, but lived in Hagar, removed the dog's head that made his scalp sweat. His light brown hair was thin which made his ears stick out like Dopey the dwarf. "Will you people get a reality check? How soon do you think the FBI would land on our asses if we let loose? The time will come to take a stand, but first we need a base. Once we get that land back we can grow from there"

Large sweat stains spread out from Berge's arm pits and he realized for the first time how hot the interior of the church had become. "Somebody crack a window, will ya?"

"So, Clever's gonna whip us into a fine military fighting unit, huh?" Ansel Smith was fifty years old and worked as a cashier at Kibble's Foodmart, the shabbier of the two grocery stores in Hagar. A career as a drunk had narrowed his possibilities and sent him running to white pride groups looking for his manhood, which still managed to elude him.

"Yes, that is exactly what he will do. With four hundred acres at our disposal we will have no limits, gentlemen!" The bit of a mustache over Berge's lip danced in excitement.

"I can't wait to try the weapons Dylan "found" for us. I am so ready for the holy war." Jones hit the air with his fist.

The small arsenal was stored in the basement below the church in several wooden crates. Clever would not elaborate on where he obtained the dozen hand grenades and ten M-16s with three cases of full magazines, but it was safe to say it was stolen from somewhere. The ex-Green Beret took the grenades with him as well as his De Lisle carbine. He had purchased over a dozen copies of the Army's Survival Manual as well as books on sniping and field medicine. Dylan Clever took the racial holy war very seriously.

At dawn, Clever returned for the fresh troops and was very unhappy at the state of intoxication evident in the Sons who lay sprawled around the church. Rage built behind those icy eyes for several minutes as he stood among the drunken men who did not even know anyone had entered the building. It was very apparent to him then that unless he wanted to find himself taking all the risks alone, some serious attitude adjustments needed to be made.

Berge was passed out near the stove, hugging his coat to his chest like a blanket. The large blond bent down until his unshaven face was but inches from the preacher's.

"Get up!" Clever's voice boomed.

Hans jerked as he was frightened out of his stupor. "Huh? What's wrong…the kid get away, the cops…"

"No, asshole, and no thanks to you!" Clever pulled Berge up by his shirt collar. "Get up! Every damned one of you, now!"

He kicked at those nearby as he shouted. "Get the hell outside now. Son-of-a-bitch!"

Snowflakes spit through the damp air as Clever made all the Sons stand in two rows, parallel to each other. They shivered as Dylan did not allow them time to grab their coats.

"Run in place." Clever barked. The men looked to each other as if the musclebound blond had spoken German. "Pick up those pussy legs! I ain't joking!" He brought his huge hands together, clapping a cadence for the confused, dazed church members to follow. After ten minutes of double time, Dylan led them through push ups, sit ups and squat thrusts which provoked a few episodes of vomiting.

"What the hell, Clever? Who pulled your fucking chain?" Jones wiped the slime from his lips as he struggled back to his feet after puking. He knew better than to mix beer and whiskey, but did it anyway. Before Officer Jones could react, Dylan slapped Dan hard across the face. The overweight cop stumbled backwards until he hit the frozen ground.

"Any of the rest of you need bitch slapped? Cause that's what you are, bitches. A bunch of whiny, drunken pussies. From what I have seen of you "men," I should just tie aprons on every one of ya and recruit your wives instead. Hear this loud and clear…I will not be left holding the bag! You assholes will pull your heads out of your asses and get with the program or I'll shoot your asses before the Feds ever get the chance! There are three men who are cold, tired and hungry out there who are waiting to be relieved and I don't have anybody to send to replace them. What am I supposed to do? Who do you suppose will pay for your mistakes? I could gut every one of you sons-of-bitches right now! What the hell did I get myself into?" Clever pulled the bush cap down over eyes and glared brutally at the sorry looking men. "I should have stayed at the compound...Berge get your ass over here!"

The Adolph wanna-be felt stupid and humiliated before his own followers. Suddenly he had taken a back seat, but Clever was right. Why should he carry most of the burden? Hans decided to save face by backing Dylan Clever. "We are the Sons of Marduk and today we start acting like an army. Gentlemen, do as the man says."

Chapter Twenty-eight

The four young women in the exercise room of the Gayle house lay on the floor in sleeping bags. Sleep had finally begun to overcome them after hours of talking about the task ahead of them. In the soft darkness each woman drifted into her own thoughts. Ethel Steeple studied the lines of the weight machine as she lay on her side. At twenty she still lived with her parents while attending junior college. She spent three nights a week patrolling the campus as a security guard, which was usually boring except for the occasional prank. She had given some thought to joining the army, but decided instead to go for the state police. In two more months Steeple could apply to the highway patrol and begin the process of becoming a trooper. Ethel was pleased that Libby would consider her a good choice to help Harry Dolan. There wasn't anything she wanted to do besides police work and she was excited about rescuing Stark Gayle.

Julie held open the curtains on the patio doors and placed her open hand on the cold glass. The snowflakes that had fallen earlier had ceased for the time being. She, like Dolan, hoped to get in and out before the ground was covered and they could be tracked like unsuspecting deer. A storm was building in the northwest that blocked the moon's beams. The only reason Cato could see the tall, dense pines that surrounded the house was the yard light attached high up on a telephone pole gave everything a golden glow. She snuggled down into the sleeping bag and felt safe inside the house with her friends around her.

While Cato had not actually been in combat, she had been in Bosnia and knew the tense uncertainty of a war zone. This was not an adventure to Julie like it was for Libby and Ethel. It was only something that needed to be done. Her life now evolved around her students.

"Anybody sleepy?" Matty Vickers rolled up on an elbow. Matty was a gun nut like her father, much to her mother's dismay. After the death of Officer Vickers, wife and daughter moved back to Mary Vickers' home town of Grangeville to escape the savagery of New York City. It was an enormous adjustment for Matty who would was used to the fast-paced, gritty atmosphere of a large city. Moving to central Idaho caused the young woman a serious case of jet lag, but the beauty of the mountains eventually worked its magic on her and Matty became a forest ranger instead of a big city cop.

"I wish...my brain won't shut off." Libby sat up and hugged her knees.

"What do you think of Harry? I liked him right off."

"Yeah, me too. Not too hard to look at either." Julie smiled in the dark.

Ethel laughed. "He's way too old for me, but hey, whatever, Jules."

"Bite me. I didn't say I would bop him, just that he wasn't that bad for someone almost fifty." Cato stretched out on her stomach. "Jesus, I feel like I'm fifteen and this is a slumber party. I must get a life."

"How crazy do you think Berge is? He's so slimy looking, who the hell would believe anything he says?" Libby took a sip of the water she kept on a table next to the forest green love seat. If she didn't drink at night her throat and eyes dried out.

"Harry thinks the guy is a real asshole and could be dangerous, and he doesn't like that big blond guy, the Green Beret, either. Clever, that's his name." Matty lay on her back staring up at the vaulted ceiling.

"Clever. What kind of a name is that for some macho military man? Wonder if anybody ever called him the Beave?" Keefe drug out the word.

"Bet they only did it once," Julie said in a deadpan voice. "I hope we can just get the kid and get out, I'm not so sure those middle-aged jerk offs won't be trouble if they get the old adrenaline going."

"Yeah, most of them were with the Christian Identity before joining ranks with Berge. They didn't think the Aryan Brotherhood was strict enough with women...my parents know Joan Brentlinger. She is a nice lady, don't know why she would put up with that loser. Anybody nervous?" Keefe wondered aloud, hoping the answer was to the affirmative.

"Of course, I wouldn't go out there with anyone that wasn't." Cato adjusted her pillow. "We should get some sleep. I know the plan is to get in and out, but it may not happen that way."

———————•—•—•———————

In the silence of his room, Dolan recalled what Alex had said about catching Albert Blue sitting up at two in the morning in his robe that Christmas after their mother died. Harry could not understand why Alex ever invited him into his home and then trusted him enough to leave his children alone with the Cheese. Al used to diddle Harry and Sarah then go downstairs to watch TV and smoke a cigarette. Dolan had no doubt about why Al was up at Alex's house in the wee hours of the morning in his bathrobe. He truly felt sorry for Alex's kids. So much for the four of them vowing that it would never happen again.

According to Alex and cousin, Becky, Dolan was going to Hell for not believing in Jesus. *Well then*, thought Harry, *I'll be seeing you there, Bro.* Dolan would rather tell God he was a Jew than have to tell Him that he peddled his children to monster for a house with a pool and threw his crippled, dying sister in the garbage. Alex was turning out to be just like Al. Albert Blue always thought he was smarter than everyone else and superior. It took a real sterling character to stick a finger up your son's ass and then an hour later call someone else a "nigger."

Hansel Berge was the same type of guy as Albert Blue. It was just something that Dolan could sense. Berge's true essence simmered just below the surface like Al's and threatened to emerge at any given minute. There was little doubt that Hans and his henchman would kill Stark if things did not go their way. The Sons of Marduk had to be crazy to think that such a shoddy plan would work or did they really just want to go down as martyrs? Dolan couldn't afford to ignore that possibility concerning Berge and Clever, but he wasn't sure about the rest of them.

There was a knock at the door and Blake peeked in.

"Harry? You asleep?"

"Good thing I'm not." Dolan sat up in the full bed that was covered with an Amish made quilt.

Gayle came in and sat in a wing-backed chair near the head of the bed. "I feel like I should be doing something...like going out with you tomorrow."

"I understand the need to help, but you know that you aren't in good enough shape for what we have to do. Time is something we do not have, Blake. If we get caught in the snow, we are going to have to haul ass out of there!" Dolan did not want to drag the doctor along.

Blake let out a deep breath. His voice quivered with a father's dread. "I know, I know...it's so hard to sit on the sidelines though."

"You just make sure that if I call you're there. You remember the codes?" Harry would take Gayle's cell phone with him and only say short phrases to communicate.

"Greensleeves means that it is snowing heavy and to meet you on Highway 14, Montego Bay means you have Stark and you're headed back, and Saigon Bride means everything has turned to shit and call the cops."

"Good. Man, let's just get some coffee. I can't sleep at all." Harry swung his legs over the side of the bed.

"Okay, I know I won't be able to."

Dolan settled down on a stool at the island in the center of the kitchen. The counter tops were covered with blue and white tiles, including the surface of the island. Laura had copper pots hanging from the ceiling for decoration and dark blue coffee cups danged from hooks on the wall. Blake poured water into the coffee maker and turned it on.

Harry glanced out the window in the breakfast nook to see if it was snowing. It wasn't and it was only three hours until dawn.

"You having a party and didn't invite me?" Cato wandered in, her hair tousled from lying on the floor.

"Coffee?" Blake asked as he watched the brewed liquid flow into the glass container.

"Our brains wouldn't quiet down enough to get any sleep." Dolan managed a lazy grin.

"I'm surprised that Laura can, being a mother and all." Julie took a stool opposite Harry.

"I gave her something, she was going nuts." Dr. Gayle served Dolan and Cato then poured himself a cup. "This isn't something we ever thought about happening. You always worry about your kids and some stranger abducting them, but at seventeen we figured we were past that risk."

"Wonder what the Sons of Marduk are doing right now? Suppose they are getting any shuteye?" Julie slowly stirred powdered creamer into her coffee.

"If they have any smarts, at least one of them is awake watching Stark and someone should be patrolling the perimeter around the site...I'm just not sure how serious the rest of them are. I haven't actually met any of the militia types before coming here." Harry really didn't consider mercenaries in the same league as the bozos in Hagar.

"They're all basically losers. They have wives and kids they could lose, but for the most part the Sons have mediocre lives and no one will miss them when they're gone." Cato seemed to know that she was talking about. "My father could have been one of them, if he hadn't shot himself. He was always blaming everyone else for his failures. It was the blacks, the Jews, the Mexicans, on and on. Dad made us all miserable....it sounds bad, but at least he didn't live long enough to turn my brothers into carbon copies of him."

Harry studied the features of the young woman whose green eyes followed the spoon as it swirled around and around the cup. "There must be a lot of that going around."

The three talked until an hour before sunrise, then Dolan and Cato checked the gear and the weapons a final time.

Chapter Twenty-nine

Stark Gayle had never been so cold in his short life. The two blankets he had wrapped tightly around him were nearly useless and he shivered until his teeth rattled. For a time he had joined his captor in doing push ups and running in place to keep warm, but eventually tired. It was impossible to tell the time of day or night that far back in the mountainside and Clever only kept two of the portable lights on at a time. His muscles were cramping and Stark's patience was running out. At one point Clever left and an old man with a shotgun took his place that was rude and nasty with the young captive.

"I want out of here. I've had enough of this shit!" Stark struggled to his feet.

"Sit down." Oval Wickers' wrinkled face made him look like an ogre when he frowned.

"No, my legs hurt. I need to walk around." Before the teenager could move Wicker took two quick strides and punched Stark in the face. He stumbled backwards, his boots getting tangled up in the blankets when they fell from his shoulders.

"When I say something, you fucking do it, understand?" The old man stood over Stark, fuming and looking very much like a Billy goat with his pointed little goatee.

"The more you do to me, you old fart, the bigger the ass whipping my uncle's going to give you." Stark used to call Dolan 'uncle' when he was younger.

Wicker laughed hard. "Yer gonna sic your uncle on me, are ya?"

"Do all your laughing now because you won't want to later, if you're still around." The young man rubbed his left arm to soothe the pain caused by landing on jagged rock.

"You're a cocky little bastard. I'll say that for ya. If you're daddy knows what's good for you, he'll do as he's told." Wicker cleared his throat and spit a disgusting looking glob.

Another two hours passed with Stark reading about how to hunt elk with a bow. Orval kept checking his watch when no relief came. He walked out to the mouth of the mine to find no sign of new people.

"Wicker?" A harsh whisper came from above the entrance.

"Yeah."

"Where the hell are they? I'm freezing and falling asleep up here." Chaney peered down at Orval who held his weapon like a Minuteman.

"Where's Brian?" Wicker suddenly felt the lucky one for spending most of his time in the mine. The air was damp outside.

"He's on the east side hoping like hell to see somebody coming to take over. Son-of-a-bitch it's cold!"

"I know. I'm starting to get pissed myself. Where the fuck are they?" Wicker growled and his neck turned red.

The sound of crackling leaves made Chaney turn sharply. It was Chester who appeared distressed. He shrugged at the lack of communication with Berge.

"Think something went wrong? Maybe one us should go back and see what the problem is?" Brain rested his Winchester over his right shoulder.

"You know what Clever said about leaving the post before being relieved. Think he was joking?' Wicker asked without expecting an answer. Large snowflakes began to fall as the three of them wondered what to do. Normally, this area already had a thick layer of snow cover, but the weather had been strange in Idaho as elsewhere that year.

A voice roared out of the mine. "Hey? Hey? It's fucking dark in here!"

Wicker chuckled. "The batteries must have run out...bet he pissed his pants." The others laughed too. Orval pulled a flashlight from his back pocket. "Better go take care of the baby."

Dolan watched the snow fall for a few minutes while the others put their packs and gloves on. While the area was wilderness and steep, there were not that many places to hide. Several ghost towns peppered Idaho County, but the only ones close were Old Ole Grande and a cluster of remains that had once been the towns of Callender, Concord and Hump Town. Harry had talked to Paul Dice whose grandfather had worked as a miner in 1905 and learned that there were numerous other mines not on the maps. Dolan didn't think that Clever would pick any of the old buildings to hold up in as they were too obvious. He had a gut feeling that Stark was in an abandoned gold mine somewhere on his father's land, but which one?

The most direct route to the first mine was out through Blake's backyard into the forest. While there were old roads and trails throughout the woods, Dolan would avoid them and take a parallel trek to avoid any booby traps that Clever might have set. The team hiked northeast toward Old Ole Grande as the sun struggled to emerge through the thick trees. Harry pulled point, Julie slack, Keefer and Steeple on either side and Vickers watched the rear. The formation of people in subdued colors moved rather smoothly for a group not used to working together.

The snow was falling harder as the troop moved through the trees. When Dolan looked to the left, Cato surveyed the right. As they approached the suspected hot zone the team became more cautious.

For some reason, snow seemed to muffle the earth's sounds and made Dolan recall roaming through the snowy woods with Sarah in Virginia. They would find old C-rations left by soldiers on training maneuvers and dig them up. The best ones were the chocolate nut roll, the cheese and crackers and the chocolate candy contained in olive drab cans with black stenciled labels. It was funny how the same cans of food lost all charm when opened in Vietnam.

After nearly an hour of creeping uninterrupted in the forest, Dolan stopped and pointed with two fingers. In the distance a speck of blue was visible as it moved down a steep slope. Harry motioned for all of them to crouch down. It was a man of about thirty wearing a blue ski coat and carrying a rifle. He kept looking behind him as he crept down the mountainside through the Aspens that had a dusty appearance through the snowflakes. The trees were close together and small saplings added to the cover that shielded the hunters from the man's view.

Chester made his way around the foot of the mountain that contained the old gold mine. His nose was bright red and his lips were tinted blue from too many hours in the frigid outdoors. Mucus ran from his nostrils and was quickly wiped away with a bright blue sleeve of his bulky coat. The group of five moved slowly toward Chester who seemed to not be as agitated as he started to run down a trail to the east. He hopped along like a jittery rabbit, was fairly sure the going was safe, but not entirely.

The menagerie of brown and green trees and swirling snow was similar to images on countless postcard scenes, scenes that are meant to depict tranquility. Vickers had spent many a day in the quiet forest searching for hunters that had not returned or a wounded deer that managed to escape its killer to die alone. There had been a time when forest rangers were mostly concerned with the environment, but now they were armed law enforcement officers who were forced suspect danger in the most beautiful of landscapes. Matty used hand signals to tell Dolan that she and Cato would move around ahead of the fleeing man while he and the other two women came from the rear. Chester stopped and bent over to catch his breath, the cold wind made his bronchial tubes ache.

"Hey!" Dolan said just loud enough for Chester to hear him.

The younger man spun around and dropped his rifle in the snow. His eyes widened as his brain decided what to do. "You that big bad Ranger Clever told us about?" Brian tried to sound unafraid, but his voice quivered at the end of the question.

"No, she is." Dolan looked to Vickers who emerged from the trees.

When Chester involuntarily turned to see who Dolan was talking about, Harry clasped the man's mouth shut with his hand and drug him off the road into a cluster of pines. Harry placed the other hand on Brian's neck. Cato kicked his shin as he tried to squirm away. "Cut the shit, boy, or I'll snap your damned neck. How many are there?" Harry's tone was curt.

Chester held up two fingers representing Chaney and Wicker. He was too tired, cold and hungry to resist.

"How many outside?" Dolan looked at the single shaking index finger.

He might be lying, but Harry thought the frightened man was telling the truth. "Here's what's going to happen. You're going to holler at the other one roaming around and tell him that you've had and it and you're leaving. You fuck up and I'll bury a knife in your back." Dolan pressed harder against the man's mouth, knowing that sharp teeth were cutting into the underside of his lip. "I'm going to take my hand away. Do as you're told or you will meet your maker before the little hand gets to twelve. Clear?" Brian shook his head yes within Dolan's tight grip.

"George....George?" Chester was terrified that the man with the salt and pepper hair would kill him anyway. "George!"

Chaney appeared on the slope. When he didn't see Chester he scrambled down, his coat flopping over his stomach in spite of the temperature and the wind that threw wet snow onto his flannel shirt. "Brian?"

"I'm over here....I'm taking a leak. Hold on." A few seconds passed then Chester yelled, "Jesus Christ, you should see this thing George!"

"See what? Your pecker? Got one of mine own!" Chaney laughed, his rifle dangling at his side.

"No Goddamn it, somebody's buried something over here."

Knowing the history of the area, Chaney had visions of some miner's long lost fortune finally discovered. He stomped through the ever deepening snow toward the sound of Chester's voice. He never saw the mythical treasure or Brian as Cato plowed the butt of her Henry rifle into the back of his skull. They gagged the two and tied them up inside the thick cluster of Christmas tree-like pines.

"Okay, there's at least one in the mine guarding Stark and we can't assume that he or they, are as stupid as the other two. We need to flush him out first. Ethel, think any of these guys would have seen you before?"

"I doubt it. I don't hang out in Hagar much and I didn't go to school here." Steeple pulled the black stocking cap further down over her ears as the chilly wind had picked up since that morning.

Dolan studied the clearing around the entrance to the mine which was now only about a thirty foot half circle. The forest had reclaimed most of it and would eventually obscure the mine altogether. He could just barely see the beams that supported the door through the small trees and bushes and the remains of an ancient track disappeared into the foliage.

"You're going to yell for help....and sound weak and helpless, okay? Keep screaming until somebody comes out. They won't expect a woman to come to the rescue, not this bunch of clowns. They'll think you need some manly assistance." Dolan's lips curled up into a grin as Ethel rolled her eyes at the other women. "You know what they say? Know thy enemy."

The other four split into two groups and positioned themselves on either side of the entrance. Dolan pumped his fist in the air to signal Steeple to start wailing. Ethel took off her cap, messed up her hair and reddened her face with snow to aid in appearing pathetic. She began pleading for someone to help, that she was lost. With each plea her voice sounded more distressed, she almost had Dolan fooled. After several minutes of crying out, the scuffling of footsteps echoing in the mine made Steeple drop to her knees in the final act.

Wicker didn't turn on the last four lights as he listened carefully to the woman who begged for help. It was probably some yuppie housewife that got separated from her old man on a hunting trip. Suburbanites really were intolerable, but he had to be sure. He gave the kid a good whack on the head just in case the chick outside was a trap of some sort. Orval felt his old heart thumping against his sternum as strained to see through the trees. The sound of his knees popping as he knelt down made him wince both at the pain and the realization that whoever was outside might have heard it.

Cold, wet circles spread out over Ethel's kneecaps as she knelt in the ever deepening snow. She wasn't able to see her companions hid among the pines, but glimpsed a bearded face peering through the trees. It wasn't easy, but Steeple managed to work up some tears which pulled the old man toward her.

"Miss, what in the world are ya doing out here? For God's sake, girl, you could freeze to death!"

"I got lost….me and my college friends went for a hike. I'm so cold!"

Wicker relaxed at the sight of the young, weeping girl nestled in the snow. He crunched through the falling snow to help her up. About the time that Orval extended his hand to Steeple, Cato slipped on some rocks slick from a thin coat of snow. Dolan sprang forth with Keefe to subdue the crusty old man and the sucker pointed his shotgun at Harry. Wicker's eyes twinkled as he hopped around and cackled with glee as he waved the gun around.

Keefe and Vickers watched Harry's expression for a clue as to what to do next. Dolan nearly laughed out loud at the comical sight.

The old fart spun around to challenge anyone who dared. The old yellow coat made him look like a giant pear.

"Girls? You brought girls to tackle the Sons of Marduk? You're one stupid jerkoff!" His voice was gravely, so Orval cleared his throat and spit.

Cato snickered. "The sons of what? Sons-of-Bitches?"

Wicker's features darkened. "Watch your mouth, you trashy slut."

Harry raised the Winchester's barrel level with Wicker's wrinkled, crimson nose. "Drop the gun, asshole." Dolan frowned at the old man.

"I ain't the only one out here…Chaney? Chester? Where the hell are ya?" Orval screeched in anger.

"They're fucked, so drop the weapon or get it shoved up your ass!" Libby was miffed over Wicker's sexist attitude.

Orval seemed to realize for the first time that he was without backup. "Just take it easy…you look like a man who is tired of the shit in this country…"

"Should we just shoot him now?" Harry did a quick poll of his team and they all agreed.

"I want to do it. I'm the trashy slut, so it won't be too hard for me to plug the bastard." Cato took a special delight in watching the old man's lip quiver. She knew he was aching to slap her down.

"Yeah, let's do him. I don't wanna cart this old turd anywhere." Vickers jabbed Wicker in the butt with a heavy boot.

"Berge is right. Women should stay mute and knocked up! Course, none of you dykes could land a man…"

"Julie and Ethel, go check on Stark." Dolan let out a breath and cradled his rifle in his arms. "Take off your clothes…down to your underwear and tee shirt" Harry smiled and looked to the ground, his face partially shielded by his black baseball cap.

The old man was stunned as he stood surrounded by women in ghillie suits with guns. "You think you're Billy Jack? You can just tell me what to do and I'll do it?"

Dolan shrugged. "Yeah."

"None a you got the balls to gun a man down. you got too much respect for the law and your cushy little lives." Wicker mocked them while copping a stance that made him appear to be doing the little teapot song. "I won't do it, you can just shoot me, you fuck!"

The Winchester swung downward and discharged into Orval's right kneecap. "Get the clothes off or I'll shoot something else for every minute that you screw with me." Harry gave Wicker his best Ranger face. His young companions were wide-eyed at Dolan's change in demeanor. The game was over.

Inside the mine Ethel smacked her head on one of round, plastic lights Clever had strung on the rope, turning on several of them. Libby yelled out Stark's name, but there was no response as the two women made their way down the dark, cold passageway supported by wood beams. The tunnel spread out into a large room after several dozen yards. Stark was on the ground with a gag in his mouth and his hands once again tied behind his back. The old man wasn't nearly as considerate as Clever who had at least seen to it that the boy could read magazines. Cato cut the ropes around Stark's feet and wrists with a large pocket knife.

Stark recognized Cato from area track meets, but never expected her to rescue him. "I kind of thought Harry would slay these dragons."

Ethel smiled broadly, her dimples cast in deep shadows.

"He is…we're the damsels sent to save the knight."

"Can you stand up okay? Your muscles have to be killing you." Julie's eyebrows scrunched together in a coach-like concern.

"They are, but I'd walk ten miles for a hot bath!" Stark let Cato help him get up from the frozen ground. "Who fired that shot?"

"The old fart got lippy with Harry..." Steeple's voice trailed off as Wicker came limping into the mine in only his underwear and a sleeveless tee shirt with Dolan supporting his left shoulder.

"Orval will need your blankets, Stark. I'll give you my coat as I have a heavy sweater on." Harry began to unbutton his old field jacket. "Tie him up. If he gives ya a hard time, slap him."

Stark ran his eyes up and down Wicker's sagging, pale flesh and shook his head. The mean old man didn't look too threatening now, but glared at all of them in a pathetic attempt to maintain his dignity.

"This shithead should do without any blankets...he wouldn't even let me use my hands to pee! I pissed all over myself!"

Dolan studied the angry young man. "Okay, we'll take his socks too."

"No, Goddamn it! I'll die out here that way, "Wicker shouted.

"No you won't. You won't be here that long. We'll send the cops back after ya." Libby made Wicker cross his hands behind him and pulled the ropes tight. "Sit down."

He hesitated a few seconds then obeyed the woman with pine branches sewn to the back of her coat. She tied his legs together then covered him with the rough brown blankets.

"Don't move and you'll stay warm enough. Okay, let's get the hell out of here before the rest of the crew shows up."

"I'm alright!" Stark remarked when he saw Harry and Julie's parental type expressions. As Wicker lay on the cold dirt, he too wondered where Clever and Berge were and what had happened to Chester and Chaney.

Once outside Harry called the Gayle's and said "Montego Bay" then hung up.

Chapter Thirty

The Sons of Marduk had been drilled until most of their alcoholic stupors were expelled. It was all Clever could do to keep himself from beating Berge to death. Hans had not seemed so educated and devoted to the cause when he was using Eddie Herman's gut as a pillow. After running the bunch until they could hardly stand up, Dylan told the teenagers to cook some eggs and toast then pushed Hans into the shower where Clever sent a stream of icy water into the preacher's face.

Hans let out a tiny screech as the frigid shower pounded his already frozen skin. A quiet rage built deep inside his chest at being treated like an underling and made to appear a fool to his own church members. He slipped the big blonde a dark glance just as Clever turned the handle over to warm.

"When I came here it was because I thought you people were serious…" Dylan spoke in a clipped tone, the veins in his neck bulging from inner stress. "I will not go to prison…I will not. Am I clear here? I take the holy war very seriously and I am willing to die to make a point, but not because you and that pack of losers in there fuck up. I will personally cave your face in if this happens again. Now you get your ass dressed! You do remember that we have a prisoner in the forest?"

Berge watched as Dylan tossed him a towel then shut the bathroom door behind him. I didn't forget anything, you mutant, Berge thought to himself. He wished that he had never gone looking for a muscle man, but in truth Hans thought that the Sons of Marduk were lame and unreliable.

What Berge needed was an opportunity to slip out to take his aggressions out on some whore, but there had not been another opportunity since that night he had killed that strung out junkie in Grangeville. He had to be more careful as Hans was sure that Dylan had heard him sneak out that night. Dumping that body close to home was stupid as well as whacking bitches in neighboring towns. When this ordeal was over, Clever was moving the hell out. He was really cramping Berge's style.

Dylan gathered the Sons in the church where the radio was kept and the rest of the militia supplies.

"Half of you will come with me and the rest will remain here. Someone needs to man the radio in case we get into trouble. Jones, you can handle that, can't ya?" Clever referred to the cop, Dan Jones.

"Hey, I wanna go with you, I'm not a sit on your ass type!" The overweight officer had removed his stained uniform shirt and argued his case in a wrinkled white tee shirt and dark pants that rode beneath his ample stomach.

"I can see that. You and your son stay here. No kingdom can stand with all of her knights away from home," Dylan replied diplomatically.

He really thought Jones was just a fat jerk off and his kid was trying hard to emulate him. "What's going to happen if that doctor won't play along?" Ansel Smith asked as he sat before the stove rubbing his hands together. "I mean, it could happen. What then?" Smith's bald head glistened with sweat though the room wasn't that warm.

"Then the holy war starts early and all you big talkers better hope that you're not full of shit." Dylan wore a deadpan expression void of any compassion for the weak.

"Just how the fuck are we supposed to fight off the whole county or the state or by God, even the Feds?" Jim Brentlinger stared at Clever and Berge.

Hans had the gleam back to his eyes. "We have Marduk, Hitler and Jesus to aid in our victory!"

Clever looked sideways at Berge. "And if that doesn't work we'll booby trap the whole damned area and shoot every son-of-a-bitch that comes onto our land. The Feds already look like Jackasses over Waco and Ruby Ridge. They won't be rushing into anything."

"Gentlemen, we can play the media too. There are many out there who agree with us and are too afraid to admit it…." Berge began and was interrupted by a glowering Clever.

"The media sucks the asses of anybody with money! We will not cater to the press, period. They will go to all lengths to make us look like a bunch of Nazi fucks with grade school educations and no agenda besides killing niggers and kikes. They know how to inflame the general public and that is all they will do for us!" Dylan's light skin flushed in his sudden anger.

Jim Brentlinger snickered. "What's a matter? Some reporter call you a "baby killer?" He stood his ground as Clever walked over to him. The man scared the living shit out of him and Jim wished he had just kept his mouth shut.

Clever plowed his fist into Brentlinger's face, knocking him into Smith and Rogers who sat behind Jim in metal folding chairs. The trio lay in a pile on the bare wood floor with blood from Brentlinger's nose draining everywhere. The tension in the air thickened as the Sons realized that some of them had been exposed to tainted blood.

"I don't want to die! Me and the old lady still go at it too…Goddamn it! Brentlinger, you sack of shit." Mike Rogers looked wide-eyed at the blood on his hand.

"I didn't hit myself, asshole…oh shit, I lost a tooth."

Jim picked a bloody incisor off his shirt. Hans stared at Clever as if the Bubonic Plague had been unleashed. "Why must you hit one of our own? We must stay united in our quest."

"Save it, Berge. Go in the house and get the bleach." Dylan said to Will Chester who jumped up and did as he was ordered. The teenager didn't have any desire to spit teeth. When he returned with the gallon jug, Clever took it from him.

"Wipe down your arms and faces, any skin that was exposed and might have cuts somewhere. Jesus, you people are pathetic! Meachem, Jason, Wayne, Herman, Rogers and you, Berge, Get ready to head out. We have a situation in case any of you dipshits have forgotten!"

———•——•——•———

It was a wintry scene worthy of Currier and Ives. The snowflakes were large and accumulated on Dolan's shoulders as he led his team through the woods back to the Gayle house. They moved quickly to beat the storm that moved in from Canada. Visibility was still fairly decent, but time was running out. Harry gave some thought to heading for the highway then decided it was a shorter distance to the house. He was also afraid that Berge and Clever might be traveling the road to access the mine from that direction and didn't care to run into them.

Once they delivered Stark to his home, Harry planned to let the local sheriffs department round up the Sons of Whatever and he would head back to his own house in Kansas. That was the plan.

The terrain was filled with steep hills and a creek that divided the land east to west. Ada creek was frozen in the shallows near the banks, but still ran through the center. A footbridge was erected about a half mile from the doctor's house to the east and Dolan guided the group toward it. Stark seemed to get a second wind as they double timed it though the forest.

In the distance there was sound that made the six stop to listen. It echoed again. It was man's voice shouting out a name. "Let's get moving, guys, I think Clever is about to discover the fate of his unfortunate soldiers." Harry winked as he resumed the parachute shuffle to home base.

Chapter Thirty-one

Clever could have slapped Rogers to the ground for shouting. He knew they were in trouble when the scene was so quiet and the snow was rapidly filling a cluster of footprints, which indicated there were more than just three people out there recently. The stupidity of the men Dylan had to deal with was unbelievable, hollering when they did not know if the cops were around?

"Where are they then?" Mike Rogers whispered to Clever after receiving a penetrating glare from the former Green Beret.

Dylan responded by placing the carbine in an offensive position and approached the mine entrance with caution. It was clear from the amount of disturbed snow that something had occurred and he really didn't expect to find the kid still in the mine. The rest of the Sons had followed him, so Clever had to instruct four of them to remain outside to maintain a watch. He placed the beam of his heavy yellow flashlight about where the rope should be to find that someone had yanked it down along with his lights.

Wicker was on the ground in his underwear tangled up in a blanket. What little hair he had was standing out to the side like Bozo the clown, small rocks and dirt clung to his cheeks and his eyeballs were bloodshot. He tried cussing though the gag making Clever grunt in amusement.

"Untie him." Jason Brentlinger rushed to obey Clever by sticking a pen light in his mouth so that he could see while Dylan took the others back outside.

"Don't ya want to know what happened?" Orval's voice was raspy as he questioned the retreating Clever.

"I can see what happened."

"It wasn't the cops. It was that asshole and a few chicks. He made us all look like jackasses!" the old man ranted in his saggy jockey shorts.

Clever turned around. "He made the three of you look like jackasses."

"Well, how am I gonna get outta here? I got no clothes or shoes?"

"We'll find them, they're out there somewhere. They had no reason to steal an old fart's getup. Wait at the entrance and somebody will toss your stuff at you. I got two people to find, you're fucking pants ain't a priority."

The sound of a greasy fart led Clever to a clump of pine trees where he discovered George Chaney and Brian Chester, tied and gagged and trussed like up hogs. Dylan shook his head back and forth. He pulled the bandana out of Chaney's mouth and pulled the knot to loosen his hands.

"Goddamn, what the hell did you eat?"

"We didn't know how else to get your attention, ya bastard." An inch of snow covered George and Chester, who in spite of his younger age, didn't handle the cold as well as Chaney.

Berge, who had remained unusually quiet, stood looking down at Chaney as he untied his feet. "What now, Adolph?" George grumbled to Hans once he was eye level.

Brian's teeth rattled as he shivered violently." I've had enough of this shit...we could have been killed."

"Quit the damned whining. You're alive and unharmed. All they did was take the kid. It isn't over...for any of you. Now the shit hits the fan and the Sons of Marduk must defend what they believe." Clever hugged the De Lisle to him.

"And what is that?" Chester moaned.

Berge appeared irritated that his sermons had not sunk in. "That we must prepare the way for Jesus by reclaiming the white man's superiority! It's up to us to put the mud people back in their place…"

"There will be cops all over this place soon. You can hide, stake your claim to this land or go to prison. Our Rahowa is now, whether any of you are ready for it or not."

"We never thought it would be this year! Rahowa was always in the future and we had time!" Chester's heart flipped in his chest with a sickening thud.

"Yeah, well, every yesterday was once a tomorrow. Berge, get these people worked up for a fight or they're screwed. Leave Herman and Brentlinger with me. Since that asshole Dolan already knows the layout of this place it will not do for field operations. We're going to use that mine over by the lake, as the cover is good and it will be easy to defend with the numbers we have…now take the poor prisoners back, get them fixed up and when you return bring the rest of the weapons." Clever referred to the M-16s in the basement under the church.

"And hurry the hell up. I'm going to start rigging the roads with grenade traps and we don't have much time."

"Don't you sons-of-bitches leave me here!" Wicker, in all his wrinkled, shriveled glory popped out of the mine. His shorts were too big for his skinny legs and his balls could be viewed swinging back and forth as the old man jumped from one foot to another to keep warm.

"God, just take me now!" Clever frowned at the group of men who looked to him for the next set of instructions. "Berge, I'm going to get you for lying to me about your cheesy ass church."

"Just give us a chance…we can do it." The Sons watched fearfully as Hans tried to plead their case.

The large, tall blonde man could have been a statue as he grew quiet and the snow piled in little drifts on the back and shoulders of his black coat. When Dylan had visions of fighting for the great cause he had not imagined doing with a handful of losers over some rich doctor's property.

The holy war Clever had dreamed of would never materialize. A pathetic showdown in Idaho County, Idaho was all the victory the Sons of Marduk would know and the only great white army Clever would ever lead. He knew that most of them would not live through the ordeal. Their proud stand for the white race would be chronicled in the newspapers as bunch of gun-loving hillbillies who died because they stole some yuppie's kid, but there it is.

"Clever!" Berge spit as he said the name. "We don't need your permission for shit…I am the leader of this movement, not you!"

"Fine, but understand this, some of you will go to prison after today and some of you will get a headstone. Those are the only two things that are going to happen. You forget those wives and kids at home because that show is over for you."

"Fuck, we're still in high school….no way, man." Jason Brentlinger waved a hand between himself and Wayne Smith.

"Your balls trying to nest in your intestines? What did you shits think would happen? Berge, you need to get your people in gear." Clever started down the path to where his black Ford F250 waited for its owner.

There was a matching fiberglass cover over the bed where the Sons would ride back to headquarters. Without turning around he said, "Unless you pussies want to hoof it I suggest you hustle." Eddie Herman, Mike Rogers, Brian Meachem and the two teenagers scrambled into the back with Wicker lagging behind them. The old man shivered and pulled the blanket tighter around his head and shoulders. They managed to find his pants and boots, but the flannel shirt and coat had traveled to some unknown location. The men grumbled and complained as the truck bounced them around like glass Coke bottles in wooden crate.

"What the hell did we get ourselves into?" Herman cradled his face in his brown work gloves. Eddie had three kids and one on the way. He thought of the many nights he lay wishing there were no wife and kids, that he was young and free again, now suddenly his boring life didn't seem so bad. A slap on the face made Herman draw in a sharp breath.

"I've about had all I can take of you whiny little pricks! We don't get to pick when the battle begins! Guess I should have told the gooks to back off in Korea, cause, sob, sob, I'm not ready to fight!" Orval's features were twisted into a mask of disgust and the sheet over his head made him appear an angry Mother Superior.

"What do you do suppose those two assholes are talking about?"

Rogers sniffed as he watched Berge and Clever in a tense conversation. "What brand of tampons they use! Who fucking knows?" Meachem's cheek was still red from the snowy face pack.

"That's enough! We have to maintain a chain of command and use a little military courtesy and discipline." Wicker cleared his throat.

"Save it, you old fuck. At least we didn't spend the morning in our underwear!" Jason laughed.

"By God, when I was boy you didn't talk to your elders that way. I would have had a razor strop taken to my backside, that's part of what's wrong with this damned country!" Wicker glared at Brentlinger.

"When you were a boy Christ was in diapers." Smith nudged Jason who unwrapped a Zero candy bar. Wayne was all for the adventure as he was thinking of dropping out of school and had no special plans.

"Berge was right…to you clowns this is just another branch of the Elks." Wicker seemed momentarily dejected.

"Well, I think we better get our heads pulled out of our collective asses." Eddie lit up a cigarette and cracked open the fiberglass door over the tail gate to let the smoke out.

"This is really it then, the shit has finally hit the fan. The Racial Holy War is upon us." Mike took a cigarette from Herman.

"Thought you quit, Mike?" Eddie asked as he surrendered one of his Camels.

"What difference does it make now?"

"Why do you think we'll automatically lose? If you aren't into the fight, then leave! We don't need your fucked attitude." Wicker kicked at Rogers's foot with his boot.

Rogers rolled his brown eyes at Eddie. "We killed that vet, or have you forgotten, you old coot? You think any of us really has a choice anymore… please. Those two up front there will put a bullet in the forehead of anybody who tries to get out."

"Maybe you're just a wuss, Rogers?" Jason Brentlinger chimed in with his seventeen years of wisdom.

"I have a life that I'm not ready to give up just yet, anybody else think we ought to be taking on the cops today?"

"I kind of wanted to be a mechanic…" Wayne looked down at his crossed legs and played with his hands.

"You got to be kidding? We have a chance to stand up for the white man, to show the bigger groups like the Aryan Brotherhood that we should be taken seriously!" Jason thumped his chest with a closed fist like a Roman warrior.

Eddie laughed. "Tomorrow's paper will be great reading over bacon and eggs and that will be the end of it. I won't see my kids graduate, get married or nothing else and most white people won't give a shit about my "sacrifice!"

"So what do we do? Wonder if the guys back at headquarters feel the same way? If we just hadn't killed Tannahill we wouldn't be in this mess…" Meachem wondered out loud, but was interrupted by Herman.

"But we didn't kill him, just Berge."

"And we helped the asshole cover it up! We took the sucker's truck back to his house, Jones and Marsh helped Jim cook him and the rest of us knew all about it. Think a jury will believe that one man could make us all do as he wished? No, some of us will do life and some will get twenty years just because we're dumb son-of-a-bitches," Rogers added.

"Maybe that Dolan guy won't call the police, hell, they got the kid back." Wayne Smith offered with hope.

"Right, the good doctor will ignore the fact that we kidnapped his son and then trespassed on his land to hide the kid out," Eddie answered in a snide tone.

Orval cleared his throat loudly. "If we're fucked anyway, then we should take as many of them bastards with us as we can!"

"By God, that's easy for you to say, most of your goddamned life is over anyway!" Mike snubbed the filter out on the bed of Clever's truck.

"How do you like that, you shit?" he said lowly. At that moment Dylan turned to glance in the back at his cargo and Rogers threw him a hard stare.

"Son-of-bitch, suppose he heard you?" Eddie joked.

"The guy gives me the creeps. He's some kind of a weird combination of Rambo and Kung Fu and Lassie." Meachem smiled as the other men laughed.

The truck turned into Berge's driveway. The lights in the church were on, the curtains drawn and Jones stood off to one side with a rifle. The snow was falling heavy now and though it was nearly noon the sunlight was dim. There was no sign of law enforcement anywhere.

Chapter Thirty-two

Libby had called her boss, Lt. Rampart, when they arrived safely back at the Gayle house. She assumed that they would ask for assistance from the State Police or the FBI, but Jack Rampart would have none of that notion. The sheriff and undersheriff were out of town at a seminar in Washington D.C., so Rampart was acting sheriff while the two were gone. It was an unfortunate situation for Idaho County.

Jack Rampart was around six foot tall with black hair, a toothy grin and a paunch that crept over his Sam Brown belt. His wife weighed nearly four hundred pounds, but was a lovely woman who liked to make cakes and pies for those who had to work in stormy weather or during holidays. Cindy was kindhearted and a good mother to their two children, but Rampart was home the least amount of time necessary to remain married. The few women who had worked patrol for the department didn't last long, but would not file harassment charges fearing they would be labeled as troublemakers, thus ending their law enforcement careers, but everyone knew Jack had something to do with their leaving.

Libby Keefe knew exactly why the other women had sought work else where as Rampart panted over her like a dog in heat.

He was always trying to meet her in some secluded spot to "share information." It was embarrassing and she knew the other officers knew he was trying to get in her pants. He made her feel like she was just a piece of ass and not a real cop and Libby hated him for it.

Jack was full of himself and wasn't about to call the state police over a few rednecks. He was a Vietnam veteran too, and could handle the problem without the state or the Feds butting in. The fact that he was in the Navy didn't seem to be a conflict with Clever's jungle experience to Rampart. He didn't appreciate Keefe assuming that they needed outside help and he was pissed that she had not asked for his assistance in rescuing the boy. Jack was also tired of her waving her tight little ass in his face, then holding out. Officer Keefe wouldn't be long for the sheriff's department if Rampart had anything to do with it. Women didn't belong in law enforcement, except as dispatchers or meter maids, and if they weren't going to be friendly they could just turn in the badge.

Libby sat on the couch at the Gayle house with Harry. She couldn't believe that she had been told to go home. "That asshole! He doesn't even want to hear about the terrain, or the mine area or my opinions at all."

"He's a fool and if I understand Clever at all, he won't be taking prisoners today." Dolan was disturbed by the lieutenant's attitude toward the small group. "If that's the way it's going to go down, then I'm glad he doesn't want you out there. Some of your comrades are going to die today, Libby, at least you won't be one of them."

"He said something about using the dogs…"

"Oh God, can you contact the sheriff at all?" Using dogs against somebody like Clever was suicide. Dogs were good for making noise and for leaving trails to follow.

"What would I tell him? That I think my supervisor who has worked for the department fifteen years doesn't know his ass from a hole in the ground?"

"Well, he doesn't!" Stark emerged at the top of the stairs, his hair still wet from a hot bath. "That Green Beret is all business…he was nicer than that old fart though. He didn't really even sleep. His eyes never really shut completely. It was kind of strange the way he let me read magazines and let me have the use of my hands."

"Clever only does what is necessary. If he had to torture you to achieve that goal, then he would. But only if that were required to complete his operation. It was to his advantage to keep you relatively happy.

Wicker is just a mean old man." Dolan shook his head at the turn of things.

"You think Berge will bring the battle here, to the land he thinks is his?" Blake looked old as he wandered in from the kitchen.

"If he can. If that idiot Rampart gets his act together he could catch some of them at Berge's place before they get dug in good."

"You don't think they will try to hold out in the woods do you? With all that snow?" Libby asked as she stirred the liquid in her cup that was more cream than coffee.

"We aren't dealing with Mensa members, remember. Plus, there could be some advantages for Clever. He already knows the layout and with the snow falling so fast and heavy he could have his people in place and their tracks filled in before the cops could find them. He could also arrange for some nasty booby traps here and there to slow the cops down too. In fact, I'd count on it." Dolan stood with his back to the fire. He liked to feel the heat seep into his spine.

"I feel helpless…I know these guys are mostly middle-aged married men with beer guts, but they seem to do what Berge wants." Libby had a tendency to think she had to save the world.

"I noticed that. I got the impression that these guys are afraid of something. The only one that really mentioned the white race thing was Clever, and he tried to convince me that we were superior to blacks and Jews, but he didn't try that hard. That old f...sorry, Mom, told me that Dad was a race traitor for treating anyone that walked in the door, but he was basically just an asshole." Stark threw Laura a crooked grin for almost saying the four letter word that she hated most.

"Well, we did what we could and Stark is back home. Libby, you can't feel guilty for whatever happens today, that is Rampart's problem."

Dolan was ready to go home and he really didn't care what sort of mess the local cops created. He was tired and still had to solve the mess with Sarah's life insurance.

Laura walked over and placed a hand on Libby's shoulder.

"Harry's right, kid. You did a brave thing today and you need to go home, take a hot bath and get some sleep. There will be other days...you did your share." The other women had already left and would be contacted later by the sheriff's department for statements regarding the kidnapping and rescue.

———•—•—•———

Clever rigged the roads that penetrated the doctor's land with grenade traps. While he could still see the pot holes through the dents in the snow, Dylan placed a grenade into the cavity then tied a thin wire from the pin to a nail placed near the rim. A vehicle tire dropping down into the hollow would pull the wire taunt and set the grenade off. Normally, one would place a tarp over the hole to conceal it, but the snow took care of that problem. He also left several pop cans near the mine where Stark was held figuring that some numb nut cop would pick one of them up. The British friend who gave Clever the De Lisle told him how to cut out the bottom of the can to cover a grenade. Once the can was removed it would trigger the explosion, a trick that worked well in the Falklands.

The field base would be the old gold mine that overlooked the lake, but only after a heated argument with Berge. Clever didn't know what the hell was up with Hans not wanting anyone around that place, but it was the easiest spot to defend, so Dylan won out. There would be no visible signs of the Sons of Marduk for the cops to see. Clever would stay high up on the mountain close to the mine and would pick off the cops as they showed up; If there were any left after the booby traps.

He would keep Jim Brentlinger with him, as Dylan didn't trust the guy not to turn traitor. Wicker and five of the Sons would wait across Highway 14 for the police to turn onto the dirt road that led to other mine where the kid was held. The men would then follow behind them on foot to finish off those not killed by the grenades. Clever was fully prepared to shoot any of the Sons that turned yellow.

Berge and the rest of the crew would approach from the ghost town of Ole Grande. It would be a blood bath, but Dylan wasn't concerned about that as none of them were walking off the property ever again anyway. Clever wanted a body count, period, and he didn't have to worry about whether any of his "troops" made it out alive. The only thing to do now was wait to see who showed up for the party.

"You and Berge are fucking nuts. We can't win, you know?" Jim brushed off the snowflakes that tickled his nose. "If my kid gets killed out here…"

Clever scrutinized the woods before for any sign of movement. When Brentlinger didn't finish he turned head toward Jim. "What? What is going to happen? You going to plug me in the back?"

"I'm just wondering what the point to all of this is?" Jim watched the western side of the slope for cops who might approach from the Gayle house.

"You dumb asses killed a man for no reason and now your balls are in a stew pot. That is the point to this whole thing. You people are not ready for any racial war, but I doubt that you ever would be. Now shut the hell up and do your job. If I get shot before I can take some of them out with me, I'll shoot you from one end of your fat body to the other, and I'll start with your little peepee!" Clever swung the rifle around and centered it on Brentlinger's zipper.

"Alright! Christ, you're an asshole." Jim made it sound like he was just kidding, but he was positive of that analysis.

Nearly a half hour later an explosion was heard to the east. Clever's lips crept into a pleasant smile.

"Guess I know what it takes to make you happy."

"By now they won't know what the hell to think. If they're smart, they will retreat and make better plans, and when they do, Wicker will meet them head on." Clever's icy blue eyes scanned the horizon.

"And if they're stupid?" Brentlinger was glad that he hadn't shaved for several days as the drifting snow was freezing the hairless parts of his face. Clever must be some kind of an android who was impervious to conditions that made humans miserable.

"They will stay off the roads and approach through the forest where at least one of them will be blown to pieces by the cans. If they head in this direction, then you and I will pick them off....not too hard, eh?"

"Fish in a barrel." Jim nodded. He looked back at the entrance to the gold mine and felt the flashlight in his coat pocket, just in case Clever was wrong.

———◦—◦—◦———

Deputy Sanders was lying in the snow with his arms and legs spread wide. Rather than drive into the targeted area, Rampart had decided to send his people in on foot. Paul Sanders had stepped directly down on the first trap and lost his right leg from the knee down. It was a gory site with a jagged portion of the femur jutting out like a dagger and pieces of bone and flesh littered the clean white snow. Blood ran from his nose and ears from the percussion. His features were frozen into a mask of bewilderment indicating that he had lived for a few seconds after the blast. Rampart knelt down on one knee to check his pulse and found none. He bit his lip as he contemplated the next move. Jack was over forty and his chances at glory were rapidly decreasing. He could back off and let the State police handle it, but since one of his men had been killed, Rampart felt it was his responsibility to capture or kill the offenders.

"What now, Lieutenant?" Deputy Hanks asked, obviously shook up over the sight of his fellow officer's remains. "Oh, man." His distress was played out in the rapid movement of his Adam's apple bobbing up and down.

Rampart stood up. The department was small, with sixteen available officers, minus two as Keefer was sitting this one out and Sanders was out period. Three officers were patrolling their regular beats, one sergeant needed to stay at the combination courthouse and jail, and the other lieutenant was on a cruise to the Bahamas. He had nine men and two were into overtime from their shifts the night before.

"Okay, Steve, put Paul's hat over his face. This is the situation. We can call in the State police and let them solve our problems for us or we can fix these SOBs ourselves. It's up to you people, talk to me." The lieutenant looked to the deputies. Half of them stared at the lifeless body slowing disappearing under a snowy blanket and the rest looked cautiously at their supervisor.

"Well?" Hanks fetched the blue ball cap that lay several yards from the deceased Sanders. He quickly covered the man's face then scampered away as if the dead deputy would reach out and grab him at any second.

"How many of them are there again?" Rick Ivandatter quizzed Rampart who looked at him as if he had just burned the American flag.

"At least ten, but we don't know for sure. He was one of us, damn it! We owe it to Sanders to try." The lieutenant weighed around two hundred sixty pounds, his shoulders were massive, his hands like small hams hooked to his belt. It was clear to the men who lingered in the blowing snow that the only honorable, professional response was to agree.

"Where's Libby? Didn't she help rescue the boy? Did she have any good info on that religious group...? Hanks had serious doubts about the small department tracking someone down who knew guerilla warfare.

"She did a stupid thing and I'll deal with her later. We'll stay off the roads, obviously. Just keep your ears and eyes open, remember your training." Rampart gestured with his right arm for the deputies to follow him.

Ivandatter kept his mouth shut, but thought privately that he did not recall any lessons about challenging right-wing fruitcakes and former Green Berets in the forest. Rick was a sergeant in the National Guard and he was used to people who did not know what they were doing running the show. Guys like Jack Rampart were everywhere and the opinions of the lower rank didn't figure into the equation. Hanks looked like a turkey on Thanksgiving morning who knew the gig was up.

"How can you be sure they aren't watching us right now?" Ryan Carter asked the lieutenant, who was bent down in a "sneaking" position. Carter's jaw showed the aftereffects of a speedy shave. His lucky quarter was safe in the left breast pocket of his government parka, right below the badge shaped patch.

"They're probably holed up in the same place they held the kid...the booby traps are to warn them we're coming." Rampart's patience was running out with inferiors who did not blindly follow orders. "Keep quiet and spread out, will ya?"

Jack keyed the mike on his portable radio and informed the dispatcher to switch to channel four in case some old busybody was listening to a scanner at home or worse, Sander's parents. He told Melva that they had an officer down, but it was not safe for the paramedics to enter the scene yet. The officer was code yellow so there was no hurry and no need to risk the life of healthcare providers. The officers moved eastward as the wind blew the freezing, wet snow into uncovered ears and clung to beards. Hanks and Ivandatter were closest to Rampart until Carter moaned about not liking the scenario, then the lieutenant ran back to hush him up.

A loud crack echoed through the woods making the cops drop and crawl behind trees for cover. Hanks spun around with his mouth hanging wide open, a red dot in the center of his forehead like a woman from Bagdad. Jack watched his officer topple into the snow like any one of the deer he had bagged throughout the years. Another crack of Clever's rifle rang out and a bullet tore a path threw Ivandatter's buttocks as he lay on the ground at the edge of a clearing.

Rampart was not sure what to do as he could not tell where the shots were coming from, but on hands and knees, he managed to get close enough to grab Rick's ankles and pull him back into the thicker trees. He knew they were in deep shit now. Two officers dead, one wounded and the rest of them were sitting ducks. Just when Rampart thought they could retreat the way they came, Orval Wicker, along with several local men, began firing on them.

Carter flattened himself against the rough bark of an old pine his hearing muffled by the rush of blood through his ears. He suddenly realized that he needed to urinate in the worst way. Between not knowing where the zealots were and the wailing of Ivandatter, Chip Carter could not think straight. He heard some twigs break and soaked his pants.

"Carter!" Rampart's voice was a strained whisper. "You okay?"

"I'm not shot if that's what you mean." The young deputy had turned down a scholarship to attend dental school and his mother had been furious and disappointed. Carter now understood her position, as he was now just as furious and disappointed in himself for doing it. "How are we gonna get out of here?"

"I don't know yet." Jack keyed the mike again. "37-19, X-ray, X-ray."

Rampart had never used the distress signal before and it seemed surreal now. The radio was silent for a few seconds as the dispatcher called Sergeant Mitchell into the command center. Stan immediately telephoned the other lieutenant at home who then grabbed his coat on the way out the door.

"19 to 37, 10-4. 38 is in route to 19. Hold on now." Melva had just told Rambadt that Lieutenant Johnson was on the way to the station.

She was relieved. Jim Johnson was an intelligent, levelheaded guy and had already told her to call the state police. Rampart held his Glock in front of him like a shield as he crouched in some bushes near an Aspen tree. He motioned to Ivandatter to stay down, not that the man had much choice with half his ass torn off. Jack saw a colorful flash dart between some trees not far away and he fired at it.

In an instant Wicker popped out and put a .223 from his mini-fourteen in Rick's skull. The lieutenant drew in a breath involuntarily at the unexpected brutality. They were all fucked. He fired at Orval and put a slug in his groin, prompting the old shit to creep into some cover.

"Jack! What the hell's happening?" Fear glued Carter to the tree. He could hear shots, but could seen nothing from his position and the snow was falling heavy now. The freezing urine was turning his hoo-ha into a popsicle. Chip began to whisper the Lord's Prayer when Rampart did not answer.

"Hi, Chip." Jason Brentlinger put his zit-covered face close to Carter's. The deputy was known for waiting just outside of town to catch students from the high school speeding home. He was responsible for many of them having high insurance rates.

"Jason, you shouldn't be out here." Carter held his weapon against his chest. In the confusion it didn't occur to the deputy that a high school student would be part of an ambush of police officers, a student he had run off from party spots many times. "Get down! People are being killed out here."

Brentlinger feigned surprise. "No?"

"What are you doing out here?" Chip glanced quickly at the teenager whose expression smacked of the smart-ass. He could not see anyone else aside from Ivandatter and his crimson backside in the distance.

"You know what my old man did to me after that ticket you wrote? He hit me so fucking hard I could not chew for two days! You do not have to be a prick, you do not have to hide in the trees and sneak up on kids...I seen you let spics and niggers fly down the road and you did nothing about it! Why do you hate your own kind?"

Carter's stomach threatened to return the early morning coffee and doughnuts as he realized the kid was one of Berge's clones. "Jason, I was just doing my job...if I don't write tickets they don't think I'm doing anything out there."

"Bullshit!" Brentlinger shoved a sixteen gauge under Carter's ribs. "I know your type, Chip. You scream at your wife and beat your kids, right?"

"I'm not married, Jason....I want." A full field load that disemboweled him silenced Carter.

Brentlinger was sprayed with blood and guts. "Fuck!"

Wicker and Dan Jones took positions behind nearby trees. Orval nearly vomited at the sight of the deputy's internal organs decorating the front of Jason Brentlinger.

"Damn it, kid! What is it with you?

"Oh shit, oh God, the smell!" When the air hit Carter's fresh innards, an odor rose out of his exposed cavity along with the steam. Jason lost it and puked on his own boots.

Rampart peered through the snow in the direction of the voices. After a few seconds the form of a lanky teenager, Jason Brentlinger, appeared. Jack did not like Jim or Jason Brentlinger as Jason was prone to pick on smaller children and Jim was prone to dismiss the behavior. Twelve-year old Roger Rampart was a favorite for after school torment from that lopeared jerk. As the lieutenant focused on the brightly colored mess on the boy's clothes and on the ground he realized it had to have come from one of his deputies. Carter was the closest to him. He leveled the sights of the Glock on Brentlingers crotch.

The force knocked Jason on his ass. Jones lined his body up with the trunk of a thick pine as the boy gripped his wounded genitals with both hands and made the strangest squeal Dan had ever heard. He unconsciously squeezed his legs together.

Wicker fired a shot back at the unseen cop. "Christ, he sounds like a gutted pig at a Cajun barbeque." Orval grimaced at the writhing teenager.

A large rock that sprouted numerous saplings provided Rampart the protection he needed to change his vantage point. He dashed from tree to tree until he could drop behind the boulder and peek at the two men who thought they were hidden from view. Jack's jaw muscles tensed as he saw a fellow law enforcement officer with Wicker and Brentlinger.

"Jones!" A nervous whisper to his right stopped Jack from unloading the weapon into Dan Jones. The five remaining deputies were scattered throughout the forest and had sent Clyde Sickle to find their supervisor.

"What do you want us to do?" Sickle was one of the older patrol officers at age thirty-eight. He sat on his heels in a way that made Jack's knees burn just looking at Clyde. "My radio is busted...I can't get out anyway."

"Fuck! We must be in a dead zone." There were certain areas throughout the county that seemed to exist in a vacuum. That explained why Rampart had not heard from his surviving men. "There are two of them over there, let's stay within sight of each other. Go get the rest of the men. I don't want any of us getting whacked in our own crossfire."

"The other four are just east of...Goddamn! Is that Jones from the Hagar department? That son-of-a-bitch! We can get both of those bastards now without hurting any of us. It won't hurt my feelings none if the name Orval Wicker disappears from the phone book." Sickle had a large, swooping mustache that made him appear as an old west gunslinger.

Wicker was a retired fish and game warden who was known for his brutality in apprehending poachers and for randomly throwing back fish that weighed much more than the legal limit.

Rampart nearly jumped out of his shorts as something thumped the ground next to his black Wellington boot. While he was safe from Jones and Wicker, Jack was now fully exposed to the sniper above them. The officer scampered on all fours toward Clyde who was far enough into the woodland that Clever could not see him. In the process of escaping, Wicker spotted him and put a bullet in Jack's left leg near the knee.

"We're gonna be on you fuckers like crabs on an old whore! You hear that, Rampart, you squid?" Orval's eyes glistened with excitement much as they had when he was killing gooks near Pork Chop Hill in Korea.

"We're in trouble, Clyde. I hope the cavalry gets here soon." Jack winced from the pain.

Sickle shouted back at Wicker. "Any whore worth her salt can cure crabs and be back to work before the hair dries!" He sent a hollow point bullet twirling at Wicker and it landed about where his stomach should be. The old man cursed and ducked out of sight.

Wicker was waiting on his own cavalry as well. Eddie Herman, Vic Marsh, Charlie Jones, Ansel Smith, Wayne Smith and Berge should all be somewhere around the lake by now. Will Chester and Jim Brentlinger were with Clever, but Orval did not know what had happened to Adam King, Mike Rogers or Buddy Meachem. He had not seen them for some time now. Wicker grunted at the pain caused by the gut wound.

Chapter Thirty-three

Libby Keefe was barely out of the bathtub when there a pounding on her apartment door. She hurriedly pulled on an old Bangles tee shirt and gray sweat pants then sprinted across the small living room in bare feet. Her first impression at the site of two big men in the blue and tan uniforms of the state police was that she was in trouble.

"Officer Keefe?" When the young woman with the wet hair shook her head to the affirmative, the older of the two officers continued. "I'm Major Whistlestop and this is Captain Roth, could we talk for a moment?"

Keefe stepped back and let the men out of the blowing snow. "Would you like some coffee or something?"

"If you have some made, I'd like a cup, thanks." Roth removed his hat and down on the dark blue sofa.

"None for me, had mine already. If you don't mind I'll just get right to it?" The Major spoke to Libby as she poured two cups of coffee. The apartment was open with no walls between the kitchen, dining area or living room.

"Yes, sir, that would be fine." Libby sat on one of her dining room chairs and faced the two cops. She noticed that Whistlestop smiled slightly. He was a handsome man whose sideburns were silvery against his olive-toned face.

"Could you give us a rundown on what the situation is with the Sons of Marduk? And what exactly occurred this morning?" the Major asked as he leaned forward on his knees.

"And who is this Harry Dolan we keep hearing about?" Roth warmed his chilled hands on the steaming cup.

"Harry is a medical investigator from Kansas who is a friend of Dr. Gayle's. The doctor asked Harry to help him out with the disappearance of his best friend, Tom Tannahill. He was getting ready to go home when Stark Gayle was snatched. Harry has been a Ranger in the army and thought we could get Stark out of there with quickly with the least amount of bloodshed...and we did. We didn't hurt anybody." Libby still thought that she was in hot water for going along on the mission.

"Libby, we know that and we appreciate Mr. Dolan's common sense. What we really need to know is how many of the Sons are there, and what sort of weapons do they have? This morning several of your comrades lost their lives or were wounded. There were booby traps set on the roads with grenades..." Roth's light brown mustache was neatly trimmed, but still managed to dampen with the coffee. His eyes were green behind gold-rimmed frames that made Roth look more like a math teacher than a cop.

"I knew it would be bad...shit..." Libby's lip quivered from anger and grief.

"Is there something you'd like to tell us?" Whistlestop prodded the young deputy. "We need to know everything before we go in there."

Tears welled up in spite of her efforts to stop them. "Harry's not some jerk-off who thinks he knows it all, he just understands what Clever is going to do and how he's going to do it, he didn't think the guys on the department would listen to him and he was right! The lieutenant told me to go home and he didn't want to hear anything I had to say about it, nothing at all!"

"Clever is one of Berge's men, right? Wasn't he special forces?" Roth asked.

"Green Berets. He was in Vietnam like Harry. Dolan told us there would be booby traps so we stayed off the roads! Nobody had to die. Harry knows how that asshole thinks."

"Libby, we'd like you to come with us to the Gayle house where we plan to set up headquarters. I'd like to hear this Dolan's assessment of the situation too."

———————

Troopers from the Lewiston division huddled around the dining room table at Blake and Laura Gayle's house. Stark sat on the couch still wore out from his ordeal, but clung to every word passed around the table amid the sea of tan shirts with pleats on the breast pockets and colorful patches on the left sleeves. The ranking officer ran the discussion with one foot planted on Laura's oak chair, which amused Stark. His mother was very fussy concerning the treatment of her furniture, but she sat on the other end of the couch with his dad intensely listening to the conversation, seemingly unaware of the abusive act.

Harry leaned against the wall next to a painting of a slain bullfighter with his arms crossed. They wanted him to go along to advice about possible traps and ambush sites and Dolan was not happy. The locals had refused all information offered and people were now dead. Libby stood next to him with a scowl on her face. If her own department had listened to her, none of this would have happened.

The six men around the table were members of a SWAT team. Most had pulled regular shifts the night before and still wore the daily uniform. They would change when the briefing was over. Dolan thought they were a good lot and should have been called in Rampart had decided to relive Missionary Ridge. He particularly liked Whistlestop who had an easy laugh and was confident in himself without being haughty. Normally Dolan would find working with these men enjoyable, but he could not keep his mind clear. There was a good possibility that he would have to fight his brother and sister for Sarah's burial policy, a mere six thousand dollars.

It was difficult to concentrate on strategic matters when he felt so betrayed and haunted by the image of the poor, legless Sarah sitting on that motel room bed crying while Alex stuffed his face in a restaurant with Al's money. The cold-blooded cruelty and hatred displayed by Alex for Harry and Sarah had knocked the wind out of Dolan. He thought he had seen or experienced damned near everything, but what had Merlin told King Author in the movie *Excalibur*? Evil is always where you never expect it.

"Harry, do you think we're looking at major artillery out there, or are they still too grassroots for that?" Bruce Whistlestop cupped his hands over his raised knee.

"Fortunately, until recently, the Sons of Marduk were mostly just a men's club where they talked big, but Berge and Clever are real problems. I suspect that Berge or Hatcher is the one that killed Tannahill and the others were too afraid to do anything about it. There is something very unsettling about Hans. I imagine he has killed many more than anyone knows. I think we can expect inexpensive jungle tricks, but deadly ones. Watch where you step and don't touch anything that looks out of place. I'll help as much as I can."

"Time is wasting, let's gear up and get out there." The Major pushed the chair back under the table and his men followed him into the family room where a temporary headquarters was set up.

Libby Keefe had only been in law enforcement for two years and was eager to experience a real hot zone, but Dolan had explained that this zone's temperature was set on char not cook. It took some coaching to convince her that she could do the most good staying at the command center, but Libby relented. If Harry thought the situation was bad, then it must be serious.

The team approached from the old mining road off Highway 14 and quickly found the body of Paul Sanders. The snow had not yet filled the numerous footprints that led into the forest.

"Looks like they crossed the highway on foot and followed the sheriff's boys into the woods." Jordy Abelard observed as his held his M-16 in an offensive position. After several years as a fire jumper, he decided to find a safer occupation.

Max Selwyn, who repaired missile systems in the army reserve, checked to make sure the downed lawman was dead. "Hope they aren't all like this."

"The last transmission from Rampart placed them near the old Hanson mine and someone was firing from a position above them. Our first objective is to take out that sniper.

"Where the hell did you find a map with that old mine on it?" Dolan asked while holding his Winchester up and away from the others.

"We've had trouble with these right wing types before, as you probably know, so the boys at the state capitol consulted maps from the turn of the century to see where abandoned mines might be. You never know when you might need to know that sort of thing around here." Captain Roth spoke quietly.

The team split into two groups. Four men would swing out around and approach the Hanson mine, Stark's place of captivity, from the northeast. Rampart said they were being hit from the north, while shots were fired from the south. They hoped to come up behind the Sons of Marduk that had the sheriff's department pinned down.

Harry would accompany Whistlestop and a Corporeal Nash Redding up the mountain to find Clever and whoever else was with him. A serious man of around thirty, Redding was the team sniper and the winner of many competitions on the combat range. He said very little, mostly because he was shy, not because he had nothing to say. Nash was very patient and could wait long hours for the perfect shot. He could also drop a bead quickly when needed.

The mountain was really more of a foothill that ascended gradually on two sides with sheer faces to the east and north. Hackbury, Elm, Blue Spruce and Aspen trees covered the slopes. Large jagged rocks could make the climbing easier by acting as natural stairs. The mine above would be rudimentary to defend with the right people, a realization that ran through every man's thoughts as he negotiated the terrain. They would emerge at the far side of the hill away from the mine, which was on the north peak and overlooked the large natural lake to the northeast. Dolan was uneasy. He expected Clever to pop up at any minute and put a bullet in his forehead. Where was he and why had the team managed to get this far without being noticed, or had they? Harry steered the troopers over to an area that was hard to climb. There was there was something about the ground beneath the stair-like boulders that Dolan did not trust. His intuition was usually right. There had to be some reason that Clever was not worried about this side of his mountain.

Near the top of the hill Dolan surveyed the area between two trees carefully as the deepening snow made searching for traps much harder. He brushed the snow off the bark of an Aspen and found fishing line tied around it that disappeared beneath the snow in the direction of another tree. Harry took out the serrated knife issued to him in Vietnam and cut the line near the trunk. He signaled to Whistlestop that there was a trip line and he passed it on to Redding. More than likely a grenade lay nearby waiting to rip them to shreds.

Brentlinger scanned the landscape below with binoculars as ordered by Dylan Clever, but he had yet to see anything. Jim could not even tell what Clever was shooting at so far in the distance. It was spooky the way that rifle of his made almost no noise at all. The gun was silent and creepy just like its owner. Dylan was off checking on Will Chester who was supposed to be guarding the two accessible sides of the rugged hill. Clever did not trust him enough to leave the seventeen-year-old on his own, nor did he trust Jim who had been told that if he was not there when the big blonde man returned, Jim would have his balls cut off.

Brentlinger glanced back at the entrance to the mine and wondered why Hans got so up tight about Clever wanting to hold up there. Berge was a weird shit, a fact that Jim had not really noticed, until after being diagnosed with AIDS. For some reason acquiring the disease had changed Brentlinger's viewpoints on most things, but now it was too late. Now he was accomplice to murder and surrounded by cops who wanted to fry his Nazi ass. He gave some thought to running or just plugging Clever and Berge and blaming it on the cops, but abandoned the idea as unrealistic. At least he had good life insurance at work and Joan would not be left high and dry when Jim bought the farm. He raised the field glasses back up to his eyes and saw something dark dart across a clearing near the lake followed by two other objects, then all three were out of view. It was either the state or the Feds. All hell was about to break loose and Brentlinger was not quite ready to die yet.

There was a heavy-duty flashlight in his right coat pocket, which Jim fingered while searching for more cops in the distance. The cops were not stupid. They would figure out that there was a sniper on the mountain and be there shortly. Brentlinger walked toward the east side where he could see around the mine entrance. The remains of a rough road where wagons had once hauled gold down the mountain ran alongside the mine. Bushes and saplings dotted the area now, but the old road was easily visible.

Maybe if he shot Clever as he returned up the road Jim would be able to escape. No, he would never get past the cops who would be crawling all over the place and he was not sure what young Chester would do. The teenagers seemed to take the whole scene more seriously than the older men did, and Will just might kill Brentlinger for being a traitor. He was positive that his own son would shoot him without hesitation. Jim wondered where Jason was and if he was still alive. He thought of Joan at home with the two small children. They were probably baking cookies, unless the media knew about the fiasco on Dr. Gayle's land, and they certainly did by now. She would be furious at him, not proud, like some of the wives and she would be right. It would be better if Jim just did not come home again. Brentlinger's only fear was that Jason would survive, get off somehow and return home to terrorize his stepmother. A firearm was discharged close by and Jim took for the entrance to the mine.

Chapter Thirty-four

Berge and his team moved slowly. They could hear the shots fired in the distance and Hans had some trouble keeping Ansel Smith and his son, Wayne, with them. The elder Smith was in poor physical shape and wheezed as if he had two rusty old bellows instead of lungs. Weakness would not be tolerated and Hans would put the old fart down before allowing desertion in the middle of their holy war. The northwest side of the lake was visible through the trees.

"Hans!" Eddie Herman whispered. He pointed to the fresh footprints in the foot high snow.

"Has to be cops or that son-of-a-bitch Dolan. Don't think any of ours would be coming from this direction or they shouldn't be." Berge wore a black BDU jacket that made him appear to be one of the SS men that he so admired. A small round, black, white and red pin with a swastika was attached to the collar. He carried one of the M-16s obtained by Clever. Some of the Sons chose their own weapons because they were more familiar with them and Dylan had not argued about it.

"Which way should we go?" Vic Marsh looked like a Native American, but denied any such ancestry. He claimed that he was black Irish, but Berge had serious doubts. Marsh was allowed to join the Sons of Marduk due to the fact that few people wanted to join them and Vic's enthusiasm made up for a suspicious heritage.

"We'll just follow the prints and come up behind them." Hans had coldness in his eyes now. Herman, Marsh, Charlie Jones, Ansel Smith and Wayne trudged along behind Berge until they reached a small rise near the Hanson mine. They lay on their stomachs in the snow watching for any movement. Whoever had left the footprints had gone around the far side of the old mine. Berge was not certain what to do at this point. The soda cans left by Clever were still there, so either the local cops had not been this far or they were not as stupid as Dylan thought them to be.

Captain Tom Roth led his troopers into a dense area of trees near the mine when he heard something odd behind them. Roth sent Sgt.Abel Zerach back the way they came but this time through the dense cluster of Blue Spruce. Zerach, like the other SWAT team members, wore camouflage BDUs that blended well with the pines. After several minutes, there was movement straight across from Abel. He signaled to Roth that he could see two men. Ansel and his son had decided to surrender, but they still had their weapons in hand. Zerach accidentally stepped on a twig that snapped and scared the two men. Wayne fired his M-16 into the trees mostly as a reflex action. Abel crawled on his stomach away from the rain of bullets until he came to a bigger tree that could provide better cover.

Roth gestured that he and Selwyn would approach from the other side. Zerach aimed for Wayne's chest and put a bullet in his heart then several more of the religious fanatics emerged and began firing. Bullets whistled in every direction. Abel was a Civil War re-enactor and he suddenly had a better appreciation for Cold Harbor.

Charlie Jones, the Hagar cop's son, proceeded to empty his clip in the direction of the noise. In the excitement, Jones hopped out into the clearing close to the mine entrance and landed in a Rambo-type stance. Abel yelled for him to drop the gun and eat snow, but the boy responded by charging forward with a steady stream of lead paving the way. A man who looked like the president of the Adolph Hitler fan club screamed at the kid to stop and turn around, but Jones kept rushing the trees. Abel could hear the bullets nick the pine that shielded him. When Zerach tried to talk the boy into giving up, his comrades sprayed the air with various types of ammo.

In the few seconds that it took Sgt. Zerach to draw a bead on the sandy haired teenager, he could see that the boy's ears stood out from his head like Dopey the Dwarf. His legs lopped along like a newborn colt's and Abel did not want to bring the kid down, but he had no choice. It was either his obituary in the paper or the boy's. The impact of the shot sent Jones backward into the snow where he slid like a bowling ball. Herman freaked and began to run eastward toward the highway where he met Roth and Selwyn. Eddie had no desire to go down in flames as Clever planned so he tossed the rifle to the ground and threw up his hands. Selwyn handcuffed him to a pine tree and smiled when the man said nothing about sitting on pinecones. Roth pulled the clip from Herman's M-16 so that it was useless in case one of Sons of Marduk should come across it. Someone shouted to Captain Roth from the south.

"Rampart! Sheriff's department. I'm hit...I have two men here with me."

Roth moved quickly from tree to tree until they reached the lieutenant and his deputies. The trooper was dumbstruck by the old prospector's appearance of Sickle and the terrified expression on a young officer named Peters.

"Are the two of you okay?" Roth asked firmly.

"Yes sir! We just stayed close to the lieutenant so he wouldn't be shot like a carp in a beer barrel...just give us orders." Clyde would have been right at home next to Wyatt Earp. Peters threw him a sideways glance that said, "Speak for yourself!"

"Come on, I've got a man pinned down over here."

Max Selywn saw three officers move toward him and took the cue to advance eastward toward the Hanson mine. The firing had stopped and Zerach emerged from the pines when saw Roth, Selwyn and two deputies sweep the clearing for perpetrators.

The Sons had divided into two groups with Berge and Marsh running like hell southward in hopes of connecting with Clever. The Smiths had just disappeared over a rise and Zerach dropped to his stomach to view their retreat. Ansel and Wayne were deserting the battle.

Roth radioed his command center at the Gayle house and ordered a squad of men to meet them near the creek.

"Wonder where Wicker and Jones are...they didn't run. I know better." Sickle's handle bar mustache jumped up and down with every word and his lower lip glowed bright pink beneath it. "Wicker's one mean bastard."

Roth frowned for a moment. "We can assume that Berge took off for the mountain...we have three good men over there now. Let's make sure those other clowns aren't going to come up behind us before we back up Whistlestop."

They began to backtrack to pump Herman for information about who was missing when the snowy air filled with several gunshots from the north. The officers advanced through an area where the trees were smaller and closer together. An angry voice echoed in the distance. The snow was trampled down as if several people had fallen then ran away. They followed the trail of footprints until they could see two men lying in the deep snow, their faces hidden from view.

"There's Wicker, Mike Rogers and that Hagar cop, Dan Jones." Peters spoke with a strain in his voice.

"Looks like the Sons of Bullshit are falling apart...they're killing their own people." Roth studied the men for a moment.

The old man looked pissed. Rogers held his rifle like it was a pool cue and then there was Jones. The way he was standing over the bodies with that arrogant look on his snaky features reminded Roth of an SS officer inspecting the corpses of Jews. Who would hire such as cold-blooded ass as a cop?

The captain shouted to the three men.

"State police, put down the weapons now!" Roth waited a few seconds as the men looked dumbfounded. Did they really believe that law enforcement would not find them?

"Drop the guns, gentlemen, or you will leave here in body bags!"

Rogers stared at his blue checked flannel shirt, as time seemed to shift into slow motion. It just did not seem real that a cop was going to kill him if he did not drop his rifle. It was like a scene in a movie that he would watch with his two sons while munching pop corn. If he did not stop this now, he would never see his family again. On the other hand, he would be seeing them in a prison visitation room for the next twenty years to life. His wife, Pam, would understand if Mike did not come back as she believed in the cause though she would not like raising two boys alone. He jumped at the sound of a loud angry voice.

Max Selwyn was losing patience with those cold-blooded killers who were leaving bodies throughout the forest.

"Drop the fucking guns or you die today…do you assholes need a translator?" Max could see Sickle grin at him a few feet away.

Wicker had no expression on his features to read. He moved only his eyes when Rogers threw his rifle into the snow and dropped to his knees, hands clasped behind his head. Orval wanted to kick the yellow bastard until his people littered the crisp, white snow.

"With cops like you, boy, we wouldn't need any bad guys!" Clyde heckled Jones whose eyes widened at the numbers of guns sites centered on his chest area. In a nervous reaction, Jones squeezed off a round that nearly hit Jordy Abelard. Wicker took the opportunity to break and run into some scraggly bushes while Jones tumbled to the ground with a round in the center of his sternum. The bullet must have nicked the aorta as he bled profusely and steam rolled off the red liquid as it soaked Dan's shirt.

"Damn, guess we can skip the spaghetti for lunch." Sickle remarked as he fell in behind the troopers in pursuit of Wicker. Peters lost the battle with his stomach and bent over to retch. Clyde laughed and Peters pointed his Glock at Rogers to regain some of his dignity then handcuffed him.

Zerach was updating the command post on the situation as the officers knelt low. There was a dropoff worn away by a creek that was presently dry. It curved around a bend and they suspected that the old man was waiting to waste the first one who turned the corner. Wicker was probably standing under the roots of a dead tree that jutted out over the creek bed.

Roth signaled for Zerach and Abelard to go right while he and Selwyn dropped to the ground for a crawl around to the left of the tree. Orval's footprints could be seen as they sent over the edge, but Roth could not see any sign of them below. The snowfall was making it harder to view the dark cavity under the tree roots. Wicker had to be there.

"Mister, you've got one last chance to come out and stop this shit. If you do not, we will open up on you and there will not be enough of your ass to stick in a pill bottle!" Captain Roth hoped the threat would work, as he was sick of playing in the snow and he was concerned about his other men and Dolan.

After several seconds of silence, Orval shouted. "Fuck you and Janet Reno and the rest of you Kike loving bastards!" He sprayed the top of the bank with .223 bullets. Selwyn watched through his scope until the old goat stepped out to fire then put several rounds into his torso. When there was no movement for several minutes, Max slid down the bank and did a quick check to be sure the perp was dead. "Don't have to worry about his one."

"Alright. We'll take the prisoner back over to where Rampart is and then see what we can do to help the Major."

Chapter Thirty-five

The mountain was loaded with traps, both lethal and of the maiming variety. It was a slow, tense climb for Dolan and the troopers. Harry peered out over the crest of the hill and could see an old road filled with saplings that jutted up through the snow. There must have originally been a bridge at the southern peak, as it appeared that the road just dropped off into nothing now. A low mumbling of voices emitted from the north side around the mine entrance. Dolan grabbed a thin tree trunk and pulled himself up into a clearing.

Several yards away fresh boot prints had worn a large spot down in the snow. He pointed them out to Whistlestop and they waited a few seconds until a young kid returned, looking unhappy. The teenager kicked at the snow as if throwing a tantrum. Harry shrugged his shoulders at the Major. They had heard Roth's transmission earlier about the Sons turning on themselves. The organization must be falling apart.

Nash Redding moved into position and placed his crosshairs on the angry man. Dolan dashed over to a large spruce to cover Whistlestop as he darted toward the kid and stuck the barrel of a .45 Glock in the middle of his back. Will Chester was warned against making any noise or resisting as the Major pulled him backward like a sack of flour.

"Don't kill me...I wanted to get away but I didn't know where all the booby traps were, Clever is really pissed!" Chester looked like a whipped pup.

"How many are up here?" Whistlestop gripped the kid's yellow parka.

"I think it's just me, Clever and Jim Brentlinger, but we could see Berge and somebody else heading this way, which is what pissed Clever off. He didn't want all of us in one place..." Will's nose was red from the cold and he looked like the high school senior that he was.

"I'm going to trust you to stay here and keep quiet, son, but if you screw us over you will never be so unhappy again, am I really clear?" Whistlestop glared at Chester knowing that the kid was too scared and tired to do anything.

Hans was more charged than he had ever been in life except for when he was killing whores. He could almost feel himself transported back in time as one of Hitler's legions, hunting the enemy in the forests of Germany or Poland. If Berge had had the chance he would have shot the Smiths for treason, but with those cops hot on the trail, he thought it best to escape. He never would have guessed that Marsh would turn out to be one of the most loyal of the soldiers, but war brought out the best in men, or the worst.

Clever was high up on the mountain so Berge decided that was the best place to be now. The west side of the slope was too steep to climb, so Hans and Marsh tromped around to the east side where they found some footprints filling with snow. Since Berge did not know if it was cops or his own church members, he avoided taking the same path.

The earth suddenly gave way under Marsh at the foot of the mountain near some rocks that were spaced almost evenly up the slope. At first, Hans wanted to laugh as he thought that Vic had slipped, but the big man moaned and cried as half of his body disappeared in the snow. Berge pulled on an arm to help Marsh up before he realized that a dozen twelve inch nails punctured his chest. Clever had placed a sheet of plywood covered with the nails into a sunken area then let the snowfall do the camouflaging for him; too bad that Dylan had not seen fit to pass out maps of his death traps to his own people.

Since the damage was already done, Berge used Marsh's body as the first step up the mountainside. The pressure forced a glob of bright red blood out of Vic's mouth. Hans stared stupidly at the clash of colors then moved on toward the ridge above. Clever met him at the top with a smug look on his Germanic features. He seemed to be pleased that someone had stumbled into his trap whether it was one of their own or not.

"What are you doing here?" the former Green Beret asked with his nose nearly touching Berge's.

"I didn't know what else to do...the cops are killing everybody and some of us ran off. Where would you have me go?" Hans was not afraid of Clever who had no idea of what Berge was capable of doing to another human being.

Dylan's cold blue eyes scrutinized Hans for any sign of fear. "Never mind now..."

Clever stopped abruptly and put a finger over his lips to Berge and Brentlinger. He took the De Lisle up the peak that rose some twenty feet over the mine and hopped like a mountain goat southward toward a noise only heard by Dylan. Taking the hint that the three of them were not alone, Hans and Jim assumed positions where they could watch the road.

Will Chester scrunched down among the trees like a scared rabbit. There was a sudden movement in the bushes near Chester, which Dylan figured had to be a cop. The snowfall made finding the target a difficult exercise, so Clever put two rounds in the general area of the motion. He could tell from Will's reaction that someone had been hit.

The kid crawled on all fours behind the brush to render aid to the enemy, which now made him a liability to Clever. The cross hairs settled on Chester's bright yellow coat and guided the .45 ACP round into the teenager's thoracic region. Whistlestop appeared confused as he looked to Dolan. He could not understand why they had not heard the shots. Harry motioned for the Major to stay down as Dolan was in a better position to hunt for Clever.

The big blonde man was somewhere just above Harry waiting patiently for any sign of life. The terrain was rocky and thick with small trees and brush that still poked through the deepening snow. The silence became deafening as each man waited for the other to make a sound. Dolan felt a jolt in his chest as he saw the flash below of Whistlestop's scope amid the pines. As if on cue, Clever fired at the Major, but the bullet went over his head.

Bruce Whistlestop found himself in a bad position. The only real solution was to make his way back toward Redding without slipping and falling off the southern face of the mountain. He hoped that Nash was not dead for Nash's sake and the department's. Redding was their best sniper. Bruce had not called for a helicopter before as the snow made it impossible to fly then and especially now. What a great help a chopper would be at this moment! Dolan was no longer visible to Whistlestop, so he must be trying to get closer to Clever. The major found a large rock and threw it in the opposite direction he was headed, but Dylan didn't fire. *Must be a smart son-of-a-bitch*, thought Bruce.

Harry watched the ridge above him, his cheek going numb from the icy rocks as he hugged the hill. Just when Dolan decided that he was going to have to force the situation, a rumble of voices rose up at the entrance to the mine. It sounded like two men fighting. A smile crossed Harry's lips, as he knew that Clever would have to deal with the problem and would be distracted where he wanted to be or not.

Berge slapped Brentlinger across his bearded face, which stung more that normal because of the frigid air. Hans wanted to charge into the action to the south, but Jim refused.

"You are a soldier for the Lord! There is no time for cowardice. Take your gun and face the enemy!" Hans had that weird gleam to his features again.

"With all the crap you pass out, you must suck a lot of shit, Berge." Jim held his M-16 in a threatening position.

"His name isn't Berge. It's Hatcher you bunch of dumb fucks!" a voice shouted out and was followed by laughter.

Jim and Hans suddenly felt like goldfish in a glass bowl. It was hard to tell from which direction the voice came. Max Selwyn, always more of a hotdog than the rest of his team, popped up from the East Ridge sending a round into Brentlinger's chest. The preacher grew wide-eyed and dashed into the dark mine. Max dropped back down. Zerach was several yards to his left and both of them searched the hilltop for Clever who was now surrounded on all sides by troopers and Harry Dolan.

Dylan Clever fought to control the natural panic that poured like a wave through his tense body. He had never thought that the police would make it this far. The top of the mine was wide enough that he could move without being seen, but it was too much of an area for one man to patrol alone. While he had talked a good game about dying for the white race, Clever was not too wild about the idea now. The spruces provided good cover while he moved toward the mine entrance.

Brentlinger was lying on his back in the snow, a surprised expression etched into features forever, or until a mortician molded them into an acceptable look of peace. There was no sign of Hans, or whoever he really was, anywhere. Roth could see Harry against the rocks as he darted over to the hill. He signaled to Dolan that he was going up. When Clever fired a shot at the East Ridge, they knew he was preoccupied enough for Roth to get an edge on him. It was getting hard to see as everything was turning white and gray. The only color was the green of the pines and the occasional flash of clothing. Whistlestop had ordered more troops to move in once they knew where the Sons of Marduk were located. The state was through playing with Hans and his church members.

When Roth and Dolan crested the hill, Clever threw his prized rifle down and it disappeared into the snow. He turned around, placed his hands behind his back and waited to be cuffed. Harry arched his eyebrows at the surrendering warrior. Dylan must have decided that it was better to live and fight another day. The Captain placed the cold, metal cuffs on the subdued man, ever cautious in case it was a trick, and then forced him down the grade to the road.

The tracks going into the mine were rapidly blurring. The old wooden gate with its faded red paint rested on one hinge, blocking half of the passageway. Berge must have run inside after Brentlinger was shot. Harry peered into the darkness using the gate for cover. When he did not hear anything, Dolan shined the beam of his flashlight around the interior.

Hans was nowhere in sight. The preacher must be familiar with the mine to have ventured deeper into the tunnels. Apparently Clever had not booby-trapped the mine. There must be an escape route that emerged somewhere below near the ground.

Boxes full of supplies like canned meat, batteries and matches were stacked along the east wall. Dolan took two D-sized batteries and dropped them into the pocket of his parka. He also took a nylon mountain climbing rope with a metal clip on one end and looped it over his left shoulder. The Winchester was laid on an olive drab colored blanket and Harry started for the bowels of the earth. The cops would not like him going down there alone after Berge, but it was something that he wanted to do. Going one on one against that murderous hypocrite would do Dolan some good.

Chapter Thirty-six

It had been over one hundred years since Bertholt Greer established the mine some five miles from Gospel Peak and ninety-five years it was last worked for gold. The walls were braced with whatever wood Greer could find. They must have done some heavy blasting as the walls were mostly rock. The remains of a rail system for hauling rubble out of the earth disappeared down a steep incline. It was possible to walk down the tracks and Hans must have done so, as he disappeared quickly.

Before taking a chance on descending the slope Harry shone the light below. He saw nothing and there was only silence from the cold cavern beneath him. Obviously, Berge was used to coming here. Hans really did not strike Dolan as the rugged outdoor type, but appearances could be deceiving. Harry studied the pathway down then focused the beam of light on the far end of the room in case Berge was watching from some unseen location.

The temperature was almost warm deep inside the mountain. There was nowhere to hide at this level so Dolan approached the tunnel ahead carefully. Where could Hans have gone so fast? There was no trace of Berge at the next level either, but here the room branched off into two directions. The air was fresh smelling, which meant there were still air shafts that channeled outside air into the mine. The tunnel to the right dropped off into an abyss just a few feet into it. Some sort of elevator type contraption had been there at one time, but only the metal framework remained.

Dolan drew the Colt 45 automatic from his shoulder holster that had been with him in many scrapes and prepared for the inevitable showdown. The passageway curved to the right and the interior grew lighter as Harry inched forward. A funny sound echoed from farther below. As he rounded the curve, light and shadow danced off a wall from a distant source. Dolan let his eyes adjust from the black darkness that was lit only by the single beam of his flashlight. He turned the light off.

It appeared that the mine had merged with a natural cavern and Harry stood on a bridge of stone with a granite panel on one side and a deep cavity to the left. The light source was coming from somewhere in that room below. Berge or something else was down there, was making a noise that sounded like the offspring of a chicken and a fiddle. A cold chill went down Dolan's spine that was unrelated to the temperature. The bridge gradually descended into the space beneath, but Harry did not want to approach Hans head on. He fed one end of the rope through the metal clip and slipped the loop around a pointed rock on the ground. The pistol was in his right pocket for easy retrieval and he began to lower himself down. Water must have rushed through this place long ago as it left strange shapes in the rock and pillars that separated the lighted room from the one Dolan was sliding into. When Harry finally felt the bottom with his boots, it was soft. He frowned at the unexpected surface. What the hell?

The smell slowly eased into Dolan's nostrils as he tried to balance himself on the uneven foundation. His left boot was on a woman's head and the right in the middle of another's back. The bodies were not frozen, but stiff from the cold. Harry could see that Hans was dancing around a fire in his underwear with some object draped over his head and an animal pelt around his shoulders. An odd chant came from his lips and he looked upward as he did a primitive dance around the flames. In one hand, he gripped a Bible, and in the other hand, he grasped an M-16.

Berge, alias Hatcher, was a serial killer and a very unusual one even among perverts. Dolan found places to step in between arms and legs, making his way over to one of the pillars. Hans beseeched Marduk, Jesus and Hitler to protect him in his hour of need. Dolan pulled out the pistol and aimed it around the pillar at Berge.

"Drop the gun, asshole," Harry demanded.

The preacher nearly did let go of the rifle, but out of shock not obedience. He sprinted into the dark shadows under the bridge then sprayed the room with bullets in Dolan's direction.
"Your mother was a whore and your daddy was a nigger!" Hans screamed at Dolan.

When the shooting stopped, Harry said in a calm voice, "My mother was a saint and daddy was a chicken hawk. Bet you like to diddle little boys too, don't ya Hans? Yeah, I can visualize you going at it…"

"You were puked out of a nigger's ass, boy!" Berge tried to lower his voice to sound powerful. He could not tell exactly where Dolan was hiding and he was terrified, as he had nearly emptied the clip in his anger and fear.

"I'd rather be a turd than what you are, Hans. In a very short while, you are going to explain to Jesus that you are a Nazi fuck, a woman hater and you like to play with hairless pee pees. In fact, why don't you say hello to Albert Blue for me since you'll be sharing a cot in the same hot place!" Harry laughed knowing that the accusation about being a child molester was getting to Berge.

"You should be ashamed to call yourself a white man! You are a nutless traitor to your race, you know NOTHING about racial pride, and you're probably a faggot! I will not leave this place until I see you gag on your own blood!" The veins in Berge's neck and forehead bulged from the strain. His underwear sagged around his skinny legs and his testicles pulled up toward the warmth of his buttocks. It made him grow even madder at the smartass who had invaded his private place of worship, then laughed at everything he said.

"You are right about one thing, Reverend Wang…you are not going to leave here." Dolan's tone changed.

"You think you're something…but the Sons of Marduk have a purpose on this Earth and you will answer for everything you do to stop our holy mission!" Hans had no way of escaping except for going into areas of the cavern that he had not explored. He should not have wasted all that ammo as now Hans had the choice of creeping through the bowels of the planet in his drawers or charging Dolan for a quick death.

"I don't think your mission could be nearly as "Holey" as them shorts."

Berge heaved a rock in Dolan's direction. "You are one infuriating bastard! You will fry in Hell, mister!"

"Yeah, I've heard that before…I'm going to ask the Devil if I can be in charge of torturing chicken hawks and Fundamentalist Christians. If I got to be there anyway, I might as well enjoy it." Harry could see that Berge was moving slowly out of the shadows. He was going to do something.

"Harry? Harry? Are you okay?" Whistlestop shouted from the room above.

"I'm fine, but Berge just hopped off into the darkness. He just threw something into the fire!" Dolan stepped near the campfire then cursed when he saw that Berge had been wearing a woman's face while he danced.

"Jesus!" Bruce remarked as he and Max ran down the bridge. "What have we got? Ed Gein reincarnated?" Gein was a serial killer that dressed women out like deer then wore their body parts in a bizarre nighttime ritual.

Max moved about in a combat ready position and Harry told him that Berge was not armed and that he was in his drawers. When they looked puzzled, Dolan said he would explain later.

"Which way did he go?" Selwyn wondered as he peered off into a blackened passageway.

"Oh, that way. He has no flashlight that I could see, unless he's got one strapped to his hooha. He can't get far."

Selwyn shined his six-battery Kel-light into the tunnel. For someone who could not see, Hans was doing all right, as Max could barely see his white jockey shorts in the distance. The Major attempted to convey the information that they had Berge, but the signal could not penetrate the mountain fortress.

Bruce pulled his baton from its hook on his belt and lifted the facial skin of the unfortunate woman from the fire. They would need to get a crime scene unit down there.

"Think you can handle that fleeing felon? I can't transmit from here…"

"I don't know, major, at any given time Hans could point old willy at me and we'd be drenched in piss. Now how would that be, it being so cold and all?" Harry feigned a concerned demeanor.

"I'll take that as a yes."

"I'll go get him, I've some this far." Harry snickered.

The passage where Berge shuffled along was manmade. The miners must have continued with the digging where the rock was softer. Berge could see a few feet ahead of him as someone had a good flashlights and was closing in on the leader of the Elder Church. Hans had no plan. He was just running. He wondered why Clever let any of these pigs live. The sound of pounding boots behind him made Berge walk faster, his bare feet smarting from sharp rocks or an occasional rusty bolt.

A few yards in the distance an opening in the mountainside allowed light and snow to enter. Hans tried to figure in his head how close they were to ground level now. If he had to jump, could he make it? Berge heard one of the men remark that he was tired of this shit and the footsteps in the rear picked up pace. It was difficult to tell where the natural light was coming from as the circles of light from the flashlights bounced around like rubber balls off the walls. Hans psyched himself up for a dramatic leap from a cave opening into the tops of trees to break his fall. That sort of escape seemed to work in the movies and Berge did not have much choice.

A large, square hole opened in the floor of a small room. Pieces of a disassembled conveyor belt lay off in a dark corner where Berge could not see them. The conveyor had once been set up at an angle and the opening to the outside was further below. Hans teetered on the edge of the trench, which was filled with broken glass and snow far below.

The beam of the flashlight made it appear that Berge was in a bizarre display of some sort. Clever knew about this place as Dolan would have expected him to, but it was too bad that he did not bother to tell the other Sons of Marduk. For a former Green Beret, Dylan Clever seemed very alienated from the team concept.

Berge pointed the weapon at Harry. He shivered in the icy draft. "It's your turn, asshole!"

Dolan pulled the pistol from his pocket and shot Berge in the genitals. Berge made a screeching sound and dropped to his knees. Blood gushed from the wound, drenching the dirty underwear.

"Thank God your wife had the good sense to terminate your horrid little bastards before they could pollute the world."

Hans gazed at Harry with wide, frightened eyes. "Help me."

"Okay." Dolan put a bullet between his eyes then kicked the corpse into the shaft.

Chapter Thirty-seven

The long drive home for Dolan allowed him to think about his future and life in general. Orphan seemed to sense he was unhappy and lay her big head in his lap. Libby had decided to apply for the State Police along with her friend, Ethel Steeple, and Harry was glad for her. The wounded trooper, Nash Redding, was going to be okay after some rehabilitation and Stark Gayle was counting the days until he could escape Hagar, Idaho. Dr. Gayle now had very mixed feelings about the beautiful land he owned and was not sure that he wanted to keep it. Dolan informed him that after all the crap they had to go through he better damned well keep it as they had all earned it.

Julie Cato had asked Harry for his email address so that they could keep in touch. At forty-seven Dolan knew he was still missing something in life, but it would be difficult to have a steady relationship and administer the type of justice that still needed administered. Pedophiles were a festering cancer in which there was only one cure: extermination.

Harry was not ready for getting close to a woman, and he had no desire to use Julie just for sexual release. She was someone that he could talk to and he encouraged the friendship.

The death of his mother, grandmother and sister in the last two and a half years haunted Dolan daily as well as the betrayal of his younger brother and sister. It was nothing to have spent over forty years with Albert Blue telling him and Sarah that they were sacks of shit, but to be treated that way by Alex and Dana was hard to stomach.

Alex belonged to a church with the same superior attitude of the Sons of Marduk and the minister there was every bit as ignorant and hateful as Berge. It had not been that long ago that Dana was completely against Alex's snake handling church, but now she was letting her son go there and Harry was no longer good enough for his niece and nephews.

The house looked bright and homey in the autumn light. While Idaho was having ice and snow, Kansas was still warm enough that Dolan could still have hanging baskets of petunias on the wrap-around porch without fear of freezing. Orphan was delighted at seeing her own territory again and ran from bush to flower sniffing and urinating. Harry shook his head at the dog that tripped on her ears. Dogs had such simple thrills.

He made himself a large glass of ice tea, then checked his answering machine. The funeral home had still not received a check from the insurance company to pay for Sarah's cremation. Dolan had tried for months to get some cooperation from the life insurance company, but they rewrote the definition of "bad faith" in their treatment of Harry Dolan. Every time that he called, he got a different answer as to why they were not paying off, then he had the funeral home call. Leonard was told that Sarah's brother and sister were accusing him of forging Sarah's signature to make himself beneficiary.

Alex threw his crippled sister in the gutter, Dana would not take her to dialysis even one time and now they wanted what little money was left after the funeral expenses were paid. Where were they when Sarah was shopping at the Salvation Army? There was no sign of Alex or Dana when Harry and his aunt and uncle busted their asses fixing up Sarah's house and there was no concern about her hurt feelings when she was put out with the trash. Yet, the selfish little bastards were out to screw Harry over too. He dialed the number for a local attorney and made an appointment. What a shame it was to fight over a lousy six thousand dollars, which Alex and Dana had no right to in the first place.

To top off the afternoon, when Harry picked up the mail piled on the floor under the mail slot, he found an envelope from Martha Ringer. It seemed that while she was investigating a guy named William Tates, she ran into a file on Willy, Dana's boyfriend. Dolan felt the blood run out of his cheeks as he read the list of child abuse and domestic violence charges. There were six, and five of them were against his daughters. The charges were dropped because the little girls could not provide dates and times the incidents occurred. It did not mean that Willy was innocent, as Dana had tearfully pleaded. He was the man Dana would be marrying in September.

Harry, of course, was not invited to wedding to be held at Alex's house on September 16. Nor was Aunt Pat invited, but her son, Jake had received an invitation in the mail. Jake was a dispatcher for the sheriff's department and was about the most laid-back person you could meet. He had said one time that Lucy Blue was a kind woman who accepted people as they are and Lucy had said the same of her nephew Jake, but everyone had a breaking point. One night long ago, Jake's life changed forever when he lost control of his pickup. He was paralyzed from the waist down and suddenly Jake was thrust into a different world where he was now a "guy in a wheelchair." Never one to be dependent on others, Jake set out to make sure that he was dependent on no one.

The journey was long and hard and he had a special place for those like him. It was bad enough when Alex bad-mouthed Lucy after her death, but when he tossed Sarah into the road like so much rotten meat it was too much for Jake to handle. The wedding invitation went into the nearest trashcan. Harry did not think that Dana was aware of everything that Alex had been up to, but he still did not excuse her. She had her head so far up Willy's ass, Dana would never see daylight again or when she did, it would be too late. Dana just assumed that if anyone was a liar or a thief it was Harry or Sarah, not Saint Alex.

Apparently Harry was guilty until proven otherwise and Alex's actions were not to be questioned. Dolan wondered how many people knew that Mr. and Mrs. God lived near Towanda Street in Golding, Kansas.

Alex already had taken over twenty thousand dollars for a down payment on his house with the swimming pool out of the estate. Dolan suspected that Willy was waiting for the money from Sarah's policy to take Dana on a honeymoon, but Harry would never let that happen, never. No one who could be so cold-blooded and cruel was going to party on Sarah. If Dana wanted money to honeymoon with that foinoff, she could damned well kiss Alex's ass to get it.

Chapter Thirty-eight

The woman's name was Nellie Price. She had worked hard since the age of fifteen doing whatever it took to survive and without a high school diploma, her choices had been few. Her reward was a small, one bedroom house with a space heater and no air conditioning, but it was hers.

It was her place and a sanctuary against the neighborhood outside that deteriorated daily from crime and vandalism. Sometime during the night, Nellie's haven was violated, along with her seventy-year old body. She lay in bed where the rapist must have surprised her while sleeping. Masking tape had been wrapped around her eyes and her cotton nightgown pushed up around her shoulders. The phone cord was pulled from the wall and a large bruise covered the left side of her face, all in an effort to keep Nellie from describing her attacker. It was all done for nothing, as the widow Mrs. Price succumbed to heart failure either during or after the rape. She lived just beyond the Wichita city limits, so Sedgwick county detectives Richardson and Ringer were there when Harry arrived.

"Christ, Harry, she could be my grandmother." Gary Richardson jotted down some notes as he studied the dead woman.

"She'd have to be a hundred and fifty years old to be your grandmother, ya old fart," Martha remarked as she asked for the crime scene techs to get a sample of some blood smeared on a wall behind the bed.

"I think she had a heart attack either while she was being raped or just after…for God's sake, she was just an old lady." Dolan filled out the basic information in a report for the medical examiner.

"I think I'll retire next year or I'm gonna go beserk and kill a few of these sick fucks!" Gary let out a deep breath.

"Know what you mean," Harry replied, a slight grin on his lips. "You guys want to get some coffee soon as we wrap it up here?"

"Yeah, I could use some caffeine. "Martha looked tired. "God, I hate ones like this."

Gary went over to a uniformed officer and told her to canvas the neighborhood for information concerning who might have seen what. "I want to know about anybody hanging around here, and that includes meter readers, the cable man, the cable man's granddaddy, everybody!"

As the three investigators left the crime scene, they walked down a sidewalk bordered by flowerbeds dormant for the winter. It was apparent that Nellie Price had cared a great deal for her yard work and gardening.

"You serious about retiring, Gary?" Martha looked to her partner who wore an old tan corduroy jacket.

"I ain't sleeping good anymore, and I can't just enjoy being with my grand kids cause I'm always thinking about what some pervert might do to them one day…I'd like to have some peace of mind before it's my turn for a coffin. I'm just tired of everything being shit colored, know what I mean?" Richardson pulled a roll of Tums from his breast pocket and popped two in his mouth.

Dolan knew exactly what he meant as Harry had been thinking the same thing for the last few months as each rape and murder victim that he saw these days made Dolan think of some relative in their place. Nellie awoke in the night to an intruder just like Abby Dolan, Harry's grandmother. He wondered if she had endured over an hour of torment as Abby had, and did she know her attacker? Her rapist did not kill Abby, but she had begun to die that night little by little as sure as if he had cut her throat.

At least Dolan had extracted revenge on Albert Blue for Abby. Who would do it for Nellie Price? The cops would try, however, in reality Dolan knew that the rapist would probably not be caught or he would not be convicted if he were caught. Justice on planet earth was a rare commodity.

"Tell you what, I'll buy the coffee. Will that help cheer you guys up?" Martha waved a five-dollar bill around.

"As soon as EMS uses the paddles on me, Jesus. Did you know that Ringer had any money? I sure as hell didn't! Damn, my chest hurts." Richardson rubbed his sternum.

"Get your ass in the car, Gary, or you will know some pain." Martha rolled her eyes at Dolan. "I don't get paid enough to work with him...you just don't know what a woman has to put up with in this business."

"I'll meet you guys there, I'm so glad that I don't work with a partner." Harry shook his head.

"And you don't have anybody to blame your fuck ups on either, Harry. Thank about that one!" Richardson made a face in Ringer's direction.

"I need an appointment with Mr. Daniels, coffee ain't gonna do it." Martha said before disappearing into the driver's seat of their Crown Victoria.

Gary put a hand over his mouth as if he was divulging a secret. "She has a lot of friends, Mr. Walker, Mr. Smirnoff, Ms. Chablis, and Mr. Schlitz...a busy, busy woman." Martha leaned over and peered out the passenger window.

"What did he say?"

Harry waved her off. "You don't even want to know. I'll meet you two at that place on Broadway."

During the next half hour, Harry found himself unloading on his two friends, something that he rarely did.

"Damn, Harry, with family like that you don't need any enemies. You got it all wrapped up in one handy little package." Martha's voice was gentle.

"That's what hurts...I thought we were close. I've heard people say that their mothers were the hub of the family, but I did not have a real grasp of the meaning until my Mom died. If she was the hub then when she broke all of us spokes went flying and the family wheel went rolling off into a shit pile." Dolan ordered an English muffin when the waitress asked if they wanted anything else.

"I'll take a stack of pancakes with bacon and a refill on the coffee." Gary smiled at the woman in a pink waitress uniform with white piping around the collar and sleeves. "You know, Harry; you just got to move on. I know it's hard, but you got friends that appreciate ya...not me and Ringer, but you know I'm getting at?"

"That's really sensitive, Gary. Remember this moment, Harry, because it is not likely to happen again. The last time I saw him show this much emotion was he blew his nose after backing over that dog when leaving a crime scene." Martha grinned at her own wit.

"I think I'll put in my retirement papers today. That's just hysterical, Martha, and I hope your next partner appreciates your sense of humor as much as I do."

"And I hope my next partner went through the academy after the Battle of Gettysburg, but we can't always have what we want. And I know you ordered that feast just because I'm paying." Ringer remarked as the waitress took the order to the kitchen.

Gary smirked. "That's why she's a de-tect-ive!"

"You should have seen that asshole lieutenant in Idaho, what a jerk off. Rampart, that was his name. He was hot to trot for a young deputy who, for some reason, was not interested in a pot-bellied married man and he refused to listen to anything she had to say because of it. He got several of his men killed in the woods...didn't want to ask for assistance from any "outside" agency. What a horse's ass!"

"Well, there's no shortage of that breed around, one of them is your own brother! It really pisses me off the way he screwed you and Sarah over. See, that's the reason I don't go to church...Alex can trash his dead mother, pimp his kids out to child molester for money then throw his crippled, dying sister in the street and yet still think he's a good Christian. I know the type, Harry. You're not good enough because you're Jewish and Sarah was gay. Now you two are going to Hell, but not the Golden Boy. If heaven is full of fucks like Alex and his old lady, then I WANT to go the other direction!" Ringer winked at Dolan. She knew he was really wounded by the betrayal of his brother and sister, but did not know how to help him.

"Yeah, Harry. You just fought a bunch just like him up there in Idaho. God help us if those right wing bastards ever get in power!" Richardson looked pleased with the pancakes placed before him.

Dolan buttered his muffin. "Martha, don't you want anything?"

"You know what a hard time I have with the blubber factor, no, I best pass."

"You let too many things bother you, Ringer. I don't need to see my worn out shoes to know they're still there." Gary stifled a belch that made his cheeks puff out.

"That's my partner, the philosopher."

"You know, Dolan. If ya just wanted to do something to feel better, there are things you could do..." Richardson remarked through a mouthful of pancake.

"Anything illegal?" Harry whispered over the table.

"Only if you get caught. Pick something that means a lot to the little shit, he's materialistic so it should not be too hard. Alex is the type that cares about what his old lady wants and what other people think, use your imagination." Gary cut a crisp piece of bacon with his fork and a chip flew off into Martha's coffee cup.

"If I'd wanted something to eat I would have ordered it." Ringer teased as she pulled the meat from the liquid. "Yum, pork flavored java!"

"You two can laugh, but some yuppie will probably market the shit." Gary looked around the cafe to see if any of the businessmen were listening.

"We better get our butts in gear, we all have paperwork to get done." Martha sighed.

"Yeah, I guess." Dolan chewed the last bite of his English muffin wishing that he were a career fisherman.

"When my son Randy worked for a security company he had this asshole supervisor who was always sneaking up on him. You know the type, bald, wearing a gun strapped to his ankle. A cop wannabe? Well, my kid worked at the phone company and they all had card keys they used to get into the building and that super had one too so he could spy on the guards. Well, my kid wanted to watch the Super Bowl without being spied on so Randy got into the computer and voided the asshole's card. He was madder than hell and they never did figure out who did it.

"There's things you could do without really hurting anybody, Harry." Gary wiped the syrup off his lips.

"Gary, I didn't know you were so devious." Martha titled her head at her partner.

"My kid is devious, I'm just a law abiding officer of the law." Richardson let out a belch. "Well, are we ready to return to crime fighting?"

"I think that syrup was fermented; now he thinks he's Spiderman." Martha grabbed the bill. "I won't be making this offer again. Damn, Gary!"

"She's completely devoted to me."

"You two are certifiable. Keep me informed about the Price case and I'll catch ya later." Harry left them at the door to the restaurant and went to his Suburban. He was going to give some serious thought to Richardson's idea.

Chapter Thirty-nine

The lawyer cost Dolan over four hundred dollars just to get a life insurance company to pay benefits Sarah had assigned to him to pay off the little house Harry bought for her. The insanity of the whole situation was unreal. He wished that he could wake up from this nightmare, but morning after morning it was still there. The lessons learned in the past three years had been hard and cruel, but he was more determined than ever to stop pedophiles from spreading their disease from one generation to the next. Albert Blue had done an excellent job of assuring that pain and conflict would continue while he burned in Hell.

The earthly remains of his mother and grandmother were buried. Some of Sarah's ashes were in a bottle labeled, Vial for Life, which she would have found very funny. He placed Sarah in front of the television that his sister bought because Alex took the one she was using at their parent's house. When Harry first brought the set home, he turned to the Discovery channel in honor of Sarah, as that was her favorite channel.

As a boy, Dolan used to have dreams where Sarah was in the middle of a river in a sinking boat. She called and called for help, but no one answered except for Harry who went to her rescue in a leaky rowboat. The dream scared him then, as he wondered why Lucy did not help her daughter. Now he knew. The only ones left to render aid to Sarah were her siblings and only one to heed the call was Harry.

At least he knew now to get his affairs in order to ensure that Alex and Dana got nothing of his estate and had nothing to say about his future if he became disabled. The mere thought of Alex's old lady and Willy going through his stuff was enough to made Dolan go ballistic. Harry had all of his mother and grandmother's heirlooms and now that he knew Alex's true feelings about Lucy, he was glad of it. No one visited Lucy's grave now except for her siblings and Harry. Alex could drive over sixty miles to pay homage to his dead father-in-law, but would not drive a mile to put flowers on his own mother's grave!

Alex had never been to their grandmother's grave at all, but Dolan suspected it was because she was buried in a Catholic cemetery. The members of the Church of the Poisoned Mind did not like Catholics, Jews or anybody else. Something had to be done to put Mr. Alex Blue in his place. He was not the family patriarch! How could anyone show nothing but hate and disgust for siblings who had gone out of the way to help him? On the other hand, trash his dead mother who thought the sun rose and set on him while at the same time glorify a sadistic pedophile and be proud of being like him? Alex was sick in the head and for his sake; he had better not be just like their father as Alex claimed to be.

Harry gritted his teeth as he thought of the lies Alex told about Harry abusing him at Vanora School, not Albert Blue. It was just as bad as Al blaming poor Lucy for his pedophilia. Some people truly had no shame. Sarah had said to listen to what Alex accused them of and they would know what he was doing. So far that was true, but then that also meant that Harry knew who was being taken to Vanora School.

If Alex knew what was good for his health, he had better walk a very straight line. They had all made a vow that the child abuse stopped with the Cheese and Dolan had meant it. If Alex and Dana did not, then Harry was sorry for their children.

So, while Sarah had been reduced to ashes after spending her last months being terrified of her youngest brother, Alex now laid around a nice swimming pool. Of course, all of his in-laws also benefited from his contract with the Devil.

It was only Harry, Sarah and Aunt Pat on the garbage heap. Harry too could languish with Alex while they barbequed and took a leisurely dip now and then, but Dolan would have to join the "I Love Albert Blue and Everything He Did to Me Club." He would also have to listen to Lucy being bashed over the head and put up with Alex and Alice trying to convince him that he too should attend the rituals at their Nazi temple if he wanted to see Heaven. Of course, basking in Alex's manly glory was also part of the admission price and Dolan would rather have puked than paid any part of it.

The house with the pool was Alice's idea as she cared about nothing as much as appearances. The place was not that great, as Dolan too had checked it out because of the swimming pool. The house was not worth the one hundred seventeen thousand dollars the owner was asking.

It was also crammed in between two other houses with a narrow driveway, but it was a gold medal of achievement for Alex. He now worked at the same aircraft plant the Cheese was retired from and could brag about the expensive house he owned. The best way to deflate the ego of someone like Alex was to financially to screw his reputation.

The first thing on Harry's list was that damned swimming pool. There was a small house for sale on the street one block east of Alex's place. Alex's privacy fence was diagonal from the backyard of the house where Dolan stood. He told the real estate agent that he wanted to pick up a rental for extra income, but he did not want to pay much for one.

The woman showed him several houses before they arrived at the brick house on High street behind the Blue house. The owners were anxious to sell and would close whenever Dolan wished.

It was not a bad place. There were two bedrooms and an attached garage, but no basement, which went right along with Harry's plans. He would build a storm shelter in the backyard for the benefit of future renters thus avoiding any suspicions when Dolan began digging in the yard. The Viet Cong had a network of tunnels the envy of any self-respecting mole, so a short passage under a pool a few hundred yards to the northwest would be no large feat. A deputy sheriff lived to the north of Alex Blue and he did not know it now, but the man was going to have a very leaky basement in the near future and so would Alex. Harry smiled wide as the real estate agent walked up beside him.

"So what do ya think?" The woman was a single mother and very happy for any sale she could make.

"Let's draw up the papers." Harry winked and extended his right hand.

Chapter Forty

About the time, that Harry Dolan had decided his life needed a face-lift, the basement walls under two houses in Golding had weakened considerably. A nice family lived in Dolan's rental house and they were very thankful that he had provided such a nice shelter from tornados. He had been back to Idaho twice to testify against Clever and what was left of the Sons of Marduk.

It was too bad that Berge had died as he had left an interesting past in California as Nathan Hatcher. It turned out that he was a suspect in several murders around the San Francisco area that were similar to the murders he had committed in Idaho. Only a few of the bodies Dolan found in the mine had been identified, but it was assumed that many had been hookers that Hans had picked up far from home.

Harry had seen many murder, accident and suicide victims since Nellie Price. The rapist turned killer of Mrs. Price had not been caught and no suspects were forthcoming, but that was typical of such cases. What bothered Harry was how many other old women had been raped and not said anything to anyone out of fear? How many were terrified to live in their own homes or be outside in their front yards? Recently a woman had been shot several times while playing golf by a man paroled from a

Colorado prison. Harvey Turnbull had raped and killed two women at a resort fifteen years ago and was then, turned loose to inflict his brand of misery on other people. Harry did not know what was worse, seeing all the pain in the world or not doing anything about it—not that he had not done his part with eliminating a few chicken hawks that could no longer hurt children.

He also hunted them down on the Internet where child porn was easy to find. One day Dolan found two pictures that really disturbed him. One was of a two-year old girl being sexually abused and the other was unbelievable, as someone had forced a five-year-old girl to orally copulate a dog. Harry Dolan concluded that he still had work to do in the administration of justice.

The sun had already set when Dolan came out into the cool night air to sit in the porch swing. A breeze reduced the temperature to around thirty, but Harry liked the cold. There was nothing better than relaxing on a covered porch when it was about to rain or snow. A sweetness came with the wind that always put Dolan in a good mood. Orphan jumped up next to him and the two of them glided gently back and forth. Harry barely heard the portable phone ring, which was under a floppy ear of his snoring Bassett Hound. He felt his good mood evaporate as calls at night usually meant a body had been found somewhere.

"Dolan."

"Harry, glad I finally caught you!" It was Sister Marcella.

"Sister, good to hear from you. How's Maine these days?"

"I wouldn't know, I was transferred to a detention camp for youth in Montana. I'm the camp nurse." She did not sound happy.

"Whose skirts did you ruffle?" Harry laughed.

"Believe it or not I was requested by the warden. He liked my style and thought that with my experience I could handle it. But that's not why I called…"

"Somehow I knew that. Just let me have it." Harry stood up and went back into the house. Orphan hit the wooden porch with a loud thump and a groan then scraped on the screen door. He let her in and closed the heavy front door.

"The state of Montana could use some help and I told Warden Cartwright about you. He would like to talk with you about a problem within the camp and offer you a job."

"I hate Montana. It's too close to Idaho." Dolan complained.

"It would only be until the situation is cleared up, then you could move on if you wanted. Please, Harry? At least come up and talk to the man." The nun's voice pleaded. "And it couldn't hurt if you would become familiar with rodeo events."

"What? I know jack shit about rodeo. Just what does he want me to do?" Dolan lowered himself into his favorite recliner.

"I can't say over the phone. Come up and see us. You can stay with me. I have a two bedroom apartment."

"Now wouldn't that look good?" He snickered.

"You should know by now Dolan that if I know how to do anything it's to ruffle feathers! You'll have your own room anyway, mister." Sister Marcella tried to sound serious.

"To tell you the truth, I was thinking of resigning anyway. I am so sick of pain and death...I could use a change. Could I bring my dog?"

"Oh, this will be a change alright. Yeah, I'm allowed one pet, bring her. I could use the company."

Harry paused for minute as the processed what she said. Wasn't his company as good as a dog? "When do you want me to come up?"

"The warden knows you work full-time, so he said the first weekend that you're not on call. We'll meet here at my place."

"Okay, I can do that. I have call this weekend, so it would be the one after that."

"Thanks, Harry. I knew you'd come through."

"I haven't said that I would do whatever it is he wants yet," Dolan teased.

"You will, I know it. I don't see you turning this adventure down. I'll see you in two weeks, Harry. Stay safe."

Harry hung up the phone wondering what in the hell Sister Marcella was up to now.

———•——•——•———

Little Tim and Brandy Blue rushed into the house after church excited because there was no school due to in-services for staff the next day. Tim, who had just started the sixth grade, peeled off his clothes and tossed them onto the floor of his room. The in ground swimming pool in the backyard was heated and the Blue family planned to have an after church swim. Brandy was chatting away as she put on her bathing suit down the hall.

"Hurry up!" Tim yelled as he ran down the hallway to the patio doors.

"I'm coming!" Brandy shouted as she came up behind her brother as he unlocked the glass doors.

Alex told them to wait for him and Alice before they got into the water. The kids mumbled their discontent then went outside to the cement area surrounding the pool. The first thing Tim noticed was that there was no steam rising off the water. He walked to the edge of the pool and peered down into the depths. The pool was empty except for about three feet of water.

"Dad! Dad! Something is wrong with the pool."

Alex stepped through the doors with a can of Mountain Dew in his hand thinking that his children were exaggerating about a minor problem.

"Oh! Let me see."

Tim pointed at the water far below. "What happened to it all?"

Alex looked as if someone had smacked him with a board. He thought for a moment then ran down to the basement, which was filled with two feet of water. The kid's toys bobbed around along with a television set, some compact discs and stereo speakers. A gospel CD floated around entitled, *The River is Wide*.

Alice gasped as she observed the scene next to her husband. "Alex, how did this happen? If those people lied to us about that pool, we are going to court. This makes me so mad! What are we going to do? Oh my God, we cannot afford this. I am calling that real estate agent right now; I do not care what time it is! She can just get her butt down here! Alex, I trusted her! This is so unfair! After what we paid for this house! I could scream!"

Alex walked back up the steps, closed the basement door and locked it. While he was very concerned about the cost of repairing the damage to the house and pool, Alex Blue wanted the answer to another question. Where did the rest of the water go?

———————————————

Sergeant Myers looked forward to his two days off, as the week had been a long one. The county had numerous drug busts and car accidents that week, and a rape not reported to the press. The deputy was tired. The wife and kids were at their maternal grandmother's house designing Halloween costumes and Bill Myers planned to watch a movie on HBO.

He was happy. His family life was good, he liked his job and their house was nearly paid off. The neighborhood was not bad and though Jake, the dispatcher, had told him about Alex Blue next door, Myers had few worries. He hardly ever saw the people next door as the privacy fence around the backyard prevented much social interaction. Bill did not want to get too friendly with them anyway, as he did not like what was done to that crippled woman, nor did Myers care for the church down the road. The last thing he wanted was some holy roller trying to sucker him into going to their church.

The microwave pinged when the popcorn was done. Bill poured the contents of the steaming bag into a large plastic bowl and grabbed a cold beer. The family room with a big screen television was in the basement. They rarely treated themselves to such luxuries, but Myers had told his small family that they deserved to have a few nice things in life. Bill's father had run off when he was a boy, forcing his mother to work minimum wage factory jobs to support him and his two brothers, so they had few extras growing up. He was pleased that he could give his wife and children a decent life.

The off-duty deputy had a big smile on his face with a bowl of popcorn in one hand and a beer in the other. Everyone he knew had already seen the movie, Hard Rain, so Myers was anxious to see it for himself. The film was shot in large vats of water for a realistic effect as the plot involved a town that was completely flooded. He flipped on the porch light with the beer can and left a small lamp on in the living room. The basement stairs were at the far end away from the front door and the stairwell was bathed in shadows. Myers had been down those steps many times in the dark as the light switch was half way down on the right.

He bent his head down and filled his mouth with popcorn then suddenly stopped chewing. His feet were wet. Using his forearm to turn on the light switch, Myers dropped the bowl of popcorn in shock. The room below was flooded halfway up the stairs. The water was chest level to a grown man and Bill could see the tip of his recliner twirling around among the hundreds of other items that were kept in the family room. The bowl joined the menagerie that floated like buoys on the surface of the water. Only a few inches of the big screen were visible and his wife's sewing machine lay on its side as it bumped into a table. Myers felt like he was on the set of the Titanic and someone would yell, "cut!" at any time.

"Son-of-a-bitch! Goddamn it! It hasn't rained in months! Where did it come from?" Bill's first thought was maybe a water main had broke, but he had just taken a shower and the water pressure was fine. He backed up the steps in shock and anger, and as he did so, it occurred to him where such a large quantity of water could have originated.

"That pool next door! I want that guy's ass!"

Printed in the United States
104338LV00004B/124/A